The
Leaving
Year

PRAISE FOR

The Leaving Year

"Ida Petrovich, wise and brave beyond her years, takes us on an incredible journey as she seeks the truth about her father's disappearance. Rich in period details of the 1960s and set against the spectacular backdrop of the Pacific Northwest, *The Leaving Year* is a lovely story of youth, sorrow, and personal growth. Truly a young adult must-read."

—Anne Leigh Parrish, author of *The Amendment*

"Pam McGaffin's thoroughly enjoyable coming-of-age novel starts and ends in the fishing communities of Puget Sound, but its landscape of imagination is really Alaska. The state's grandeur and largeness of spirit are echoed in the richly drawn characters that fight and feel their way through this story of caring, loss, and the price of self-awareness."

—Steve Lindbeck, former CEO of Alaska Public Media

"In Pam McGaffin's exceptional debut, emotion bubbles right below the surface and weaves an addictive tale of mystery and forgiveness as Ida's search for a missing father takes her on a remarkable journey to find herself."

—Jan Von Schleh, author of *But Not Forever*

"*The Leaving Year* takes the reader to a time and a place that is not only singular but also beautifully familiar. Author Pam McGaffin has written a powerful story of loss and its unknowns, rife with grief and confusion, and woven it into an empowering journey of self-discovery and promise."

—Emily Russin, writer and editor

The Leaving Year

A Novel

By

Pam McGaffin

Published by SparkPress, a BookSparks imprint,
A division of SparkPoint Studio, LLC
Tempe, Arizona, USA, 85281
www.gosparkpress.com

Published 2018
Printed in the United States of America
ISBN: 978-1-943006-81-6 (pbk)
ISBN: 978-1-943006-82-3 (e-bk)
Library of Congress Control Number: 2018936842

Book design by Stacey Aaronson

To Mark, for giving me time and a room of my own

———

PART ONE

CHAPTER 1

Mayday
*An international radio distress signal
used by ships and aircraft*

August smells of fish and creosote, sun-warmed and oily. People wrinkle their noses at the stink, but I like it. It's the smell of boats returning. I've got my lucky Minnie Mouse beach towel, a can of Diet Pepsi, and my transistor radio. I've got the binder I started when I was six with "Homecomings" written on the cover inside a border of blue stars. Nine years. Nine fishing seasons in Alaska. Trollers in one column, purse seiners in another, writing in my best cursive all their clever, sentimental names, even though the only one I really care about is the *Lady Rose*, the beautiful red troller Dad named after me.

The west end of the Port Dock offers me a clear view of the channel. I kick off my flip-flops, spread my towel over the bull rail, and sit straddling it, my right leg dangling over the water. It's early, but the families have already started to gather. There's Mrs. Baldwin in her wheelchair being pushed by her grandson. And Mrs. Thompson, who usually spots the first fishing boats through the binoculars she keeps on her windowsill. The pregnant clerk at Tradewell is here with her little boy. And there's my old Sunday school teacher, Mrs. Ward, with her daughter-in-law. Some kids are playing tag. I'm not sure who they belong to.

Mrs. Ward waves hello and walks over, casting me in her ample shade. She cradles a big bunch of flowers—carnations, I think. Should I warn her that flowers are bad luck? Or maybe that's just flowers in the water. She's probably okay.

"Is your father coming in today?" she asks.

"No, not yet. Maybe this weekend."

"Bet you're counting the minutes." My grin must give me away because she laughs. "How's your mother doing? I haven't seen her in a while."

My mother is probably still in her bathrobe, but I don't tell her that. "She's fine . . . ready for the season to be over."

Mrs. Ward cups her mouth with her free hand and leans in as if to tell me a secret. "The only thing harder than living with a fisherman is living without him."

I giggle at that. "Pretty flowers," I tell her, but her attention has shifted to Mrs. Thompson, who comes over to chat. The two women walk off together and I'm free to switch on my radio. Before I do, though, I make up a test. If the first song I hear is happy, I'll see Dad this week. If it's sad, it'll be longer. From Ketchikan, Alaska, to Annisport, Washington, is three to five days, including fuel stops. Dad called Tuesday night, and today is Thursday, so he'll probably get in this weekend. Tonight he's supposed to call again and tell us where he is.

I turn my radio on and get what I think is a song, until I hear *Things go better with Coca-Cola.* Damn. I hate it when they fool you. I have to wait through advertisements for Doublemint Gum and Rice-A-Roni and finally a station-identification before I hear a familiar big-band intro and the Beatles singing, "Love, love, love." Nine loves. I've counted. I close my eyes and sing along, trying to send Dad all the love I can. Then I pop open my Pepsi—take that, Coca-Cola!—and turn to a fresh page in my notebook. At the top, I write August 17, 1967.

I look up just in time to see Mrs. Ward and Mrs. Thompson taking turns glancing back at me—this plump and desperate girl who obviously has nothing better to do with her last precious days of summer. What they don't know is that summer is purgatory when you're an only child stuck with a moody mom. Talk about desperate. The year I was born, she spiked Dad's dinner with powdered milk because she'd had a "death dream" about him. He got so sick he had to postpone his departure for Alaska by a whole week. I don't know how my grandparents found out. Maybe Mom felt so bad she confessed. But they weren't sympathetic at all.

Thank heaven I came along because I brought everyone together in a way that only a baby can. Now Grandpa Bill and my uncles laugh about the "Lac Attack," though Grandma still hasn't completely forgiven my mother. That's according to my cousin, Dena, who knows everything.

I flip back to the first page in my notebook. *GRACE*, the purse seiner my uncles named after my grandma, is written in big, blocky letters on the back of the grocery receipt Mom gave me out of her purse. The scrap is starting to lift away from the notebook paper I pasted it on. I press it down and turn the page, reading back through boats named for luck and strength and ladies.

Logging the names started as a way to kill time while I waited for Dad. Now it feels like an important ritual, a reverse blessing of the fleet. Dad understands. He's the one who taught me all the nautical sayings and superstitions, including the "red sky" saying everyone knows. "Never leave port on a Friday." That's another one. And women are bad luck unless they're gracing the bow as a figurehead. A boat is always a she, never a he, because captains love their ships more than the sweethearts they leave behind. Dad denies feeling that way about the *Lady Rose*, but I have to wonder when he seems so excited to get going each spring.

He says naming the boat after me is an honor. Mom says it's yet another example of guilt talking because he's away so long. Either way, I feel an almost human love for the *Lady Rose* and all the other lady boats, with their pretty names:

Miss Sharon
Lizzy Mae
Ma Cherie
Little Queen
Rebecca

I'm not sure why Dad chose my middle name instead of my first. I guess Rose sounded better to him than Ida, which is Mom's favorite girl name. She says she got to name me because Dad saddled us with the last name Petrovich, which in Croatian means "son of Peter." I don't know if there's a surname ending for "daughter of." I'll have to remember to ask Dad about that when he gets home.

The channel sparkles with little waves that turn into a thin band of light at the horizon. Past where I can see, the water widens into Rosario Strait, which connects to the Strait of Juan de Fuca, which then leads to a rugged and stormy stretch of Northwest coastline known as the Graveyard of the Pacific. Dad won't be out there. He'll be on the protected east side of Vancouver Island, coming home early so we have some summer together before I start high school. The purse seine fishermen, including my Uncle Alex, are still up in Alaska, scooping up the salmon that are returning to the rivers to spawn.

"Easy over-fishing," Dad calls it, which always makes me think of eggs. If my uncles are over easy, Dad's scrambled, because he fishes out in the open ocean, where the weather and waves toss him around like a cork. It's dangerous out there, but the payoff, he says, is a hold full of the most beautiful fish you ever saw. He's shown me pictures of kings, the biggest and most prized salmon. He once caught and lost a fish that he said weighed well over a hundred pounds, more than I did at the time.

"Now your spring salmon has a choice," he'll say. "He can bite on your line or not. The purse seine fishing your uncles do is different. They circle a net around a run of homebound salmon and trap them. The poor things get all bruised and battered thrashing against each other in the net. That's no way to treat a fish."

He'll go on and on about the virtues of trolling versus net fishing even though it's a lost cause. All Slav fishermen are purse seiners and proud of it. How did that Thanksgiving argument start? I don't remember, but Dad must have had just enough dandelion wine to accuse all net fishermen, including my uncles, of being too greedy. "We have families to support, not to mention get back to," Uncle Pat shot back. He accused Dad of "playing cowboy" with his own life, which made Dad so mad he slammed his fist on the table, spilling his wine.

The wind shifts and I'm hit by a strong, spicy smell. Tabu. The only perfume I know that can compete with fish and win, which is probably why Mom wears it.

"I thought I'd find you here."

I turn to find her standing behind me. She's all dolled up—navy blue dress, gold pin in the shape of a clam shell, and bright red lips that bring out the strawberry-blond curls peeking out from the edges of her white chiffon scarf. Most of the other women here are wearing housedresses or pants with simple tops. Except for the scarf around her head, Mom could be working the perfume counter at Frederick & Nelson. And that can only mean one thing.

"Is Dad coming in?" As soon as I ask the question, I realize the impossibility. He's still at least a day away.

"No, but the Mackeys are."

Behind her, Mrs. Mackey raises her hand from the shoulder of her younger son to wave hello. I wave back, and my insides, which have been perfectly calm all morning, do a somersault. She looks so much like David, the boy I've been in love with for three years running. I knew I'd get to see him when he returned from fishing with his dad. I just didn't think it'd be this soon. I'm still summer-sloppy, with grimy clothes and unwashed hair, a lovely combination of greasy roots and frizzy curls.

"Do I have time to run home and take a shower?"

"I don't think so." Mom looks over my head toward the channel. I whip my head around. In the distance, I can just make out three trollers by the sun glinting off their outrigger poles.

Mrs. Thompson, peering through her binoculars, bellows this news to those gathered on the dock. All at once I'm surrounded by mothers, wives, and kids straining to see. The kids sit in front of me on the bull rail, partially blocking my view—not that there's much to look at yet.

When the boats get closer, Mrs. Thompson announces them: *Fin's Folly*, *Oceana*, and the *Jumpin' J*. My heart races when I hear *Jumpin' J*. That's the Mackey boat. I take a deep breath, trying to calm my nerves enough to write down the names. Then I close my notebook and look for a way to escape. Mom's talking to Mrs. Mackey, who's underdressed by comparison in jeans and a gingham shirt. And *she's* the one who's actually meeting family. Whatever they're talking about must be funny, judging from Mrs. Mackey's smirk. Could Mom be telling her that I'm in love with her son? Suddenly I'm conscious of my oily, frizzy hair, my notebook of lists, and my radio playing a Dippity-Do commercial. Could I be any more of a square if I tried?

As they approach the dock, the boats honk like a trio of very loud geese, drowning out the sounds of my radio. And there's David at the rail of the *Jumpin' J*, looking tanned and handsome and . . . oh my God, is that a mustache? He's seen me. I flutter my fingers at him in what I hope is a sophisticated wave. I think he's waving back until I see his mom and younger brother behind me wind-milling their arms. There's no escaping now.

God, I wish I'd showered. Of course, he'll be reeking of fish.

They all do when they come back, but no one cares. After four months of separation, Mrs. Mackey will attack her son and husband with hugs and kisses even as she checks to make sure they have all their fingers. Then it'll be, "How'd you do?" and "What price did you get?" and maybe even, "Did you beat so-and-so?" When I was younger, I had a hard time understanding how fishermen could be so competitive and chummy at the same time. Many of the troll fishermen, including Dad, fish alone, but they're always talking to each other on the radio. When they come home, they'll often come in pairs or groups of three. The purse seiners are even more clannish, coming in as a fleet to much fanfare. There's still a dent in the dock where the captain of the *Liberty* rammed it. Dad said he shouldn't have been showing off. All that wood crushing and splintering sure got everyone's attention, though.

The three boats come in slow and steady, barely making a ripple in the water. I turn around to follow them, knocking my empty Pepsi can into the water. Sheesh. Hope no one saw that. The *Jumpin' J* slides alongside us, goes into reverse, and nudges up to the rail. I have the thrill of watching David step onto the dock. His arm bulges as he secures the line. He's all muscle, not an ounce of fat left on him, which makes me more conscious of my own. Twiggy I'm not. I tug on the legs of my cut-offs before giving up and placing my beach bag strategically over my lap.

The Mackeys are having their hug fest. Mustn't stare. Look at the other boats tying up, the other families, the wheels of Mrs. Baldwin's wheelchair bumping over the planks of the dock. But David is facing me. Is it possible for someone's eyes to get bluer? They seem to hold the entire sky and then some. Blue is recessive. But then, so is green, I think. We learned that in science class. Maybe our children will have blue-green—

"Hi, Ida."

"David. I didn't see you . . . um, so, how was fishing?"

"Tough."

"Really?"

His left shoe has a hole in the toe and his pants are covered in fish scales, but his T-shirt is clean, and very white against his brown skin. Close up, I notice the start of a beard in addition to the mustache. His lips are sun-chapped. That's okay. I still want to kiss them. He's saying something about fish.

"What?"

"It was hard to find fish," he repeats. "And when we did, something was always going wrong with our gear."

"Well, congratulations on surviving."

He laughs. "Thanks. I think I'm going to sleep for three days."

I'd like to kiss you to sleep. You could sleep in my arms for as long as you like.

" . . . your summer?"

"What?"

"How was your summer?"

"Oh, you know, pretty boring. Not like yours."

He's got his mother's smirk under that shaggy mustache. "So, you're going into tenth, right?"

"Yep . . . Annisport High." As if it isn't obvious. We only have one high school.

"Well, I'll see you there." He turns back to his family and I let out my breath. I need to do something, anything, to work out my jitters, so I fiddle with my radio dial even though it's already tuned to my favorite station. After hitting some embarrassing mother-music stations, I switch it off and stick it back in my bag. Now I can't get out of here fast enough. I get up, put on my flip-flops, stuff my towel in my bag, and look for Mom.

Ugh. Just my luck, she's talking to David's dad, and it looks like they could go on for a while. I could slip away and head home. I came down here alone. But Mom would be mad if I left without telling her. So I walk up to them and stand there like a doofus. Fortunately, David has turned his attention to his younger brother, who's jabbing him and running away before circling back and doing it again. David just laughs. Aw, what a guy. He even plays with his brother.

Okay, mustn't stare.

Mr. Mackey's sunburned nose is peeling. "We don't call each other as much when we're heading home," he says to my mother. "There's not much left to talk about."

"Oh, I'm not worried," Mom says in a voice I know as forced cheer. She uses it around my grandparents. She turns away from Mr. Mackey. "Oh," she says to me. "Are you ready to leave?"

"Yeah, whenever."

She throws a *see-what-I-mean?* glance Mr. Mackey's way. Did she tell him about my crush too? God, now David's going to find out for sure.

Is it my imagination, or is there sympathy in Mrs. Mackey's eyes as we say our good-byes and congratulations?

"It won't be long now," she says to Mom. What? Until our children are married? Until we're in-laws?

"I hope," Mom says.

"Well, let us know. We'll come down to help you welcome him."

Duh, of course, they're talking about Dad. I've got to get my head out of the clouds.

"Thanks," Mom says. "Thanks so much."

I steal one last glance at David and his bluer-than-blue eyes and a zingy sensation ripples through my body, leaving a pleasing tickle.

"I was kind of thinking," Mom says after settling herself behind the wheel of our station wagon. "Would you like to get lunch at the A&W? I'm craving one of their root beer floats."

If I nodded my head any more enthusiastically I'd give myself whiplash. The A&W is perhaps the only thing that can get my mind off David. We turn down Commercial Avenue to go through the middle of town, passing under a street banner advertising the annual Summer Salts Festival.

"Oh God, that stupid festival," Mom says.

"Dad likes it."

"Well your dad's just a big kid."

"Yeah." When I was little, he got me over my fear of Salty, the salmon mascot, by making me "shake fins" with it. Up close, I could see through the black mesh in Salty's mouth that it was just a man in a gray foam-rubber suit.

"Salty looks more like a shark than a salmon," I say, which makes Mom laugh as she pulls into the A&W parking lot. The stalls still have those speaker boxes that let you place orders from your car, but Mom insists on sitting inside at a table. Her tolerance for fast food only goes so far.

We hardly ever eat out when Dad's gone because Mom likes to watch expenses and calories. But this small splurge has

become a tradition to celebrate the news of Dad's homecoming.
Mom orders her root beer float and a plain hamburger, no
cheese. I order a bacon burger with cheese, and she cringes a
little but doesn't say anything.

When we get our food, Mom spoons up a dainty amount
of the ice cream froth in her root beer. "Oh, my," she says,
closing her eyes. "That is *so* good."

"I wonder where he is right now." I take a big bite of my
bacon burger.

"I guess we'll find out tonight." Mom cuts her burger in
half with a plastic knife.

"Do you think he's through Johnstone Strait?"

"I don't have a crystal ball, honey. And don't talk with
your mouth full."

I swallow and think of that scene in the *Wizard of Oz*
when Dorothy is in the fortune-teller's tent and sees her
Auntie Em calling her name.

"I wish we did . . . have a crystal ball. Then we wouldn't
have to worry all the time."

"I don't know. I think I'm better off not knowing what
your father's up against."

Waves as high as the Majestic. That's Dad's description of
what happens when high winds meet high seas in the Gulf of
Alaska. The Majestic is Annisport's only hotel and its tallest
building. Three stories, with a cupola on top.

"So what were you talking to Mr. Mackey about?"

Mom blots her lips with a napkin. "Oh, the usual stuff."

"You said you weren't worried. Worried about what?"

She clears her throat. "I'd simply asked him if he'd heard
from your father."

"So, had he?"

She hesitates. "No, not since Tuesday, which is when he called us. I'm sure we'll hear from him tonight." Her voice has that bossy edge that means she's done explaining.

"Okay, I was just curious." I eat some more of my hamburger, making sure to swallow before I speak again. "David says it was hard to find fish."

"Hm, I'm not surprised. They've been catching less and less every year."

"And staying out longer," I add. "David says he's so tired he's going to sleep for three days."

Mom doesn't say anything, and I feel myself blush despite every effort not to.

"You've got quite the crush on him, don't you?"

I can't help my grin.

"He's cute. I have to admit." She sighs long and slow. "But you don't want to get involved with a fisherman, trust me." She wipes her hands with her napkin and leaves it crumpled on her plate. She digs her lipstick and compact out of her purse and applies a fresh coat of color. She rubs her lips together and checks them in the mirror.

"We really should do this more often, you and me." Her pretty coral mouth spreads wide and thin.

"Can you take me back to the dock?"

"Hm, I could really use your help getting the house ready," she says, shaking her head. "And you'll want to be there when Dad calls."

I know that he usually doesn't call until well after dinner, but something tells me that now is not the time to argue.

I wish we lived in one of the big houses on the ridge with a view of the channel. That way I could watch the boats through binoculars like Mrs. Thompson does. But our house is on the Slav side of town. Mom calls it "modest," which I think means it's unremarkable in every way except for her climbing rose bush, which, in early summer, looks like a pink polka-dot blob that's eaten half the fence. By now, though, most of the blooms have started to brown and fall apart. Dad has never seen Mom's pride and joy at its best.

We park behind his truck full of rusty boat parts, Mom going through her checklist of stuff that still needs to be cleaned, including my room. So that's where I start, while she goes to hers to change out of her too-dressy dress.

My room isn't that bad. Sure, there are clothes on the floor, but that makes it easier to tell what's dirty and what can be worn again. I figure I'm saving on laundry by wearing the same T-shirts, jeans, and cutoffs over and over. The only people I see during the summer are my cousins, and they don't care. I scoop up an armload—it smells of sweat and Coppertone—and carry it to the clothes hamper in the hallway. Three more trips and my floor is clean.

Now for my shelves. I wet one of my dirty socks and wipe around my collection of troll dolls and the big glass snow globe Dad brought back from Juneau with a mother polar bear and her three cubs inside. I dust around my books and put back the copy of *Moby Dick* I started in June. It's been buried under my clothes for weeks. Someday.

When I get to my dresser, I take the sock off my hand

and look in the mirror at a face too fleshy to be pretty and hair too frizzy to stay down. It frames my head like a Christmas tree. Dad has the same thick, dark hair, but short, of course. In the one family photo I've tucked into my mirror, the resemblance between us is obvious—same hair, same longish nose, same tall, broad body, except his is muscled from hard work. The three of us stand on the Port Dock. Dad has his arm around my shoulders. Mom's on my other side, arm around my waist. Next to my tan, Mom's pale Irish skin looks almost ghostly. She's pretty, in a delicate way. Dad used to call her his blue fairy because he thought she looked like the character in *Pinocchio*. I don't know about that, but the only thing I seem to have inherited from her are my green eyes.

Dad's eyes are brown. Warm. I take the photo out from the mirror and pinch a little slit on the edge between Mom's head and mine. Working my way down, I tear her part of the photo off so it's just the two of us, me and Dad. I slip the two-thirds photo under my pillow and lie down on my unmade bed.

The clock on my nightstand says it's only a quarter past one. I thought it was later. Six more hours till we hear from him. Then what? Two days? Maybe three? What's three days when I've already waited four months?

"Love you, Dad. Please hurry." I say the words out loud, hoping, through some miracle, that he can hear them. If telepaths can bend spoons with their thoughts, then maybe, if I concentrate really hard, I can help pull the *Lady Rose* home.

AT seven o'clock I take a seat next to the telephone and watch Mom wait without obviously waiting. She putters around doing other things—wiping down counters, pushing in chairs, watering the plants. When seven thirty ticks by and he still hasn't called, she sits down across from me and straightens the pile of magazines covering the state of Washington. Our coffee table, with a map of Dad's route to Alaska preserved under a thick coating of clear plastic, was his gift to Mom after they were married. My finger makes a long, greasy smear as I try to feel where along that twisty waterway he might be.

"He's late tonight," Mom says.

I grab the deck of cards that's next to the phone for just this purpose. "Want to play some five-card draw?" We don't call it poker because we don't play for chips.

Mom sighs. "Sure."

Dad taught me how to shuffle, and I do it three times before dealing our cards. I get a pair of kings and discard three. Mom discards four.

"Pair of fives," she says placing her hand down.

"Two kings."

We play for an hour, me winning most of the hands because Mom's heart isn't really in it. Outside, it's starting to get dark. The sun is setting earlier every day as we head toward fall.

"I'm done," Mom says putting down her cards and picking up one of the magazines she straightened earlier.

At ten o'clock, she gets up to go to bed. "He'll probably call once I've fallen asleep. You should get to bed, too. Readjust your clock for school."

I nod. "In a bit. I'm going to have a little snack."

She shoots me a little look of disapproval but doesn't say what I know she's thinking—that I shouldn't eat before bed if I really want to lose weight. She must realize that tonight we have more important things to worry about.

I fix myself a PBJ with extra jelly and pour myself a glass of milk. If Dad were here, he'd have one, too—he loves PBJs—but I don't know how he can eat them without milk. "Simple," he says. "I'd rather not get sick, thank you." I think of all the wonderful things he's missed out on—cheese, ice cream, whipped cream, gravy—and thank God I didn't inherit his lactose intolerance, if such a thing can be inherited.

I finish my sandwich, put my glass in the sink with the dirty knife, and head upstairs. If Mom were still up, she'd remind me to brush my teeth. Since she's not, I go straight to my room. It's 10:13.

THE mast is as big around as a tree. I try to hold on as my boat gets tossed by the waves. A bell buoy rings, warning me that I'm too close to the rocks. But I can't let go. And I can't steer. The bell keeps ringing to warn me, taking on a shrill tone, like a fire alarm.

That's no bell. It's the telephone in Mom and Dad's room. He's calling. I roll out of bed and run to answer it, but Mom's already there. I find her sitting on the edge of the bed in her nightgown.

"Okay," she says into the receiver. Her voice is soft and slow. Then her face goes slack and she drops the receiver to the floor. It lands with a thud. She collapses next to the bed. My stomach flutters—softly at first, then in a rush, like a flock of panicked birds. They fly into my lungs, those birds, threatening to choke me as I ask the question: "What happened?"

"Dad's not answering his radio. They've called a search." Her chin quivers. She picks up the receiver and throws it. "God damn it!" It clangs against the hardwood floor, just missing my feet. I pick up the receiver and return it to its cradle on Mom's nightstand. She starts to cry.

I'm frozen. This isn't real. I'm still dreaming. I'm not conscious of forming the words, the same words Mom has used with me when I've cried, words I don't really believe, but I hear myself speak: "It'll be okay."

She leans over and strokes the top of my bare foot. I slide down next to her. My blood whooshes in my ears and the birds beat themselves silly in my stomach. I don't move.

I don't know how long we sit like that, but it's long enough for the soft shadows of morning to turn sharp.

I was five when Dad gave me my first boating safety lesson. We were listening to the strange language coming over the ship-to-shore radio, and I asked him what a "vessel" was. "Pretty much anything that floats," he said, launching into an explanation of the CB. After that, I could expect a quiz whenever I came aboard.

"Okay, what do you say on the radio if you need help?"

"Mayday! Mayday!"

He'd always plug his ears in anticipation of my high-pitched shouting. It was a routine we had: him plugging his ears, me yelling way too loud, using comedy to lighten up a serious subject. He wanted me to be prepared but not worried. It worked. I came to think of *Mayday* as an all-powerful word unlocked by the magic of a silver box.

Dad never sent out a Mayday.

CHAPTER 2

All Hands
*Entire ship's company, both officers
and enlisted personnel*

My family and Dad's trolling buddies, whose homecomings I missed, pace the floors of our house drinking coffee and smoking cigarettes. The Mackeys are here, but no David. This is an adults-only gathering. I probably wouldn't be allowed if I didn't live here.

Sitting at a kitchen table full of snacks people brought, I don't eat. The hollowness inside me can't be filled with food. Or reading. *Moby Dick* rests, unopened, in my lap. Mom's in the living room, sitting next to the phone with Grandpa Bill and Grandma Grace. They seem to be shielding her from a stiff wind. On any other day I'd be amazed by this show of closeness, but today we're all united in worry. Not that anyone's being obvious about it. My relatives hug me and ask about school starting, as if I would be thinking about that right now. They don't say anything about Dad. They know how these stories usually end. As someone who's grown up in a fishing town, I do too. But I refuse to give up. As long as he's still missing, there's hope.

All this sympathy food concerns me, though. When the freezer in our refrigerator can hold no more, Aunt Janet hands me a couple of casseroles wrapped in grocery sacks and asks me to put them in the spare ice box in the basement.

The stairs creak as I make my way down into what Mom calls "Dad's Lair" because he'll spend hours down here in the winter making his nautical-themed creations. He has a vast collection of knick-knacks—ropes, lures, maps, old coins, and stuff—that he "floats" in plastic tabletops, trays, and coasters. I never come down here in the summer. There's no reason to. He's gone and his workshop is cleaned up and closed for the season, the smell of curing epoxy replaced by a musty staleness.

What if they don't find him? What if he doesn't come back?

I can't think like that. He *will* be found. He *will* come back.

My shadow breaks the squares of light thrown by the windows. The freezer box is in the corner, next to the sinks and the washing machine. I open the lid and place the donated food on top of the packages of frozen fish left over from Dad's last fishing trip in Puget Sound. The lid makes a hollow *whump* as it closes. As I turn to leave I see something stir out of the corner of my eye, but when I look back the only thing moving is a swirl of dust motes. I take the stairs two at a time and burst out of the dim into the brightness of a sunlit kitchen.

"Whoa, there!" Uncle Pat grabs me by the shoulders, steadying me. "Good thing my coffee cup was empty." He walks over to the stove, picks up the still-percolating pot, and pours himself a fresh cup.

"You and Dena will be in the same school again," he says. "She's going to be graduating." He whistles through his teeth. "Seems like last week you two were babies. Where'd the time go?"

I don't think he means for me to answer. I shrug and smile.

"Listen." He leans in, the lines around his mouth turning down. "No matter what happens, your mother's going to need lots of help getting through this. You know you can call on us any time, day or night."

I nod even though I can't imagine a reason to call someone in the middle of the night.

"Good girl." He pats my shoulder and leaves to join the other adults in the living room. No one seems to be eating the food.

THE telephone rings three times that day. Each time, everybody stops talking and hangs on Mom's timid "Hello?" They try to read her expression as she listens to the voice on the other end. It could be the marine operator calling with news. But each time all Mom says is, "Okay, thank you," because the only news is that they still haven't found anything despite the widening search for my dad.

THE following evening, the fishermen's wives hold a candle-light vigil on the Port Dock. Mom can't bring herself to attend, but everyone else goes, including all five of my cousins. Gregory and Jonathan, Uncle Alex's boys, are too young to really appreciate the gravity of the situation, but they're here because they love Dad. All my cousins do. He's the fun uncle who plays Santa every Christmas and doesn't mind making the more than two-hour drive south to Seattle for a matinee. If he were part of our sad procession down to the waterfront, he'd try to lighten the mood with a funny story or a comment to remind everyone how lucky we are to be alive. He'd definitely stop to appreciate this sky, glowing pink as the sun slips behind a bank of purple clouds.

Red sky at night, sailor's delight.

But Dad's not here, so no one says anything about the sunset or anything else, not even Dougie, my motor-mouth middle cousin. I walk with his sister, Dena, behind Uncle Pat, who leads the way, suit tails flapping in the wind. The air smells faintly of wood smoke, the first sign of fall.

At the dock, we're each handed a candle in a Dixie cup and a mimeographed copy of a poem with a picture of Dad on the *Lady Rose* under his full name, "Stephen James Petrovich," as if he's dead, though in the picture he looks so alive. He's wearing his lucky sweater and grinning like he couldn't be happier. Seeing that smile just makes me hurt. So does the size of this crowd. Even the mayor of Annisport is here, standing, because there aren't enough folded chairs. I get the seat of honor, center front, between Aunt Janet and Dena. What I'd give to be someone on the fringe, a friend of a friend.

I spot something red at my feet; I bend down and pick up

a carnation that must have fallen off of Mrs. Ward's bouquet. I sniff its sweet scent and let the flower drop through my fingers. The sun slips below the horizon as Father O'Neal takes his place facing us, his back to the water. It's strange seeing him out of church, but he actually appears holier against this bruised sky, his robes rippling in the wind. His eyes scan the crowd, landing first on me, then on the other members of our family. If he's asking himself where my mother is, it's not obvious. He says a few words about my dad and God and His love, leads us in the Lord's Prayer, then directs us to the poem on the sheet we were given. Turns out, it's a hymn to be sung. I've never heard it before so I try to follow along as best I can. Most of it doesn't make much sense, but there's a repeated line I kind of like: *O hear us when we cry to thee, for those in peril on the sea.*

With no houses or roofs to contain them, our voices fly straight and true up to God, who has to know where my father is. The hymn starts people sniffling. Aunt Janet takes out a package of tissues and hands me one. I crumple it in my fist. *Dad come home. Dad come home. Dad come home.*

A wail from a woman behind me makes me stop my silent prayer and turn around. She must be one of the fishermen's wives. I'd probably recognize her if her face wasn't buried in a handkerchief. Dena glances back too. She gives me a private eye roll and grabs one of my hands in hers. Her fingernails were painted red at one time, but almost all of the polish has chipped off.

The stars come out as we walk home. There's no moon. I find the Big Dipper and draw a line to the North Star like Dad taught me to do. The same combination of stars is on the

Alaska state flag, which Dad says was designed by a thirteen-year-old Aleut boy.

When I turned fifteen June 20, Dad had been gone almost two months.

Before he left, he kissed my forehead. "Happy almost-birthday, Ida Rose," he said.

The weather was beautiful that day, clear and calm, and all the fishermen were in good spirits as they made their predictions from the decks of their freshly painted boats. With their outrigger poles in the upright position, trollers remind me of scrunched up daddy long-legs spiders. It's like they want nothing more than to stretch out and get to work. I suspect the fishermen feel the same way when they leave Annisport each spring.

The last time I saw Dad, he was waving from the wheelhouse of the *Lady Rose*, his "good-bye" lost in a blast of boat whistles. He and the other trollers left the marina as a fleet, carving white Vs in the water as they picked up speed down the channel. The families watched them until they disappeared and all that was left were lapping waves and the smell of diesel.

I'VE ridden on the *Lady Rose* many times, taking that same route to the west, going far enough for Dad to tell me some interesting bits of maritime history or a new folktale. He loves the Native Alaskan myths, with their wild explanations of how things in nature came to be.

I was little enough to fit on his lap, even with a bulky life preserver, the first time he told me how Raven brought light to the world. We'd gone out on the *Lady Rose*, just me and him on a clear September night after he came home. His clothes smelled of tobacco and brine, and his words vibrated in my ears.

"Raven was a sly, crafty fellow who used trickery to get what he wanted, and he wanted that box of stars."

I asked him lots of impossible questions that night. *Did Raven know God? How'd all the stars fit into a box? Why doesn't the North Star move?* I kept asking him questions, not to hear the answers so much as the happy sound of his voice when he talked about the things he loved.

CHAPTER 3

Adrift

A loose boat that's at the mercy of
the wind and current

Today—August 23, only five days after Dad was reported missing—the Coast Guard called off its search. Dad is *presumed drowned*. A Foss tug returning from a fuel run to Alaska reported an oil slick west of the Dixon Entrance, his last known location, but that was all. There was no body, no boat, no pieces, nothing.

That word *presumed* bothers me, but not as much as *drowned*. *Drowned* can only mean one thing: he suffered. First the cold, like a thousand electric shocks, then the struggle to keep your head above the waves and the horror of knowing you can't. I bury my face in my pillow, cutting off my air. *One Mississippi, two Mississippi . . .* At twenty-eight Mississippi, I gasp for breath. What was he thinking as he went under? Did he pray for himself? Did he pray for Mom and me?

People have started coming to the house again, but not

all at once. They come in twos and threes, to comfort and be comforted. One lady who says she knew Dad in high school gets so blubbery talking about him that Aunt Janet has to hug her for five minutes. After she leaves, my aunt tells my uncle to take over so she can go to the bathroom to "freshen up." Pat walks in from the kitchen, grumbling and rubbing his lined forehead.

Mom doesn't come out of her room, so it's hard to know what she's thinking. Is she cursing the Coast Guard like I am? Is she wondering how they could just give up? Five days is nothing. In all that water, you could easily miss a small boat . . . or a man. Oh, God, what if he was floating around in a life preserver waiting to be rescued? How long could he have lasted before dying of exposure? I try to stop the awful thoughts by squeezing Boo, the giant stuffed bear Dad got me when I was smaller than his gift. The dusty smell of Boo's fake fur pulls up my tears, and I cry into his soft middle until I can't cry any more.

I dream of dark water. It pitches and churns as it collects into a huge funnel, running down, down, taking everything. The dock, the boats—

I wake up with a start and pinch myself, hard, just to make sure I'm still here. Then comes the second shock: my father really is gone, not down a giant funnel, but gone. The jolt of that truth steals my breath. I gasp and roll over, curling into myself. My chest feels as if it's been hollowed out, leaving a sharp pit at its center. Is this what it's like to have a broken heart? It's not really broken; it keeps right on beating. But each beat hurts, really hurts, like pounding on a bruise.

The sudden roar of our Hoover vacuum cleaner rips me

from my quiet cocoon. It fills the house like a swarm of angry bees, back and forth, back and forth. I throw off my covers to find that I never changed out of my shirt and jeans. Downstairs, Mom's going over the living room carpet with herky-jerky strokes that threaten to suck up the corners of her long bathrobe. She sees me and turns off the machine, but the noise still echoes.

I have my cereal in the kitchen and head back upstairs, only to lie down again. This becomes a pattern. Bed, bathroom, snack. Bed, bathroom, snack. And dreams. Awful, watery dreams. Mom is like a passing shadow, her slippers *shush-shushing* across the floor like she's too tired to lift her feet.

IT'S been about a week since they called off the search, and today Mom goes on a cleaning binge. I walk past her room—it's just her room now—and she's in there, throwing Dad's clothes on the bed. Some of hers as well. Soon there's a mountain of discards ready for the Salvation Army.

"I should have done this years ago," she says.

Years ago, you still had a husband and I still had a father. I think it but don't say it.

Mom reties the belt of her robe and pushes her hair out of her eyes before diving into the closet again. I take a seat on the edge of the bed next to a green satin dress, still on its hanger, its form-fitting shape collapsed on the heap.

"This is pretty," I say to her stooped backside.

"The green dress? I got that for my eighteenth birthday," she says without turning around. "There were still ballrooms then." From the guts of her closet, she tosses out a black satin circle skirt. It slides off the bed and onto the floor. "I hear the Acropolis is a roller rink now."

"The Acropolis?"

"Where I met your father." She comes out hugging an armload of dress shoes—strappy and rhinestoned—and a single pair of clear plastic rain boots. She dumps them on the bed on top of the gown. Then she bends over to pick up the circle skirt and throw it back on the pile. As she turns toward me, her eyes travel vacantly to the ceiling. She cocks her head as if trying to make out a faint and distant tune, but the only sound I can hear is the cawing of a crow outside. "He sure could dance."

She breathes out heavily and turns back to the task at hand. "If that dress could talk . . . but I'm never going to wear it again."

NO speck of dirt is safe from Mom's wrath. My eyes tear from all the Pine-Sol she's using. I can't eat with that smell in my nose—not that I have much of an appetite. Mom isn't eating either. When she takes a bath, I worry that the warm water will wash away what's left of her. But she comes out whole, her wet hair combed back, the scent of Johnson's No More Tears competing with the smell of Pine-Sol. Pine-Sol always wins.

What will she do when she runs out of house? She's doing a lot more cleaning than we're doing dirtying. If Dad were here, he'd tell her to relax. "Perfection is the enemy of the good," he'd say. His calm was the cure for her nerves, the buffer for her temper. She'd still get mad at him for leaving his boots in the kitchen or his dishes on the table, but life was allowed to happen. We had meals that messed up the counters, board games and puzzles in the dining room. We had fires in the fireplace. Now our fireplace sits swept and empty next to a perfectly stacked pile of wood that appears to be just for show.

The too-clean house is just another sad reminder in my day. I'll be numbly going along, not really thinking about it, when the sight of Dad's empty chair at the dining room table punches me in the gut. I think I can't go on, but I do. Time somehow passes. I somehow stay alive—but it's not a good alive. I can't even lose myself in books. I read the same paragraph over and over. And television just makes me mad. Those kids on *American Bandstand*, don't they know what happened? Don't they care? I stare at my posters for *Mary Poppins* and *My Fair Lady* and the pattern of pink blossoms on my wallpaper. I stroke the long, fuzzy hair of my troll dolls; I arrange and rearrange my stuffed animals without making my bed. Sometimes I feel guilty for doing normal things, like eating. Then comes the next reminder that Dad's gone, the next shock, and it's a relief in a way. I never knew pain could be so comforting.

MOM and I would probably go on like this, existing but not living, were it not for school starting. The first day is Tuesday, and ready or not, I must go.

"You need shoes and school clothes. I think you've outgrown your old ones." Mom stands in the doorway of my room. Her hair is fixed and she's wearing lipstick, a lavender cotton blouse, and beige pedal-pushers. I even catch the familiar scent of Tabu.

Normally I'd be excited to make this shopping trip to Seattle, but it takes all my energy to change out of my grimy clothes and into clean ones. When I slide into the passenger side of our station wagon, I realize I'm sitting where Mom usually does. Now she's the driver, the only driver. Her narrow shoulders seem to sink with the responsibility. She turns to me, her expression pained, like her pants are too tight.

"I know I've been . . . absent," she says. "You deserve better. The truth is I can barely take care of myself right now. I know it's not much, but I'm yours today. Maybe we can have some fun."

I smile for her sake. "Okay." Maybe it will be okay. I'm willing to try.

She takes the scenic route along the waterfront. We pass the canneries and the shabby homes and dormitories where the workers live. Outside Pacific Packing, I see a group of women in gut-splattered aprons taking a cigarette break.

"*That*," Mom says, pointing, "is why you get a good education. You don't want to end up on the slime line."

But the women don't seem unhappy to me. Except for the cigarettes and aprons, they could be a group of girls talking at recess.

"I want to go to college," I say.

"Good. Don't waste that brain of yours." Mom drives up the hill towards a tree-lined bluff overlooking the harbor. On the edge of the drop-off is a ragged line of dwarf hemlocks. I call them "old man" trees because of their bent, wind-whipped backs. No one knows—not even Dena—about my secret place, my special tree. My heart tugs as the bluff recedes in the side-view mirror.

We pass the fancy view homes where the mayor lives, as well as a doctor or two. Midway down the street is Marine Heritage Park, which isn't so much a park as a fisherman's memorial surrounded by a circle of grass. On top of a pedestal, with names listed according to year, is a bronze statue of a mother and child. The woman holds a lantern, presumably to search the seas for her lost husband. The boy hangs on to the folds of his mother's skirt. She stands tall and strong, like she will carry on no matter what.

Reality isn't so noble. Reality is a closed bedroom door and a mother in her bathrobe, emptying closets. When will Dad's name be added to that pedestal? Does there need to be a body or a wreck so they know for sure? Do they add the names as they get them or wait until they have a few saved up? I remember visiting the memorial with my elementary school class. Around the base, the ground was littered with wilted wreaths and bouquets that had long since turned brown. Someone must have to pick them all up when the pile gets too big. What a depressing job. I think I'd rather work the slime line.

The harbor road connects with Main Street just before the spur that leads out of town. We're on the short end of an upside down L, going east for a while before turning south for the long, straight shot into civilization. Mom has the radio tuned to her station, which is playing "Theme from A Summer Place," a "pop favorite." Ugh. I'm so busy trying to close my ears that I forget to roll up the window. The smell of manure from the valley's dairy farms is with us until we get the sulfur smell of wood pulp in Everett. Then more farms.

The air clears by the time we reach the county line and pass the Krip's Eats sign. If Dad were driving, he'd ask if we wanted to stop for pie—fresh berry in summer, cream in winter, though he can't have the cream. I can see him now, one hand on the steering wheel, the other resting on the seat behind Mom's shoulders, driving just to drive. If there was something to see, like a field filled with snow geese or the rain-swollen Skagit River, he'd point it out. Aside from that stuff she calls music, Mom hates being distracted when she drives. In fact, she doesn't like to drive at all unless she has to. It seems selfish to mourn a future with fewer and less-fun car trips, but I do.

We pass the new Northgate Shopping Center north of Seattle. Everybody's talking about it, but Mom prefers to go downtown to the places she's always gone.

Our first stop is Nordstrom Best for shoes. I usually get saddle shoes one size up, which make my feet look enormous. But today, Mom asks if I want to look around for something different.

"What?" I'm not sure I've heard her right.

"Why don't you go pick out the nicest practical shoes you can find," she says in a voice hushed with drama.

It doesn't take me long to settle on a pair of shiny brown penny loafers. They cost a bit more than the saddle shoes, but Mom willingly hands over a twenty-dollar bill.

Those loafers give me hope as we walk to the Bon Marché. In the girls' department on the second floor, I see another mother and daughter flipping through a display of miniskirts.

Apparently, we're not the only ones to wait until the last minute. The girl looks familiar, but I can't remember her name. She sees me and lifts her hand, cupping her fingers in a shy wave. I give her a baby wave back.

"Can I try on some miniskirts?" I ask.

"You can try them on, but I'm not going to buy you one."

Mom heads to a rack of jumpers and pulls out one in plain navy blue. She also picks out a couple of skirts in dark neutral colors, along with some coordinating blouses and sweaters. I try them on, and, after a few exchanges to get the right sizes (her) and colors (me), we head to the counter with the two skirts, three blouses, two sweaters, one jumper, and four pairs of knee-high socks.

"What grade are you going into, young lady?" the saleslady asks as she starts ringing up our items.

"Tenth."

"They grow up so fast!" Her eyes peer at Mom over a pair of cat-eye glasses attached to a chain around her neck.

Mom doesn't respond. She's too busy digging through her purse.

"I could have sworn . . . ." A blush creeps up her neck. "I seem to have left my checkbook."

The saleslady waits with a frozen smile.

Embarrassed by Mom's embarrassment, I turn around to see the girl I sort of know coming to the counter with her mother carrying a stack of clothes bigger than ours. My mother pokes me in the shoulder to get my attention. In a half-whisper, she asks me which sweater I want because we can't get both.

"Hmm."

"Pick one, Ida, or I will."

"Okay, the green one, I guess."

The saleslady isn't smiling anymore. Her long pink fingernails clack as she pushes the buttons of her cash register. "Sixty-eight-ninety-four is your new total."

Mom doesn't respond. She's going through her wallet. The blush has reached her cheeks. The sound of someone sighing makes me turn around. The girl whose name I can't remember is standing there waiting. Her mother adjusts the pile of clothes on her arm.

"I'm sorry," Mom says. "We'll just get two of the blouses."

"Which two?" The saleslady taps a pink-nailed pointer finger on the counter.

"Which two, Ida?" Mom asks me, as if I need a translator.

They're all white so it hardly matters. I point to one of two long-sleeved blouses. "Take that one out," I say.

The saleslady goes through the button-pushing process once again. When she gives us a third total, I pray to God Mom has it. Dark crescents of sweat bloom under her arms on her sleeveless lavender blouse. That's when I know it's too soon, too soon to go out in public, too soon to deal with snotty sales ladies, too soon to jump back into what grownups like to call the rat race.

Please, please have the money. Mom takes out two twenties, a ten and five dollars in ones and change out of her wallet and gets back six cents in change. The saleslady folds my new clothes in tissue paper and, noticing that I'm already carrying a bag, asks if we'd like a shopping bag to put everything into.

"Yes, please," I say.

Her smile is back as she hands me a giant white bag that

says "Bon Marché" across the middle in bold black letters.
"Have a good school year," she says.

I say thanks but Mom just turns on her heels and brushes
past the mother standing behind us. The woman glares at her
before plopping her items down on the counter. Mom heads
for the escalator, leaving me to carry the heavy shopping bag.
Its handles dig into my right hand, and I have to switch sides
as I walk. I step on the escalator just as Mom's getting to the
bottom. I expect her to stop and wait when she gets off, but
she just checks to make sure I'm behind her and then keeps
on going. My anger rises with the pressure of that bag handle
slicing my fingers. The ground floor is more crowded, and I
actually have to try to keep her in my sights as we head for
the exit. By the time we're outside, I'm so mad I want to
throw my new clothes in the street and run away, maybe
hitchhike to California and become a hippie. See how Mom
likes that.

Oh my God! She's actually running to cross the street
before the light turns. I enter the crosswalk with others hur-
rying to get across. Then I stop. The light changes. One car
lurches forward and brakes a foot away from hitting me. The
driver beeps his horn, which starts a chorus of honking and
shouting. I ignore it.

"Ida!"

I don't move.

Mom runs over and grabs my arm. I shake off her grip
and hold my ground. People on the sidewalk have turned
around to watch. An old man shakes his head. But I don't
care if they all think I'm crazy.

I start walking again, but slowly, taking my time. When I

finally step onto the curb, the cars roll forward behind me. "Jesus, lady!" a driver yells as he drives past. Mom grabs me by the shoulders. I let the shopping bag drop to my side. The whites of her eyes have red veins running through them. Her glare says she would slap me if all these people weren't around, and part of me wishes she would. Her face is so red, it looks like it could explode.

I can't help it. I laugh.

"Don't you ever, ever pull a stunt like that again!" We stand toe to toe in the middle of the sidewalk, Mom's fingernails digging into my skin.

"What about you?" I shout back. "You just left me back there."

She says nothing as the fury drains from her face. She lets go of my shoulders and her own shoulders shudder like she's about to cry. "I'm sorry. I had to get out of there. This isn't working . . ."

I remember her vow to make things up to me, starting with the brown loafers. We might have had enough money if I'd settled for saddle shoes.

"It's okay," I tell her.

We both grab for the shopping bag at the same time. "Here," she says, fishing out the sack with my shoes. "You carry these. I'll get the rest."

My mind continues to sift through the afternoon as we walk to the car. I shouldn't have scared her like that. But then, she shouldn't have left me in the lurch. She *did* say she was sorry. I should apologize too, but something deep inside of me won't let me say the words.

CHAPTER 4

School

*A group of fish swimming in the
same direction*

In third grade, there was Marcie Horvat. In fifth, it was
Zach Ribarevic. They weren't really friends, but I played
kickball with Marcie and said hello to Zach in the halls of
Washington Junior High. After they lost their fathers in fishing accidents, I stopped talking to them. I didn't know what
to say, so I didn't say anything.

Now I'm that kid getting the sorrowful stares, but only a
few. Most of my schoolmates are too wrapped up in their
own nerves to pay me any mind. The heel of my left loafer
rubs as I walk through Annisport High's main entrance past
wall murals showing Indians and explorers and men sawing
through big cedar trees. "Welcome to the home of the Annisport Lumberjacks!" says a big banner over the doors to the
auditorium. This is where all the sophomores are supposed
to meet for an orientation.

I sit in the back middle section of seats, close enough to see but not so close that I'm sitting with the super-smart kids with their tight braids and stinky, Brylcreemed heads. Scattered as we are in pairs and small groups, everybody talking and craning their heads, our incoming class must be a pitiful sight for the adults on stage who have the job of teaching us.

I'm content to sit by myself, though I do see some friends I recognize. They're not close friends so I just wave. I don't go over. And they don't come to me, thank goodness. I don't want to have to talk about what happened to my dad and endure them feeling sorry for me. Maybe, if no one says anything, I can almost pretend it didn't happen.

Almost.

The screech of the microphone makes all heads turn to the stage, where a man in a black suit and thick, black-rimmed glasses stands at a podium. He introduces himself as our principal, Mr. Hargrove, and says he's proud to be welcoming the "class of 1970" to Annisport High School, which sounds momentous, it being a new decade and all. Behind him, sitting on either side are the tenth-grade teachers, the vice-principal, and the school nurse. He introduces each one, and we clap, then he talks about "our proud Annisport High School family" and its "tradition of excellence," and we clap some more.

The assembly takes about fifteen minutes. We get five minutes to find our first-period classes. Should we get lost, we can ask for help from one of the "student guides," seniors wearing felt vests in our school colors of green and gray.

I have US History first period. So do a couple of my friends from junior high school. Janet Brand is one of the super-smarts, but nice. And Shelly Ford was in my PE class last year. I became her friend for life when I gave her a dime for the Kotex machine. The three of us claim neighboring desks in the back corner on the window side just as the bell rings.

Our teacher, a squat older woman with a wide mouth like a frog, writes her name—Mrs. Holland—on the blackboard before taking the roll. Being a P-name, I'm always toward the end, along with the other Slavs, all of whose names start with late letters and end in "ich" or "ic."

After Hayley Zanich says "here," the door opens, and a girl in a green and gray vest walks in and hands Mrs. Holland a note.

"Ida Petrovich?" She looks straight at me like she already knows who I am.

"Here," I say again.

"You're to go to the principal's office."

THE girl's vest reflects off the floors of the empty halls I just walked. What could the principal possibly want from me? In my old school, being called to the principal's office meant you'd done something seriously bad. Even if I was the type of student who gets into trouble, which I'm not, I haven't been here long enough to do anything, right or wrong.

A secretary escorts me back. When he sees me, Mr. Hargrove stands up from the chair behind his desk, which is huge and covered with glass, and asks me to take a seat. My knees shake as I lower myself into a wooden chair with an indented seat for my butt. The man I just saw on stage sits back down, folds his arms in front of him, and looks me in the eyes.

"I was very sorry to hear about your father."

Oh. Now I understand why I'm here. "Thank you."

"You need to know that the loss you've experienced is about the biggest you can have in life, and you're just a teenager," he says. "You're probably feeling a jumble of emotions and a whole lot of sadness. And you're probably going to feel that way for a good long while. I'm not going to say 'until you get over it,' because I don't think anyone gets over the death of a parent. But you'll start to feel better after a while. I just want you to know that we're here for you if you need to talk to someone, so please don't be shy."

"Okay."

His face brightens. "Your mother says you like to read."

My mother talked to you? is what I want to say, but I just nod.

"That's great. That's just great. We have an excellent library." He pauses. "You have a relative here, don't you? Diana?"

"Dena. She's my cousin."

"Oh, yes, Dena Petrovich. Nice girl. She can help you get settled in. Welcome to high school, Ida. We're happy to have you. And remember, don't be shy."

Mr. Hargrove reaches for a small pad of pink permission slips. He scribbles his signature, tears off the slip, and hands it to me. "This will get you back to class."

He may give boring speeches, but Mr. Hargrove is a pretty nice man. Maybe high school won't be so bad.

WHEN I get back to class, Mrs. Holland stops talking and everyone turns. As I take my seat, I catch Shelly's sympathetic stare.

"Ida, we're discussing the question, 'What is history?'" Mrs. Holland says. "Bridget, would you care to repeat what you just said?"

"It's when important things happen," says a small girl with a cute upturned nose.

"And who decides what's important?" Mrs. Holland asks.

"President Johnson?" offers a boy with grease lines through his hair.

"Yes, certainly the President, but he's just one man. Who else?"

A girl named Connie reads the names on the cover of our new history textbook. "James Maxwell and Dean Cornish?" she asks hopefully.

"Well, okay." I can tell by Mrs. Holland's smirk that she's not getting the answer she wants.

I raise my hand. "What's important to one person may not be important to another person," I say. "Anyone can decide what's important, what's history. I mean it can be as small as, um, starting high school . . ."

Several kids laugh.

"Or as big as the Vietnam War," I continue. "President Kennedy getting shot."

Mrs. Holland's mouth spreads open in a silent "aah." "Do you agree or disagree?" She scans the room. Several hands shoot up. Soon we're debating what's important and whether or not anyone knows if something's important at the time. One girl, whose parents collect antiques, points out that everyday objects gain value over time, which prompts a boy in back to hold up his Pink Pearl eraser and say, "You mean a hundred years from now, this will be worth something?" More laughter, more hands. The bell rings, and the kids whose hands were up groan. As I pass Mrs. Holland she gives me a grin with that frog mouth of hers, and my lungs fill with the rich air of recognition.

I start to relax. In math, I actually catch myself yawning. Then comes lunch, and my self-consciousness pops up like a jack-in-the-box. So far no one but Mr. Hargrove has mentioned Dad, although everybody must know. Annisport's a small town, and it was all over the front page of the *Annisport American*. Dena showed me. There were our names in black and white: "Petrovich is survived by his wife, Christina, and daughter, Ida." Damn newspapers. I wish they wouldn't do that. I really don't want to go through high school as "the girl whose father presumably drowned."

Sorry, Dad, I know I'm being selfish worrying about such things. You know I'd do anything to have you back. I feel that sharp pit of sadness well up inside of me. There's nothing I can do to stop it. With my eyes full of tears and my tray full of food, I search the crowded cafeteria for a place to hide. No such luck. All the tables are filled or almost filled. Then I spot Dena. Or rather, she spots me. Only Dena would wave me over like I was a taxi cab to be hailed. And only Dena would wear a Day-Glo pink and orange dress and matching head-scarf the first day of school. Surrounding her are more conservatively dressed girls, all with sack lunches.

I blink away my tears, but there's no wiping them from my face with this tray in my hands. Dena's friends make room so I can sit across from my beautiful, older, and more popular cousin.

"Oh, dear," she says when she sees my face. She hands me a crumpled napkin that smells of bologna. I blot my eyes and cheeks, and feel something cool on my skin.

I expect more sympathy, but Dena starts to giggle. "You've, um." She points at a spot below her right eye. I wipe my fingers over the spot and come away with a glob of mayonnaise.

"Sorry about that," she says. "I didn't mean to give you a facial."

I giggle.

"Well, at least you're not crying anymore."

She introduces me around, but the only names I remember are the two girls sitting on either side of her—Sophie, a long-faced blonde with pale blue cat-eye glasses, and Gerry, short for Geraldine, a plump redhead. I take an immediate liking to Gerry when she asks me if I want my garlic bread.

"No," I say, "you can have it." As I hand it over I think about offering her the rest of my lunch, too, but decide against it. She may take it wrong.

Dena delicately unwraps a Twinkie with her hot pink fingernails, then leans forward and asks how I'm doing.

"Okay," I say. "I had to go to the principal's office." I get the raised eyebrows I expect from everyone but Dena. I didn't want to talk about my family, but now I have no choice. "He told me to ask for help if I need it."

Several of the girls nod. And one, who somehow missed the news, asks if I'm Special Ed. "I mean, it's okay if you are."

For her benefit, I fill everyone in. "My dad drowned in a

fishing accident last month. At least, that's what they think happened."

"So they're still not sure?" Gerry asks in between bites of my garlic bread.

I shake my head. "They didn't find anything."

"Wow," Sophie says.

Dena folds her plastic Twinkie wrapper. "Steve was my uncle, and a super-cool guy. It's been *so* hard. Ida's been *so* brave."

I'm not as brave as I'm trying to appear. God, am I really using my father's death to impress Dena's friends? My shame must show because she asks me if I'm going to cry again.

"No. I'm okay," I lie.

I finish the fruit cocktail but only manage a few bites of spaghetti before the bell rings. I give Gerry my milk. As I stand up to take my tray back, Dena stops me.

"I almost forgot to give you this." She takes a folded piece of paper from her math textbook and tucks it into the pocket of my blouse.

"What is it?"

"Don't get too excited," she says. "It's from Grandma."

"Thanks . . . I think."

Dena giggles and walks away, calling, "See ya later, alligator."

"After a while, crocodile," I answer, but she's already disappeared around the corner.

ON my way to my fourth-period class, I hear a familiar voice.

David.

He's standing next to his locker talking to a couple of buddies. The Mackeys must have been among the first non-family members to find out about Dad. What will he say to me? What do I say back? He turns around. I duck into a classroom and get a startled look from a teacher sitting at her desk eating lunch.

"Sorry," I mumble, backing out into the hall. I muster the nerve to say hello to David, but he's already walking away with his friends.

As I pass by the spot where he was just standing, I catch a whiff of something sugary, familiar. But it isn't David's lingering sweetness. It's just a girl sharing a box of Dots with her friends. They were Dad's favorite candy when we went into Seattle for Sunday matinees. He'd even eat my green ones. Oh, God, don't let me cry again.

THE second half of the day goes better than I expect, though I have PE. I get some sympathetic stares in the halls but I also reunite with two good friends from ninth grade: Alice Peters, who was always right ahead of me in the alphabet, and Kathy Simon, another big and tall girl. Alice is in my Home Economics class, and Kathy is in PE with me.

Kathy gives me a hug when we meet in the girls' gymnasium before class starts. "If you need a shoulder to cry on . . ."

I tell her thanks and fix my eyes on the lines bisecting the polished floor.

There's an awkward pause, then she says, "I'm sure glad we have PE last period. We won't have to shower or even change out of our gym clothes."

"And today we won't have to change *into* our gym clothes," I add, stating the obvious. None of us have them yet.

Our teacher, a tiny, unsmiling woman in grey sweats, tells us what to bring and gives us a hygiene lecture before distributing combination locks for the baskets where we will keep our things.

All in all, it's a remarkably easy first day, except for the now broken blister on my left heel where my shoe has been rubbing. I take the shoe off as soon as I sit down in the school bus, then I hobble with one shoe on and one shoe off for the block and a half between the bus stop and home.

"SO, how was it?" Mom sits at the dining room table, reading glasses on, shuffling through papers.

"Fine." I walk past her to the kitchen to make myself a couple of peanut butter and jelly sandwiches. Now that I'm home, I'm starving.

"Why are you limping?"

"Uh, I have a blister on my foot."

"Are those shoes going to be okay?"

"Yeah. I think so."

"Because I'm not getting you new ones."

I hear the bait in her voice. She wants me to argue with her, but I know better. As I make my sandwiches, her loud sighs vie for my attention. She wants a fight. Maybe she has been waiting for me to get home, her anger building. I sit down at the kitchen table to eat. When I'm done, I try to ignore her as I cross the dining room to get to the stairs, but she pounces before I can take the first step.

"Do you know what these are?" she asks, picking up the papers in front of her.

"No."

"No, of course you don't. These are *bills*, Ida." She throws them into the air. They flutter down around her and onto the floor. "You see, the city doesn't care whether your husband just died. They still want their money. And you know what? We don't have any."

"Not any?" That slipped out. I've just thrown a log on her fire.

She turns toward me, not bothering to pick up the fallen bills. "Let's see. We have this house, which Dad mortgaged to the hilt to buy the boat. We won't be able to get insurance to cover the loss because he isn't legally dead. He won't be legally"— she makes quote marks in the air—"dead for another seven years. Meanwhile, we have to pay for the water, the lights, and the garbage. Thank Heaven it's warm and there's no heating bill, because I don't know how we're going to pay the utilities *and* buy food, *and* clothes *and*, oh yes, shoes that don't fit!"

"They fit okay."

Her angry eyes fall to my loafers, which aren't so shiny anymore. They have creases where my foot bends, and the right toe has a scuff. There's a pause. She rubs the side of her head with the tips of her fingers. The bills remain scattered around her.

"What did you have for lunch?"

"Spaghetti. But I wasn't all that hungry." Now that we're off the subject of shoes, I think I'm in the clear. I'm wrong.

"I suppose you spent all the money I gave you even though you didn't eat."

"I ate some."

"I can't afford to buy you food you don't eat, Ida! I'm not sure I can afford the food you *do* eat." She holds her head in her hands and I hear the whimper of her crying. I'm beginning to hate that sound.

"Maybe I should just starve myself to death!" I run upstairs to my room and slam the door. Then I kick off my shoes and throw them at my closet. They bang against the door and drop to the floor. I hope Mom hears every thud. I pull my blouse over my head without undoing the buttons and hear something crinkle. Oh, yeah, the note from Grandma. I take the piece of paper out of the pocket and read, "ISAIAH 41:10 and 13 and CORINTHIANS 4:16-18. For the service. Love, Grandma Grace."

I set it down on my nightstand. A service, as in a funeral? I picture our family, all dressed in black, gathered around Dad's grave while Father O'Neal talks about how great and kind he was. But how can you have a grave for someone who's been lost at sea? Do they just put up a stone with nothing under it? Maybe that's why they have memorials for fishermen, to make up for the empty graves.

I'm still thinking about this when Mom brings my dinner up on a TV tray two hours later.

"Are we having a service for Dad?" I ask.

The meal is a peace offering. She's made my favorite: pork chops, Tater Tots, and applesauce. I sit up in bed and she places the tray across my lap.

"Why? Are people asking?"

"Yeah, Grandma." I point out the note on my bed stand. "Dena gave that to me at lunch."

She reads it and rolls her eyes. "Grandma hasn't said anything to me, but that's no surprise." She sighs. "Like I don't have enough to deal with."

I watch her tear up the note and toss the pieces in the trashcan by my dresser.

"I didn't see anything suggesting Bible verses. Did you?"

I don't say anything, but I kind of like being in on Mom's secret, for a change.

"Anyway, I came up to apologize." She moves my stuffed animals and sits down on my bed. "I don't mean to take my worries out on you. I'm just a little scared right now."

I suspect she's more than a little scared, otherwise she wouldn't admit to being scared at all.

"I know," I tell her. "Me too."

CHAPTER 5

Ballast

Heavy material placed in the hold of a vessel to provide stability

My shoes just took some breaking in. School is more comfortable now too. Well, except for the gymnastics unit we're doing in PE. Fortunately, I'm not the only klutz in there. Kathy couldn't do a handstand if her life depended on it.

My tragedy doesn't come up again, with her or with any of my other ninth-grade friends. Most of them seem to have overcome their fear of talking to me, and some have even joined Dena's orbit at lunch. I'm more than happy to let my cousin hold court while I eat my low-calorie sack lunches: carrot and celery sticks and sandwiches light on the mayo. I'm determined to lose weight, but I don't make a big deal of it around Gerry. Her face fell when she saw that I wasn't buying the school lunches anymore. Now she just sneers at my "rabbit food" and tells me I'm not fat.

I could kiss her for saying that. Speaking of wanting to

kiss people, I have yet to have a real conversation with
David, but I see him in the halls and we've exchanged hellos,
which is better than nothing.

"Does your nana get here soon?" Dena asks, checking her
painted nails for a chip. Today they are dark coral.

I nod since my mouth is full of sandwich and I don't want
to spit food. Mom's mom, who I call Nana, is coming this
Tuesday and will be staying with us through Thanksgiving. I
can count on seeing her once a year. Either we go to Montana or she comes here, but never for this long. This time we
get her for two whole months.

MOM calls her mother Kooky Kathleen, but even she seems
to realize that we need to bring some life back to the house.
Just preparing for Nana's visit has helped her mood. Today
when I get home, she actually hums as she prepares the spare
bedroom. I help her put fresh sheets on the mattress—white
with yellow roses to match the walls.

"Ida, get that corner would you?"

I pull the fitted sheet around the end so it's tight and
smooth. Then I help her fluff the pillows, shake out the gold
throw rug, and cut chrysanthemums from our garden for the
top of her dresser. When we're done, the room's so pretty I
want to move in myself.

I'M in school when Nana arrives. I come home to the sweet
smell of cinnamon and cloves, and Nana running in from the
kitchen wearing one of Mom's aprons and an oven mitt. Her

hair has changed color since I saw her last. It used to be light brown streaked with gray. Now it's orange.

She gives me a giant hug. "Let me look at you," she says, holding me out at arm's length. "What a beauty you're becoming!"

"Thanks." I hug her back and the smell of cloves hits me harder. My mother is stretched out on the couch with a book in her lap, looking more comfortable than she's been in weeks.

Nana and I talk about high school, miniskirts, and Lady Bird Johnson's wildflowers. She's going on about how we need more color in our lives when I smell something burning.

"Are you baking something?" I try to be delicate about it.

"Uh-oh." She rushes off to pull a tray of very dark brown cookies from the oven. "I thought you'd like an after-school snack." She flips the cookies upside down on a cooling rack and hands me three that aren't completely black on the bottom. "Charcoal's good for you. Absorbs gas."

I'm always so hungry after school that I'll eat almost anything, including things that aren't on my diet. Grandma's cookies are hard to bite into but the molasses taste isn't bad.

As I sit at the kitchen table eating, I can't help staring at her hair.

"It came out a little too brassy, even for my taste," she says. "Some things you shouldn't do yourself. Clairol Nice 'n Easy, my fanny."

I laugh.

"Oh, I brought you a belated birthday present. Have your mother show you what's in that cardboard box in the living room. It was too bulky to wrap."

The box sits on the floor next to the couch where Mom is reading. She watches with anticipation as I walk over and kneel down next to it. Inside are books. Most of them are old, slightly musty hardbacks, with embossed titles in silver and gold. I pull them out one by one. *Pride and Prejudice, The Scarlet Letter, Treasure Island, The Swiss Family Robinson, Little Women, Journey to the Center of the Earth,* and *The Railway Children.* There are also two new paperback books with funny names: *The Phantom Tollbooth* and *From the Mixed-Up Files of Mrs. Basil E. Frankweiler.*

Nana comes in from the kitchen, wiping her hands on her apron. "I was wondering what to give you now that you've outgrown trolls and stuffed animals, and your mom suggested her old books. To think those have been sitting in my attic all these years! Well, all except for the two new ones. The saleslady at the bookstore recommended them."

Mom hands me the book she's reading, *Jane Eyre.* "This is yours too," she says. "It was my favorite, but I loved them all."

I get up and give them each a hug. "Thank you."

"You're welcome," Mom says.

"That should keep you reading for at least a week," Nana adds.

I grin. "I'll try to make them last."

"You *are* your mother's daughter. I had to yank books out of her hands to get her to go outside. Not that I have any-thing against reading, mind you, but kids need to run around and get dirty."

"Oh, she does a fair amount of that too." Mom winks at me.

A small gesture, but that wink warms me to the core. I read. I run around. And I'm becoming a beauty. I don't really believe that last one, but I want to hug my grandmother for helping my mother see that I do have good qualities.

NOW I look forward to coming home, if only to discover what Nana's cooked up, whether it's slightly burned baked goods, thick soups full of mystery seasonings, or plates heaped with crackers and cheese and peanut butter and celery—protein for growth, celery for nerves. Mom doesn't mind. They make the perfect pair. One likes to cook but not clean. The other likes to clean but not cook. Between the two of them, the house feels lived in again.

The other day, I walked in the front door to find Nana using all our dining room chairs to untangle a big shopping bag of leftover yarn she brought. Each chair appeared to be wearing a thick, brightly colored woolen belt, and the effect was so cheerful I wanted her to leave them that way. But she had other plans. She hopes to make us an afghan before she leaves. "I'll have to knit like the wind," she said. I thought she was exaggerating, but she wasn't. Her needles move so lightning fast that I could stare at them for days and never figure out exactly what they're doing. So she gave me a lesson, slowing the process down into steps so I could see that knitting is just row upon row of interlocking loops. She even gave me my own yarn and needles so I can practice, but my hands are slow and awkward. And, anyway, I'd much rather watch her.

While Nana's cooking or working on the afghan, she listens to my mother. After weeks of mostly silence, the dam holding back Mom's emotions has given way, releasing a torrent of talk. They don't have these conversations in front of me. They go into the kitchen and close the swinging door behind them. But that door doesn't latch, so I can pretty much hear what Mom and Nana are saying if I stand with my ear cocked up to the line of light between the door and the frame. What I've learned from this eavesdropping is that, more than anything else, Mom is afraid. I'm afraid, too, but it's just a sensation of panic that comes and goes like fever spikes or hiccups. Mom's afraid of specific things, like bills and debt and the prospect of having to get a job to support us. She's afraid of me coming of age without a dad. She's afraid she's not up to being a working, single mother. And she's afraid of being alone.

"But you're not," Nana points out. "You have us." I can't make out Mom's response to that, but I can hear Nana loud and clear. "And you have Ida. Let her help out, share the burden. It will be good for both of you."

Listening to what I'm not supposed to hear, I learn that I have a powerful ally in my grandmother. Funny how understanding skips generations.

IT'S late on a Saturday night, and I just came downstairs for a glass of water only to find my way to the kitchen blocked. So I've taken up my usual position behind the door, ear to the opening. Mom and Nana are drinking wine, and Mom's making no attempt to keep her voice down.

"Ida doesn't know," she says. "She thought Steve walked on water."

"That's probably for the best," Nana says.

What's for the best? That I don't know? Or that I thought my dad walked on water?

"One more reason not to have a funeral," Mom says.

"Honestly, you think the women are going to come up and introduce themselves? Besides, there would be so many people there, it wouldn't matter."

"That's what his folks want. A big Catholic whoop-de-do! Well, I won't be pressured! They're nothing to me. They never liked me. To hell with 'em."

"They've lost a son, honey," Nana says.

Mom doesn't say anything to that.

"If not for them, then for Ida," Nana adds. "She needs to say good-bye to her father. It might be good for you, too."

I hear a cupboard bang, then footsteps.

"I can't." Mom's voice cracks. "I can't have a funeral when I'm not even sure he's dead."

What? Did I hear that right? She's not sure Dad is dead? Does that mean she thinks he's still alive?

I peer into the crack, waiting for her to say more. She's right next to the door, her body blocking the light. But she doesn't say more. She pushes. Hard.

A silver flash. The room goes white. I fall back. My face, I can't feel it. Something warm and salty runs into my mouth. I touch the wet. Blood.

Mom gasps and drops down next to me. "Grab a towel!" she yells to my grandmother. "And some ice!"

The trip to the car is a frenzied blur of words and arms and hands fluttering about me, holding me up, pushing me forward. My nose throbs under a cold and bloody tea towel. I nearly throw up as Mom and Nana ease me down onto the cold vinyl of the backseat. Nana folds her sweater for a pillow to keep my head propped up. Then she gets in the backseat with me and continues to hold the towel of ice to my nose while Mom drives.

At the hospital, we're led back to a curtained-off space with a bed and a sink and anatomy charts on the walls showing people front and back without skin. A young doctor shines a light in my eyes and tells me to follow his finger as he moves it from side to side and up and down. He examines my head and neck and has me tilt back so he can stick a tube up my nose and look inside. It hurts more than the little bit he says it will. Once he's satisfied that my head's okay and my nose took the brunt of it, he says there's not much he can do until the swelling comes down.

THE pain pills the doctor prescribed give me weird dreams. I am sifting through sand, trying to find Dad in the granules. Not a drop of water anywhere. When I wake up, my mouth is so dry that my tongue is a thing apart, the tongue of a shoe. In another dream, Dad's telling me a story about clams. I interrupt him to tell him he's supposed to be dead, and he just keeps talking. The dream is so real, I wake up thinking my waking life was the dream, that Dad never was lost or drowned. The delusion pops like a soap bubble, and I mourn all over again.

The next couple of days and nights melt together in a fuzzy half-sleep. The afternoons, when I should be in school, are the worst. I can't read my books because the pain pills make me too drowsy, so I watch soaps—*One Life to Live, All*

My Children—even though the characters are too dramatic to be believed.

Nana and Mom take turns bringing me ice to pack on my nose and moist, non-chewy, non-crunchy food to eat. Nana insists I eat lots of broccoli, which she cooks and mashes into a paste that makes me glad I can't taste anything. "It's high in vitamin C, great for healing." She also starts some home remedies for my bruising. After all that ice, I enjoy the hot washcloths she puts on my nose, but I'm not so keen on the soaked cabbage leaves and crushed parsley.

"You're getting the green-glop treatment," Mom says, making me laugh. It hurts to laugh. She looks at my nose without looking at me—the cotton tubes caked with blood that are sticking out of my nostrils, the red-purple bruise curling below both eyes. "I think the swelling's come down."

We go to our doctor to reset my nose. This time, when I'm told it might hurt, I brace myself. The pain makes my eyes water.

"Young bones heal quickly," he says. "But it was a bad break, so she'll have a slight crook in her nose."

Nana says it gives me character, which I guess is a good thing, but I'd rather not have it—the crook, that is. Mom feels so bad about the accident that she lets me use her makeup before going to school, but no amount of foundation can hide the rainbow of colors under my skin. Funny thing is, way more people come up and ask me about my nose than ever asked me about my father. Apparently, a hurt you can see is much easier to talk about than one you can't. I don't tell my friends what I was doing behind the door. I don't tell Mom, either, and she doesn't ask. She's probably hoping I didn't hear anything, or else that I'll forget what I heard. But I plan on asking her, when the time's right, why she thinks Dad might be alive.

CHAPTER 6

Heel
The lean of a vessel to one side or the other while maneuvering or sailing

It takes about two weeks for the bruises to fade away. Not so the memory.

Mom's in our basement defrosting the freezer box. Her ponytail wags from side to side as she chips away at the ice. On the floor beside her is a pile of frozen lumps, the last of the fish and all that sympathy food we've yet to eat.

"What is it, Ida?" she asks without turning around.

I walk around her so she can see me. Her skin is flushed and slightly puffy around the eyes from bending down, but her expression is open, not angry.

"You know when I broke my nose?"

"How could I forget?"

"Well, I heard you and Nana talking about Dad."

I wait for her to volunteer something, anything. She stands up but doesn't say anything.

"You said that he maybe isn't dead." There, it's out.

She bites her lip. One rubber-gloved hand balances on the edge of the freezer. "Ida . . . you've *got* to stop taking things so literally. That's not what I said or what I meant."

"But I heard you!"

A stray tendril of hair falls into her eyes. She fumbles with her rubber-covered fingers to get a hold of it and tuck it behind her ear. "I know you're grieving," she says. "So am I. But I think this is wishful thinking on your part."

Am I really hearing this? How can she pretend she didn't say what I clearly heard her say? How can she act like *I'm* the crazy one?

"It's *not* wishful thinking on my part! Maybe *yours*."

The slow shake of her head, her eyes, half-lowered in pity . . . the lie. Damn her!

"Why did you say it, then?" My voice rises. "Why?"

"Ida, stop. I know you want answers, but I don't have them. I may never have them. I'm sorry, but that's just the way it is."

"I'm not asking about Dad! I'm asking about *you*, why you said what you said."

"Said what?"

"Oh, my God!" *That. He. May. Be. Alive.*

Mom flinches, recovers, expression hardening. "Don't you yell at me!" she hisses through her teeth.

I scream, right in her face, before I dash up the stairs. Anywhere would be better than here.

A raw, gusty wind sweeps the last of yesterday's rain clouds from the sky. I walk headlong into it, relishing the sting on my skin. Good thing I packed a blanket.

I left without telling Mom where I was going. She'll be mad but I don't care.

I walk all the way over to the marina on the east side of town. I don't go to Dad's mooring on J dock. I don't think I could stand the sight of his empty berth. Instead, I just take in all the idle fishing boats, their sharp angles and pointy masts broken and bent in reflection on the water.

How many photos of Dad do we have with this scene in the background? There must be dozens, all from the deck of the *Lady Rose*. Departures and arrivals, both. In spring, he was always fresh-faced and humming as he tended to last-minute details. I never knew the names of the songs he hummed because he never sang the words, but I might recognize the melody if I heard one again.

Was there anything different about the morning he left for Alaska? I can be sure of certain things because they never changed. Like all fishermen, Dad had his good luck ritual. He would wear his red sweater because it matched the *Lady Rose's* red hull, and he'd put up the Croatian flag. He'd give two long toots of his horn to signal leaving port. Before all that, he'd hug and kiss "his girls" and tell me to take care of Mom with a wink in her direction. Then he'd climb on the boat, and Mom would take his picture with our old Brownie camera. I don't remember the wink this time, but he must have done it. He always did.

I walk north toward the Port dock then turn west and follow the channel. The giant maple tree outside Sound Seafoods is shedding its big yellow leaves. The wind sends them spiraling down to the sidewalk to be trampled into squishy brown sludge. The windows to the cannery are dark except for a couple of dim lights here and there.

If he's alive, where is he? And why hasn't he come home?

Did he have a fight with Mom? Was it over me? The one I'll never forget was over me, or rather the gifts Dad brought back for me. I never found out what happened to that coat. It was a beauty, too. Real fur, and pure white—the softest, most elegant thing I had ever seen, let alone worn, and it was mine. Until Mom took it away. One day, it was hanging in our closet in its plastic garment bag. The next day it was gone.

When I asked Mom where it was, she couldn't look me in the eyes. That's when I knew.

So did Dad. He threw down the newspaper he'd been reading and stomped over. "You didn't get rid of it, did you?"

She held her finger up to her mouth and glanced in my direction, but Dad wouldn't be silenced.

"Did you?"

She nodded, and I started to cry.

"Why?" Dad was yelling now.

Mom squeezed her eyes closed, as if trying to shut him out. "Because it was completely inappropriate and impractical for a six-year-old, that's why." Her eyes popped open. She wheeled around to face him. "You buy her these expensive gifts that she's just going to ruin or lose."

"I still have the jade bracelet," I protested, tears streaming down my face, but they weren't listening.

"Honestly, where's she going to wear something like that?"

"I don't know," Dad said, throwing his arms in the air. "Outside, maybe?"

"And white!"

"Ida deserves to have pretty things. What's the harm?"

"Ida deserves to have a father who's actually around on her birthday. That coat was nothing but guilt talking."

I'll never forget what Mom said next. It was just an off-hand comment. She didn't need to say it, but she couldn't stop herself from telling the truth—her truth.

"Besides," she said in a low voice. "It makes her look ridiculous."

I think Dad might have forgiven her about the coat were it not for that comment. I might have, too. After that year, he hid my special gifts.

I reach under my parka and finger the gold locket he got me for my tenth birthday. He had it inscribed: *For my sweet Ida Rose, Love always, Dad.*

I guess I was old enough to appreciate it, because I never lost it. And today, I hope it will help me find out what really happened to him. I've also brought the torn photo of the two of us.

When I get to the turnoff that snakes down to Sunset Beach, I realize I've just walked the entire width of town. I keep going straight, onto a dirt path that skirts the bluff. Down below is where kids like to carve their names, graduation years, and the initials of girlfriends and boyfriends, but I ignore all that and go straight to my special tree. Older and bigger than the other dwarfs, it arches over a rock shelf, making the perfect little shelter. I take my blanket out of my backpack and spread it underneath. With the wind howling off the harbor and the waves crashing against the shore below, this sap-scented cocoon feels like love.

Once I'm comfortable, I reach into my coat pocket, take out the photo, and set it down on the blanket in front of me. Next, I pull the locket out from under my shirt. Gazing skyward through the branches, I ask the universe for a sign, something obvious that will tell me whether he's dead or alive. I count to ten, but nothing happens, no thunderclaps or lightning bolts, just the wind, the waves, and the agonized cries of a seagull.

I must be going crazy. The wind coming through the trees is starting to sound like voices. Wait. Those *are* voices. Male voices.

I stand up and wait for the blood to prickle back into my legs. The voices seem to be coming from the woods behind me. I venture into the trees until I spot the whites of their T-shirts. Ducking behind a fat hemlock, I keep myself hidden while I count one, two, three . . . six boys standing around in a circle. The two boys I can't see are in the middle, fighting. I hear the scuffle of their feet, the huff of their bodies, the slap of skin on skin.

"Hey, Chink," yells one of them.

"He's no Chink. He's Charlie," says another. "Where'd you learn to fight? Vietnam?"

The circle parts just enough for me to see two bodies grappling. The smaller of the two has straight black hair. He must be Charlie. The boys push off each other, and the bigger one throws a punch the smaller one manages to block. The circle closes again, and I hear a loud *uulf*, followed by a thud and then the wet, guttural sounds of someone being pummeled.

They're going to kill that poor kid if I don't do something. But what can I do? There are seven of them, not counting the kid being pummeled. What would Emma Peel on *The Avengers* do if she didn't know karate? . . . Create a diversion. I pick up a pinecone from the ground and throw it as hard as I can. It bounces harmlessly off one boy's shoe. He doesn't even feel it. I pick up another and throw it. And another. Finally, one of them turns around.

"Hey, who's doing that?"

Behind his shoulder, I see the black-haired boy standing. Our eyes meet. His face is flushed, but you wouldn't know he's been fighting. Not so the kid on the ground, who's holding his stomach. As I turn to run, I hear one of them say, "Anyway, he's down. Fight's over. Time to pay up."

Pay up? What? Was that fight *a bet*? Just goes to show, you can't tell a book by its cover, as Dad would say. Maybe that was the sign from the universe. But what does a fight in the woods have to do with anything?

I get back to my tree and pack up my stuff. Where's the photo of me and Dad? It was right here on my blanket. I shake the blanket, but nothing falls out except for tree needles. I scan the ground. Nothing. Heart in my throat, I walk to the edge of the outcrop and look below.

No photo. But I do see a crow lift off from the rocks. Its blue-black wings catch the light as it flaps and glides, riding the wind up and down and finally away, out of sight. I think of a story Dad told me about Raven stealing the light—first the stars, then the moon, then the biggest prize of all, the sun. Crows are like ravens. I've heard they like to collect shiny objects. Did that bird make off with my photograph? Or is *this* the sign from the universe I was looking for?

If so, I have no idea what it means. What I do know is that all this thinking and wondering is making my head hurt. I wish I'd never heard Mom say what she did. Hope is cruel. I pack up my blanket, searching one last time for Dad's photo. It's getting dark when I start the long walk home.

I know I'm in trouble when Nana opens the door without me having to knock. "Thank God in Heaven!" she says, shooing me in. She closes the door behind me, takes me by the shoulders. "You had your mother very worried."

Mom's tennis shoes squeak on the linoleum as she rushes in from the kitchen. "Where the hell have you been?"

"I took a walk."

"For four hours?" Mom's hands are clenched in fists on her hips. Her eyes are wild. "Did it ever occur to you that we might wonder where you were? This I don't need, Ida. I've already had a husband disappear on me."

My eyes travel from her angry face to her hands, balled into fists, dripping soapy water onto her pants. "Who could blame him!"

She strikes. Her wet fingers sting my cheek. My tongue tastes the soap from her hand. I ball it up on my tongue and spit it out on Mom's clean carpet. Before she can go after me again, I run upstairs to my room and slam the door. Belly on the bed, face buried in my pillow, I ask myself why he left us, why he left *me*, and without so much as a phone call or a letter. He obviously doesn't care. I hope that's not true. I hope I'm dead wrong. But try as I might to imagine something different, that's the only meaning of "alive" that makes sense.

CHAPTER 7

Groggy
*Drunk from having consumed a lot
of grog, a watered-down rum*

I just got a D on an algebra quiz I didn't study for, and I don't even care. Equations and homework are for my friends with normal lives, friends with two parents and nothing to worry about but grades and what they're going to wear tomorrow. The stuff of life all seems so small and separate to me now, like I'm looking through the wrong end of a telescope.

I can't stop thinking about Dad living somewhere else with another woman or maybe another family. I tie my brain in knots wondering how he might have done it. Was his life with us so awful that he had to escape? I know Mom can be a bitch at times, but I thought he loved me. Was he just biding his time until he could run away? Do I really want him to be alive if it means he's left us? Do I want him dead if it means the opposite? God, stop these questions!

"Ida? Are you with us?" Mrs. Smith, my English teacher, stands in front of the class with the attendance book in her hands. She's staring at me, waiting.

"Here," my voice croaks.

She goes through the rest of the Ps and the Ss and then says a name I don't recognize. "Samuel Tap-o-sok. Am I pronouncing that correctly?"

"Top . . . o . . . soak."

I've been so wrapped up in thoughts of Dad I didn't notice we have a new student in class. I turn around to see the owner of the voice—a boy with shiny black hair. Oh my God, could it be? He's much tidier than the last time I saw him. His hair has been cut and his white shirt has those just-bought crease marks in it, but I recognize the eyes that locked onto mine that day in the woods.

"I go by Sam," he tells the teacher. He looks at me, and I realize I'm staring at him with my mouth open. I shut it and turn around.

Mrs. Smith tells the class that Sam's family came here from San Diego and that his father's in the Navy. She asks Sam if there's anything he'd like to add, and he says no.

Because he seems shy, Mrs. Smith makes a point of calling on him as much as possible for a new lesson she's introducing: American poetry. No, he doesn't have a favorite poet. Yes, he likes poetry okay, but sometimes finds it hard to understand. He doesn't say anything earth shattering, but he speaks in such a way that he sounds thoughtful, with clear words and distinct syllables, not all mashed together and lazy like most people talk.

We finally meet when our teacher breaks the class into

study groups and puts us together, along with Ralph Tucker and Julie Simon. Each group is given a list of poets. We are to choose one and give a report to the rest of the class, reading and interpreting one of our poet's works and giving a short biography that includes when and where the writer lived and some major events and influences in their life. This will count as 30 percent of our grade.

Julie immediately takes charge of our group, reciting the list of poets and poems as if the rest of us can't read. When she gets to Edgar Allen Poe and *The Raven*, she stops. "Ooh, we should do *him*," she says. "It's almost Halloween."

I don't much care who we do. I'm just watching Sam. He nods his agreement, so I shrug and say, "Okay."

We find the poem in our English anthology, and Ralph whimpers when he sees how long it is.

"We're going to read this whole thing?" he says.

"I'll help you with it, Ralph-ie," Julie says like she's talking to a toddler.

That leaves me and Sam to work on the biography.

I assumed that meant "together," but he makes no move to even talk to me. Days go by. Okay, if he doesn't want to work with me, I don't want to work with him. This whole assignment is stupid. Why do we have to learn poetry, anyway? Poetry, like math, is for kids like . . . like Julie Simon. She doesn't lie awake at night wondering if her dad is dead or alive. She doesn't wonder if anyone gives a fig about her. She knows.

"ARE you mad at me?" Dena is in the next stall in the girls' bathroom. If I didn't know her voice, I could surely identify her by her white go-go boots. "You seem mad."

"I'm not mad."

"Then what?"

"I'm just—I don't know—confused. It's . . . confusing."

I flush. Dena flushes. We meet at the mirror. She puts her arm around my shoulders. "It's okay. You don't need to explain." Her face brightens. "Hey, Sophie, Gerry, and I are going to this party Saturday night at the haunted house. Wanna come?"

The haunted house out on Highway 20 is a notorious drinking hangout. Everybody knows this. "My mom would never let me go."

Dena's frosted pink lips curl into a grin. "That's why we have the cover party."

"The cover party?"

"Jill's having a Halloween party. We tell our folks we're going there—"

"And go to the haunted house instead," I finish.

"Bingo."

"I don't know." I puff my cheeks in and out, mulling it over. "It's . . ."

"What?"

"Well, Halloween feels . . . different. It's like death and ghosts and stuff aren't funny anymore."

"Aw, Ida." She leans over and gives me a hug.

"On the other hand, I'd really like to get out of the house," I say over her shoulder. We part. "I'll think about it."

She claps me on the back so hard I cough.

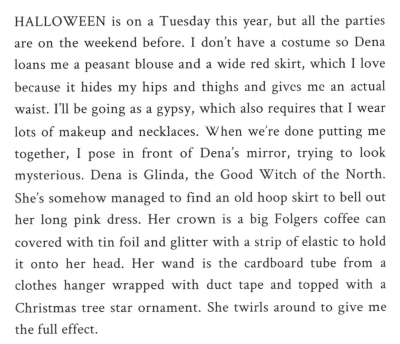

HALLOWEEN is on a Tuesday this year, but all the parties are on the weekend before. I don't have a costume so Dena loans me a peasant blouse and a wide red skirt, which I love because it hides my hips and thighs and gives me an actual waist. I'll be going as a gypsy, which also requires that I wear lots of makeup and necklaces. When we're done putting me together, I pose in front of Dena's mirror, trying to look mysterious. Dena is Glinda, the Good Witch of the North. She's somehow managed to find an old hoop skirt to bell out her long pink dress. Her crown is a big Folgers coffee can covered with tin foil and glitter with a strip of elastic to hold it onto her head. Her wand is the cardboard tube from a clothes hanger wrapped with duct tape and topped with a Christmas tree star ornament. She twirls around to give me the full effect.

"Wow!"

"The only thing is I can't sit down." She sits on the end of her bed and her skirt pops over her head, revealing her flowered underpants in all their glory. We both collapse in giggles. Then Dena gets the hiccups. This makes it difficult for me to apply lipstick to her lips. I end up getting some on her teeth and nose, which triggers another round of hilarity, and I almost lose myself in the moment before I remember. *Oh, yeah. Dad's gone, and I'm acting all happy.*

"Are you girls just about ready?" Uncle Pat calls through the door.

When we emerge, he hands Dena his keys and tells us to be careful. Now that she has her license, she jumps at any opportunity to drive, even if it's just Uncle Pat's rusty truck. She puts her hoop skirt, crown, and wand in a big garbage sack, which she throws in the space behind the front seats. Now she's a deflated good witch, but much more comfortable for the drive over to the school to pick up Sophie, who's dressed as Raggedy Ann, and Gerry, who's also a witch, but the black kind.

I lose at rock-paper-scissors, so I have to ride in the bed of the truck on the way out to the haunted house, but the weather is so mild, I don't mind. Sitting against the back of the cab between Uncle Pat's crab pots, it stinks, but I'm mostly out of the wind. As we roll down the highway, I'm reminded of the view from the stern of the *Lady Rose* and that strange sensation of going backwards while you're going forwards. Mom, of course, would die if she knew I was back here rattling around with the crabbing gear. That just adds to the thrill of watching the pavement unspool before me.

We stop at the end of a long dirt road behind a line of haphazardly parked cars. The house is across a mushy field overgrown with tall weeds and blackberry bushes.

Before we set off, Dena ducks behind the truck and assembles her costume. Then she reaches into the cab and grabs her dad's massive flashlight.

"This way, we'll see the ghosts before they scare us," she jokes.

I don't remind her that my ghost is real. He's in my dreams, my thoughts. He's always there, if not front and center then in the background. Of course, I'd probably wet my pants if I actually saw Dad's ghost, especially if he came back bloated and covered in barnacles. What an awful thought.

But it's just as awful imagining him happy with another family. *If you're dead, I'm sorry. If you're alive and don't care what happens to me, then I don't care either.*

DENA'S belled dress keeps popping up in the wind, so we have to go back to the truck and ditch the hoop skirt and crown, which also isn't staying put.

"Damn," she says.

"You still look great," Sophie assures her as we make our way through the mud and brambles.

I've only ever seen the haunted house from our trips down Highway 20. Standing tall and alone in the middle of flat nothingness, it's a familiar landmark. Up close, it looks even lonelier, but you can tell it used to be a stately thing. "A once-grand Victorian lady," Dad would say when he pointed it out on our drives.

All that remains of that lady now are pieces of trim hanging here and there and an ornately carved beam fallen like a warning across the missing front door. Her most remarkable feature is a squat, round tower that hangs off the southeast-facing corner. It's suspended as if a strong breeze could take it down, but no windstorm has been able to. I think that stubbornness has fed the rumors.

"It must have been beautiful before the murders," Gerry says.

Sophie's Raggedy Ann eyes narrow. "Is that a true story?"

Gerry nods while Dena shakes her head. "Not true," she says. "It wasn't murder that caused the house to be abandoned."

Sophie turns to her. "Do you know the real story?"

"Yep. Dad told me."

"Well?" Gerry waves her hand, signaling for her to get on with it.

"Well, it's kind of sad," she starts. "A farmer named Bell homesteaded here, but he didn't know that the land floods, like, every other year. This one winter, it flooded really bad. All the fields were underwater. They lost cows and chickens and stuff, but the worst part was the family dog. He got trapped underneath the house. The family was inside and could hear him struggling and whimpering right below them, but they couldn't save him."

"That's *really* sad," Sophie says.

"They abandoned the house after that," Dena says. "They couldn't get the sound of their dog drowning out of their heads."

Gerry gives a fake cough and nods her head in my direction.

Dena claps her hand over her mouth. "I'm sooo sorry. I'm such a dope."

"It's okay," I say, and it is. "It's not something I haven't already thought about a million times. Besides, my dad knew the risks. That poor dog didn't know anything."

We stand there, staring up at the hanging tower, until our solemn reverence is disturbed by a girl falling backwards into our group, crushing her fairy wings.

"I think we have some catching up to do." Dena grabs me by the elbow and we thread our way through the bodies to a plastic tarp where someone has set up a makeshift bar with a beer keg and a big basin of "punch," a mysterious red liquid that smells like cherry cough syrup. Dena scoops a full cup of it and hands it to me. "Drink up."

It's as sickly sweet as it smells, but I take a second sip, then a third. Once the others get their drinks, we fall into a line of kids who are stepping over the fallen beam to go into the gray skeleton of a house. "Just to say we did," says Dena, shining her flashlight on floors littered with bottles and trash too rotten to be identified. The house smells of mildew and piss, and the wood under our feet is so spongy I'm amazed it holds our weight. Tumbling three stories would probably kill a person, but we go upstairs anyway because everyone else is going upstairs. Someone I can't see keeps making *OOOO* sounds, and I hear a girl say, "Here's where the children were killed." Dena clucks her tongue and yells, "Not true!"

From the third story, the strong beam of Uncle Pat's flashlight illuminates the squinty-eyed, red-lipped faces of those stumbling around below, as well as some of the feature-less landscape beyond. If the sun were out, we'd see snow-capped mountains to the east and the waters and islands of Puget Sound to the west. It would be spectacular. No wonder the Ball family wanted to build here. But it must have been terrible when it flooded. They must have felt trapped.

A dark shape flits by what used to be a window. Sophie screams. Then Dena and I scream. Then everyone else on the third floor screams. "What?" yells a guy wearing a Superman costume. A whistle pierces the din. Gerry is holding her arms up. In her witch dress, she looks like she's fixing to cast a spell. "Calm down, you boobs," she says. "It was only a bat."

We leave the house as more people pour in, having heard the screams. Dena skips away to say hello to a friend dressed up as a cat, and Sophie and Gerry wander off to talk to people they know. I continue to drink my drink to make up for the fact that I am now friendless at this party of seventeen- and eighteen-year-olds. A fuzzy numbness seeps in as I watch the flow of kids going through the front door. I wish they'd stop laughing and making fake ghost sounds. This used to be someone's home.

I walk around the back, almost stepping on a couple making out in the grass—at least, I *think* it's a couple making out. Without Dena's flashlight, I can't see a thing. My skirt catches on a blackberry branch. To free myself, I have to gingerly lift the thorns off the fabric. Half of my drink spills down Dena's white peasant blouse, leaving what I'm sure will be a big pink stain. Crap.

I drink the rest just to get rid of it. The taste isn't so bad now, and I kind of like the numbness taking over my body. A pleasant buzz blots out all but the now, the sensations of moving through space. There's a fingernail moon tonight, and the stars are out. I turn around, looking for the North Star, and I feel my center of gravity tilt. Whoa, better watch where I'm going. Don't want to step on or in anything.

Soon I'm back at the tarp, where someone has helpfully set out several filled cups for people to take. I grab another and find a place to sit on a wide tree stump. Two couples are already taking up most of the space. One of the girls, a much thinner and prettier gypsy than me, moves to let me sit and then tosses her long thick braid into my face. She's in the tight grip of a boy dressed like a hobo.

The other couple is kissing. The guy leans back with the girl on top of him, bumping me. I spill more punch on Dena's blouse. She's going to be so mad. Where is she, anyway? I scan the silhouettes around me, looking for hers, but it's all just shapes and noise, punctuated by the occasional scream or shrill laugh. I gulp my drink down. It's better if you don't taste it. Maybe I should go look for the others, but I'm kind of afraid to get up. My body is one big buzz with a sloshy liquid middle. I really want to lie down, but there's no place to do it. Is this stump swaying? I feel like I'm on a boat.

A bubble of sour cherry rises from the pinch of Dena's skirt. Oh-oh, I try to hold it down. God, don't let me throw up. I try to stand, but my legs collapse beneath me, and what must come up does, in a heaving gush of red.

CHAPTER 8

Trolling Spoon
*A fishing lure with a large spoon
that's trailed behind a boat*

I'm grounded. Dena's grounded. Mom's furious, and Nana's none too pleased either. She wouldn't even come to my defense when Mom said I couldn't see Dena outside of school. The punishment came with no time limit, but I assume family gatherings are exempt with the holidays coming up. Mom also said nothing about telephone contact.

As soon as I'm feeling up to it, I call my cousin to apologize for getting us in trouble and ruining her peasant blouse.

"Aw, that's okay," she says. "It was my fault. I should have warned you about that punch. Everyone was getting sick, not just you, so don't feel bad."

"Still, I'm sorry you had to face my mom."

"You remember?"

"Actually, no. But she's really mad at me today, so I can only guess."

"Yeah, she pretty much had a cow. But then she needed my help getting you up the stairs."

"God, I'll never drink again. It hurt to move my head, but you have to move your head to—"

"Spare me the details."

"Anyway, I'm sorry you got grounded."

"I'll survive . . . You know Gerry and Sophie got off scot-free? Those snots. Gerry says her dad snores so her mom wears earplugs. She could do a tap dance in their bedroom and they wouldn't wake up. She'll tell you all about it at lunch, I'm sure."

"Um . . . I may not be coming to lunch for a while."

"Jeez, your mom must really hate me."

"No, it's not that. It's my grades and this project in English. It's due Thursday and I haven't even started."

"Whoops," Dena says.

I find the 800s and look for Poe, Poe, Poe. Where can he be? Uh-oh. I'm gonna . . . monster sneeze! I wipe with the only thing available, my sleeve, and when I look up, David has appeared out of nowhere. All I can think about as we stand there staring at each other is whether or not I have snot on my face.

"Hi," we say at the same time.

"Jinx!" My voice squeaks.

He grins. "So, how are you?"

"I'm okay." I take in air, let it out again. *Don't let that nose tickle come back, please.* He's wearing black Converse tennis shoes. Even his feet are cute, the way one's rolled out, balancing on the outside sole.

"That's good," he says. "Hey, I've, um, been wanting to

tell you how sorry I am about your dad. Steve was a great guy."

Maybe not so great—present tense. David obviously thinks he's dead. I wonder what he knows. I dare to stare up into those incredibly blue eyes. His fishing tan has faded and his mustache is gone, but his face still has that lean ruggedness that comes from a summer of hard work. His mouth is moving, but the only word I hear is "Alaska."

"Huh?"

"The Salty Dog," he repeats. "It's a tavern in Ketchikan your dad . . . uh . . . liked."

"Oh." Dad never told me about a tavern, not that he would. So how does David know about it? He's only two years older than I am.

"The fishermen would meet up there," he adds. "Us younger guys all had fake IDs."

Question answered.

"Your dad could tell some wild stories."

I wait for him to give me an example or explain, but he just bows his head and shakes it slowly back and forth, as if he can't quite believe his memories. I want to ask him about a million questions, but he adjusts his backpack on his shoulder and moves to leave.

"Well, I'll see you later," he says.

As he turns around, I see my one chance to learn more about my father slip away in black Converse tennis shoes.

"I'd like to hear more about my dad." My desperation hangs there between us, grotesque and waiting. "In Alaska, I mean."

"Sure," he says. "Although, there's this saying among fishermen that what happens in Alaska stays in Alaska . . . but sure. Any time."

I watch him disappear around the shelf of books. God, what were the chances? Here it is, October, almost two months since school started, and we connect by chance in the stacks. Is this fate? What was he doing here? What am *I* doing here? Oh, yeah. Poe.

I get to the shelf where the books on him should be and find the section has been picked clean. The only book left is a slim volume with the super-vague title *Rhyme and Reason*. This is what happens when you wait until the last minute.

I ask the librarian if anything on Edgar Allen Poe has been returned and she points me to a table in the middle of the room and a stack of books hiding a person with black hair.

Sam.

I don't remember seeing him when I walked in. Of course, he's not one to draw attention to himself. I approach his table and scan the titles in his pile. Sure enough, he has the book I want, *The Life and Times of Edgar Allan Poe.*

"Can we share?"

He jerks his head up, startled.

"Hi. Sorry. Can I look through your books?"

He nods.

I sit down across from him and ask him how much he's done on our assignment.

"Not too much," he says with his pretty articulation. He shows me three pages of neatly written notes.

"I haven't even started."

Sam's eyes widen in surprise, but he doesn't scold me.

"Maybe we should work together," I tell him. "It might save us both having to read the same stuff." I dig out the worksheet Mrs. Smith gave us, a list of things the biography needs to include. "How about we split up this list? You do the first half, and I do the second half?"

He takes my worksheet. "I will mark what I've done." He starts making check marks down the page. He's left-handed, I notice. Scabs and small white scars riddle his knuckles. Another scar cuts his left eyebrow in half. Could that be from fighting? Other than that, his light brown skin is flawless. No bruises, no pimples. I decide he has cute lips. They form two perfect peaks on top.

He looks up, catches me staring. My eyes shift to the worksheet. About the only things he hasn't marked are "bibliography," "end of life," and "lasting influence."

"That doesn't leave a lot for me," I say.

"That's okay. Poe is interesting."

In-ter-rest-ting. I can't help but smile at his crisp diction. "Oh, good. I'd hate to study a boring poet."

His laugh takes me by surprise. It's soft and musical, like his voice. I take out a pen and open my binder to a fresh sheet of notebook paper. I'm about to grab *Life and Times* when I spot something more intriguing, *Edgar Allan Poe: The Man, The Mystery, The Magic.* I look inside the jacket and read, "Lies, spread by a competitor, helped tarnish Poe's reputation near the time of his death, the exact circumstances of which remain open to speculation."

The exact circumstances of which. "Are you using this book?" I ask Sam. "I'd like to check it out."

I can't help comparing Poe's mysterious death to Dad's. Then, as I'm changing for gym class, I remember a key detail from Mom's conversation with Nana that night I broke my nose. There's something I don't know about Dad that could have tarnished *his* reputation. And because I don't know it, I *still think he walks on water.* Running around the track, I don't even notice how hard I'm breathing. My mind is too busy turning around all the little invitations that have been dropped in my lap. The English assignment. Julie choosing Poe. Running into David. Poe's mysterious death. The book that's in my backpack. Forces are at play here. In some strange way it's all leading to this thing I'm meant to find out about my father. For once, I can't wait to get home and do my homework.

I stay up late to finish the Poe biography. His life makes mine look like a cakewalk. He was orphaned at two. First his father leaves. (Hmm, another coincidence?) Then his mother dies of tuberculosis. He marries his thirteen-year-old cousin, which is a little gross, and loses her to the same disease. He can't really support himself off his writing, though "The Raven" was an instant success. He spent years planning his own journal but died at age forty, before it could come out. His death was attributed to alcoholism, but some say he may have been murdered. If that's not enough, this editor with a grudge sets out to destroy Poe's reputation by portraying him as a depraved madman. Sheesh! It's depressing stuff, and I can't wait to share it with Sam. We're going to ace this project!

SAM and I meet in the library and divide Poe's life into four sections. We agree to trade off on the presentation, with him starting and me ending.

"Oh, good, I get the mysterious death," I say, drawing some five-sided stars next to the notes I took last night. "Know all about those," I mumble.

"What?" Sam looks up from his own notes.

My first thought is to say, "Oh, nothing," but something inside me wants to tell him. He's different from my other friends. He's had some hard knocks—literally. He might understand. "I know all about mysterious deaths," I repeat. "My dad . . . I guess you wouldn't know, being kinda new here."

"Know what? Was he killed? In 'Nam?"

I shake my head, but he's on a roll. "My dad's over there. Gulf of Tonkin. He's been gone almost five months now."

"No, my dad's a fisherman—was—a fisherman. He went missing this summer. They think he had a boat accident and drowned."

"Oh, man." Sam looks down at the table and bites his lower lip. "That's terrible. Crap, that's worse than terrible. How can you stand it? Not knowing for sure?"

"I'm not sure I can."

OUR Poe presentation went great, but Ralph, of all people, stole the show with his growly and ridiculously drawn out *ne-e-v-e-r-r-m-o-r-r-e*s. Voicing the Raven was his sole contribution to our group project, and everyone praised him like he's the next Laurence Olivier. Even Mrs. Smith looked impressed.

I'm trying not to let Ralph's unearned A bother me. If I've learned anything from these last two months, it's that you can't count on anything in life, including life. It's time to "fish or cut bait," as Dad would say. I need to find out about that part of him I never saw, and the one person who can tell me will be graduating this year. First chance I get, I'll pin David down and get him to tell me about my father, Alaska, and all those wild stories.

CHAPTER 9

Cannonball
A weight that carries lines and lures down to the depth where fish are feeding

Istake out a small reading table by the window and wait for David. I skipped lunch—too nervous!—but he probably didn't. To keep myself from watching the doorway, I stare out at the view of the channel. Water and sky are two shades of the same gray. When I was little, I'd watch Dad's boat disappear into that line and imagine him falling off the edge of the earth. When you can't see the end, you assume it's there, like all those people who thought the earth was flat.

The way Dad talked about it, Alaska may as well have been off the edge of the earth. "They don't call it the Last Frontier for nothing," he was fond of saying. There was always work to be done and money to be made, and nobody caring how you made it. "A man can start over there."

I never asked him to explain what he meant by that, whether he might have been talking about himself. It never mattered to me what he did when he was away, so long as he came back. Now that he's gone, I want to find out all I can.

My head jerks up as an Army-green book bag thunks down on the table. David pulls out the chair across from me, making his own breeze. It smells of spearmint, fresh like the blue of his eyes.

Get a hold of yourself, Ida. You're not here to ogle David.

"So, whaddya want to know?" he asks.

"Everything."

"Hmm, okay." He shifts in his chair like he could just as easily bolt as settle in. I shouldn't have said that. He can't tell me what happened, or even what it was like on the *Lady Rose.* He only saw Dad a few times in that bar.

"Tell me about the Foggy Dog."

He snickers and the muscles in his neck and shoulders soften. "The *Salty* Dog is an interesting place. It's as much a museum as a bar. I swear, every square inch is covered with fishing stuff. There's even a hammerhead shark hanging from the ceiling. Man, that's one ugly fish."

"I can see Dad in a place like that. He loved anything having to do with the sea . . . and probably that ugly fish, too."

"Actually, he liked to sit under the moose head."

"Moose head?"

"Yeah, a moose head with Christmas lights strung through its antlers. I think it was the only thing in The Salty Dog not fishing related. Your dad always claimed the table underneath it. Funny guy, Steve. I loved his stories." He flashes me that lopsided grin.

"Fishing stories?"

"Yeah, a few of those. Along with some history, maybe a

tale or two about Raven. He liked the Native Alaskan myths. He'd read from this book he carried around."

Book? I don't remember any book. I'm stung by the thought of Dad sharing a book with David and not with me, but I let it pass. "He loved the creation myths," I say, "even though Raven was a bit of a scoundrel." *A bit of a scoundrel,* the exact phrase Dad used. It sounds fake when I say it, like I'm trying to sound smarter than I am.

"I think he liked Raven *because* he was a scoundrel," David says. "His scoundrel-ness made the stories funnier."

"And Dad loved to entertain people."

"Yeah, he was a joker. I think I only saw him get real serious that one time."

My ears perk up. "Oh?"

"Yeah, kind of took me by surprise because fishermen are always swearing and saying rude things."

"My dad said something rude?"

David shakes his head. "No, one of the guys from another boat did. He was talking about a knife fight he saw, no big deal there, but he called the men"—David lowers his voice —"f-ing 'drunken Indians,' and your dad just laid into him."

"What'd he say?"

"Um, I don't remember everything, but he basically talked about the bad things the white men did to the Natives in Alaska, like bringing disease and taking their kids away to live in boarding schools." David's Adam's apple goes up and down as he swallows. "I guess it was really horrible for those kids. First, their parents die of TB or whatever—"

"TB, like tuberculosis?" I flash back on the women in Poe's life.

"Yeah, then they're stuck in these schools that force them to become Christians. Imagine being taken away from everything you know . . . forever."

"Did Dad turn that guy around?"

"Who knows? I've never forgotten it, I can tell you that. I think the reason he got so mad was because he had friends up there. Natives. There was this one Aleut lady he talked about a lot. She . . . uh, worked on Creek Street." He pauses, like that's significant. "Do you know about Creek Street?"

I shake my head.

"Well it's pretty famous for . . . a certain activity. The joke is that it's the only place where both salmon and men come to spawn."

It takes me a while, but when I finally get it, heat creeps up my cheeks. David's too wrapped up in his story to notice.

"Anyway, this lady had a nickname that her own people used against her. It was really rude, but she started using it herself to show she wasn't . . ."

"Ashamed?"

"Exactly."

"So what was it?"

He gives me that lopsided grin of his. "Two-Bit."

His next words are lost to the deafening jangle of the school bell. He waits for it to stop. "It means almost worthless. But, as your dad said, she was anything but. I think she was retired from"—he searches for the word—"her *work* by the time your dad got to know her. Now *she's* an interesting story."

"Can we meet for lunch again tomorrow?" I imagine I must look like a dog begging for treats. "Please?"

Hours pass in that moment before he opens his mouth. "Sure," he says.

I wait until David has left before I do a little dance. Mrs. McDaniel, the librarian, sees me and just shakes her head like I'm beyond hope. And maybe I am.

I go to class. Physically, I'm in the seat, but my head is lost in space, like that goofy TV show. I don't remember the bus trip home or the walk to my house. Nana's burnt goods never tasted so delicious. I compliment her baking, getting a flabbergasted, "Why thank you!"

That evening, I set the dining room table without Mom having to ask me, and I offer to wash dishes. As I scrub, rinse, and hand off to her to dry, I whistle a made-up tune.

"What's gotten into you, anyway?" Mom holds her free hand up to my forehead.

"Nothing."

After retreating to my room, I spend about twenty minutes doing math and twice that long figuring out what I'm going to wear tomorrow. I finally settle on one of the skirts we bought in August and a fresh white blouse.

After washing my hair I go to bed early, but it's hard to sleep. I spend half the night wondering whether or not David likes me, and the other half trying to think up questions to ask him, starting with how my dad became friends with an ex-prostitute.

DAVID doesn't show. Either he forgot, or he really doesn't want to talk to me. Even if he just forgot, it's crushing. I do the math. Minus the short night's sleep I got, I've just spent about eighteen hours thinking about him while he's spent zero thinking about me.

I wish I could go home, sneak up to my room, and take a nap, but that's out of the question. As I'm mustering up the will to go class, I hear my name.

Could it be? Better late than never. I turn around, but it's just Sam. When did he slip in? He walks over to my table carrying a heavily doodled Pee-Chee. For a moment he just stands there as if trying to remember why he came over. Finally, he says, "I have something of yours."

I think that I may have left a pencil behind or something, but he opens his Pee-Chee and pulls out a small, slightly soiled envelope.

"Sorry. I had this a long time," he says.

I feel his eyes on me as I open the seal and pull out the photo of me and my dad that I lost. "Oh, wow, where did you find it?"

"The bluff," he says, exaggerating the "F" sound. "I found it that day I saw you in the woods and kept forgetting to bring it. Then you told me about your dad, and I put it in my school stuff so I'd have it next time I saw you."

"Thanks, Sam." I finger the photo in my hand, running my thumb over the rough edge where I tore it. "I was sure I'd lost this." The sensations of that strange afternoon come back to me—the bracing wind, the smell of sap, the fight, and the pinecones I threw in my feeble attempt to stop it. "So you *did* see me. I thought you were getting beat up."

Sam winces. "None of them can fight worth a damn, but they keep betting me." The muscles in his forearm tense as he clutches his Pee-Chee to his chest.

"Who are they? Do they go to this school?"

"No, they're older."

"What was that name they called you?" I ask him.

"Which one? Chink or Charlie? Both are wrong. I'm not Chinese or Vietnamese." He looks up at me and I stare into his eyes. They're dark, almost black, and restless, like he's watching for predators.

"You're Filipino, aren't you?"

"Yeah." He drops his Pee-Chee to his side. His other hand braces against the edge of the table. "Those guys were too stupid to know we're on your side."

"Oh, right, your dad's in Vietnam on a boat."

Sam smirks. "He would not like you calling the USS Constellation a boat."

"I know more about fishing boats." I feel my cheeks flush. In my rush to tell Sam about my dad, I realize I never asked him about his. "So how do *you* deal with it? The worry. The not knowing . . ."

"I read the newspapers and magazines about the war. Every day."

"You must know everything there is to know," I say.

He shakes his head. "No one knows everything."

"But you know more than . . . a lot of people." I almost said "me." The only things I read in the newspaper are the horoscope and the funnies. "I should read more . . . of the newspaper. I read a lot of books—"

"Come here after lunch," he says. "Mrs. McDaniel brings

mc her *Seattle Post-Intelligencer* and *Time* magazines after she's done. I'll share them with you."

I'm not sure I want to commit to coming to the library to read the news. It sounds boring, but Sam's smile is hard to resist, and I kind of like talking to him. "Sure . . . I mean, if I don't have to research any more interesting poets."

CHAPTER 10

Aloof
A ship that sails higher into the wind so that it draws apart from the rest of the fleet

I somehow manage to get through my first quarter of high school with two A's, three B's, and a C. I explain to Mom about the gymnastics unit in PE, but she doesn't seem to care about that. "Not bad," she says, "considering."

Normally I'd be pleased, too. My favorite time of the year is fast approaching, but I can't seem to get into the spirit without Dad, who went crazy over Christmas.

And now Nana's gone, too.

Her afghan brightens our living room like a sunburst, commanding cheer, but it just makes me miss her more. She finally had to get back to Montana and her "other life," as she put it.

I wrap myself up in that blanket, smelling her talcum, as I watch Mom go about her busy work of picking up and straightening. The house is shockingly still. I think Mom notices, too. She's quick to snap at me over the least little thing, like leaving the lights on. I know we're trying to save on our electric bill, but it's like she's trying to obliterate all joy and memories of Dad, which I can see if he walked out on us, but still.

Christmas was his time to shine, literally. Not only was he the designated Santa impersonator, he also had an out-of-control light fixation. It'd take him several days to decorate our house, the shrubbery, and all his homemade plywood figures. It started with a sleigh and reindeer set; then, every year, he added something new—an elf, an angel, a penguin with a bowtie, whatever inspired him. This year, our house looks forlorn, not a scrap of Christmas to be found inside or out.

Once school lets out for holiday break, it's too much sadness to bear, so I spend most of my time over at Dena's now that we can see each other again. At my cousin's house, there's a tree, a nativity scene, and felt stockings with each person's name in glitter. There's also a color TV. We watch *Rudolph the Red-Nosed Reindeer*. The color is off—Rudolph's nose is more orange than red—but it still beats black and white.

When we're not watching TV, we're in the dining room listening to Dena's records while playing an epic game of Monopoly with Dougie. Danielle had a tantrum after landing on Dena's hotel-fortified Marvin Gardens. Dougie, who is leading, sprays the board with droplets of spit as he demands his $75 rent for my boot landing on one of his three railroads. I mortgaged St. Charles Place to buy the fourth railroad, The Reading, just to prevent him from getting a monopoly, and now he's out to get me.

The day Dougie finally wins is the day I come home to find an artificial tree standing in our living room. It's a bristly silver thing that comes up to my shoulder. Mom bought it at Tradewell.

"At least it will be easy to get the star on top," she says. "And we never have to water it."

This "tree," which doesn't smell and appears like it's made out of tin, is worse than no tree at all, but I don't say so. I don't want to hurt Mom's feelings when she made an effort, however pathetic. Still, it's all I can do to act upbeat as I help her decorate it. We only hang the smaller ornaments because the big ones would topple it. The whole process takes about ten minutes.

"There, you see?" she says, standing back to take in the room. "Much better."

I don't know if she means the room or the tree, but neither is true. If Dad were here, he'd snicker at it. If Dad were here, we'd have a six-foot noble fir that actually looked and smelled like Christmas.

Mom's only doing these Christmassy things to check them off her to-do list. We spend a quiet Christmas Eve, just the two of us, eating roasted game hen because a turkey would be too much food. Then we plug in the lights on the silver Christmas tree and open the few gifts scattered underneath. I got Mom a coffee table book I bought at Woolworths on famous rose gardens of the world. She likes roses, and she likes books, so I thought it would be perfect. She makes a show of appreciation but doesn't even crack it open before setting it aside.

The rest of the gifts are for me. From Nana, I get a hat,

scarf, and mittens she knitted in my favorite color, spring green, with the exception of one pink thumb. From Mom, I get the usual socks, slippers, and underwear, but then she surprises me with a record. When I tear the paper and see the half-shadowed faces of John, George, Paul, and Ringo, I scream just like one of those crazy girls on *The Ed Sullivan Show.*

Mom beams. "I'm not a total square."

"Wow, we needed a new one. Dena's record is all scratched."

I've listened to *Meet the Beatles!* so many times at her house that I know all the songs and the exact order they come in, but I still can't wait to play my record, which I oh-so-carefully take out of its crisp paper sleeve. Touching only the outer rim with my palms like Mom taught me, I place it on our stereo turntable and wait for the needle to drop on "I Want to Hold Your Hand." Mom bobs her head to the beat while reading the back of the record cover.

"It says here that the Beatles' first visit in Dublin caused a mob free-for-all and *unnumbered broken limbs.* Can you imagine? At London Airport, fans repeatedly kissed the gloved hand of a reporter after it touched a Beatle."

"Which one?" I ask.

"Doesn't say."

"Must have been Paul. He's the cutest."

"Oh, I don't know. I think George is pretty handsome." Mom studies the photo on the back of the cover. "And I just want to hug Ringo!"

"Honestly, Mom."

She giggles. We listen to the entire record twice through,

and side one a third time, before she tells me it's time to go to bed. "Big day tomorrow," she says, then adds under her breath, "God, I'm not looking forward to it."

WE get up early Christmas morning to go to mass. Mom clomps around the house in her heels, muttering "okay" as she completes one task and moves on to the next. Finally the presents are all wrapped and sitting next to the door in a shopping bag. The food we're bringing to my grandparents' house is tinned or cellophaned in another bag. Mom checks her hemline in the closet door mirror to make sure her slip isn't showing. I guess she doesn't care that her fancy fur-collared coat smells of mothballs.

I wear what I call my popcorn dress, with bumpy white knit fabric that resembles popped kernels, and nylon stockings with a garter belt. I hate wearing stockings. They're always sagging around my ankles, and I can't go for more than half an hour without snagging them on something. But Mom says I look nice, and I guess that's what matters.

After mass, we head straight over to the big family gathering that Mom's dreading. My grandparents live about a mile away. Red and white Christmas lights outline the main roof of their white house. The lights are Grandpa's homage to the Croatian flag, which has a red-and-white checkerboard pattern in the middle, but most people would just think candy cane. Mom parks the car, pulls the emergency brake, and stares at the house.

"Okay, let's get this over with." She used to act enthusiastic for my benefit, but now that I'm older and well aware of her feelings, she probably figures there's no point. I guess I prefer her honesty, though it makes me nervous.

Uncle Pat answers the door and we exchange hugs and greetings with Dad's side of the family. The men sit on the sofa cracking and eating walnuts and talking politics, while the aunts in their Christmas aprons help Grandma in the kitchen.

"Oh, good, good, you came," Grandma says as if our arrival were in doubt. She hugs Mom before turning to me. Taking my chin in her damp, onion-smelling hands, she plants a kiss on each cheek and then steps back to take me in, head to toe. "You've lost weight," she says. She turns to Mom. "Are you feeding her?"

Mom frowns, letting the question hang there unanswered. If Dad were with us, he'd give Mom a private roll of the eyes and she'd shrug off "Grandma Graceless," but he's not here to be the buffer, and I don't know how.

We're relieved of our coats and dishes of food. Mom's hand gently presses my back as we move toward meal-prep central. She asks if she can do anything to help and is told there are too many cooks in the kitchen as it is. "Just relax. We've got it covered," Aunt Janet tells her. I know Mom would rather be put to work. It would help her nerves to be doing something, anything, but she's stuck wandering back to the living room with Grandpa and the uncles. I hear Uncle Pat joke, "So they banished you, too, huh?" as I leave to join my cousins.

They're all sitting in the den watching a Bob Hope Christmas special on TV. I sit next to Dena and compliment her on her earrings—dangly red balls, like Christmas ornaments, to match her fuzzy red sweater and red plaid mini-skirt. The look is subdued for her.

I'm not sure why they're watching some old guy swinging a golf club and telling a bunch of jokes they can't possibly understand, but I've watched Gregory and Jonathan watch one Road Runner cartoon after another, so I know they're not terribly picky.

Then I hear "Gulf of Tonkin" and perk up. I wonder if Sam is watching this. I bet a lot of families are, hoping to spot their men in the crowd. They seem hungry, those soldiers—not for food, though maybe that too, but for attention, any attention. Bob Hope makes them go crazy, hanging from poles and cramming together on hot hillsides with no shade. I feel sorry for them. Most of them appear so young and eager, you can't help but wonder if they really know what they're over there for.

When Bob Hope calls up on stage a sixty-nine-year-old Navy Chief, I think it must be a joke. But then the man says that he signed up to stop Communism, and I realize he's real.

"What's Com-moo-zizzm?" Gregory asks.

"It's when you turn red," Jonathan says, trying to push his brother off the beanbag chair they're sharing. Gregory pushes him back, starting a shoving match.

"Knock it off, you two," Dena says. "Communism is what they have in China and Russia, and we're fighting it in Vietnam because we don't want it to spread."

Danielle rocks forward on the couch. "Oh, so it's a disease?"

"Um, not exactly." Dena locks eyes with me and tilts her head toward the door, motioning for me to come with her. "We'll leave you brain surgeons to your program."

She leads me back to the spare bedroom, where our grandparents have shut away their toy poodle, Lassie, jokingly named after the beautiful collie on the TV program. Lassie is being confined because she jumps on people. She jumps on us, threatening my stockings, but I don't care. I pity her being all alone with the sounds of celebration just out of her reach. She wiggles over on her side so Dena can scratch her skinny belly.

"I'm going north to Alaska!" Dena says. Then, without warning, she starts singing, "No-r-r-th to A-las-ka," and I don't know if she's serious or pulling my leg.

"What?"

"It's only for the summer. I'm going to work in a cannery. Dad said I could after graduation. It's a great way to earn money for college, and it's a lot safer than fishing. Maybe you can come too."

Her suggestion is so ridiculous I let out a loud snort. "Mom won't even let me work at a cannery in town. She thinks it's 'lowly,' her word."

"Of course it's lowly! And boring and slimy and gross! But it's money, and it's just for one summer. And I would be there to keep an eye on you."

"Then *for sure* Mom wouldn't let me."

Dena pretend pouts. "You know, if we were boys, we'd be out there fishing already. Dad started fishing with Grandpa when he was sixteen. I bet Uncle Steve started about the same age. Dougie's already talking about it."

"Somehow, I can't—"

"I know, my brother. Maybe he can talk the fish to death."

We both crack up, startling Lassie out of her belly-scratch bliss.

"I'm kind of glad I'm not a boy," I say. "I'd be afraid to go out after what happened."

"Yeah, can't say I blame you."

"But I'd like to go to Alaska," I add, surprising myself. "I want to find out why Mom thinks Dad may still be alive."

I hadn't meant to tell Dena. Why shatter her good memories of Dad with something that may or may not be true? But it slipped out, and now her face is frozen in shock.

"What . . . did you just say?"

Now I have to explain. I take in a deep breath and tell her about the conversation in the kitchen, including Mom saying that there's something I don't know about Dad.

"Hmm, she's not really saying that she thinks he's alive, only that she can't be sure that he's dead. There's a difference." Dena stares absently at Lassie, who's rolled over on her back again, inviting more belly rubs. "What do *you* think happened?"

"I don't know. If he's alive, he's a jerk for not calling us. On the other hand, I don't want him to be dead, but he probably is."

"I think you're right, sad as that is. I just can't imagine Uncle Steve leaving you all."

"I know. Me neither, unless it has to do with this thing I don't know about him. What do you suppose it is?"

Dena shrugs. "Beats me."

"See, that's what I need to find out, because whatever it is, it's shocking and bad and super-secret. I can tell by the way Mom's acting."

"Are you sure you want to know?"

I meet her eyes. "Yes."

"Well, you could talk to my dad. He's not going to snitch on his own brother, but you may pick up some clues."

"You really think Uncle Pat will talk to me?"

"Sure, why not?" She must sense my nervousness because she adds, "Do you want me to ask him for you?"

"Would you? Really? God, that would be great."

I didn't mean that Dena should ask him right now, but she says, "Just hold on," like it's an emergency and rushes out of the room. After a few minutes, I hear the doorknob turn and she's back, beckoning me to get up and join her. She deposits me in Grandma's sewing room, which at the moment is cluttered with boxes and ribbons and rolls of wrapping paper, and disappears back out the door.

I stare at Grandma's sewing machine. I've always been fascinated by it. It's an ancient one with a back-and-forth pedal you have to pump with your feet. At first, I think I'm alone in the room, but then I hear a shuffle and Uncle Pat backs out of a closet cradling a big, leather-bound book. He wipes the dust off the top with his arm.

"It's been a while since I've looked at this," he says, more to himself than to me. "So, you want to know more about your Dad. That's understandable." He sits in the chair next to the sewing machine and pulls up another chair next to him. The leather-bound book is a photo album.

"I was jealous of him." His tone is matter-of-fact. "He got the looks, the smarts . . . the girls." I expect him to go through the pages of photos starting at the beginning, but Uncle Pat opens the book in the middle, and I'm startled by a picture of my dad as a teenager, dressed in a tuxedo and standing next to a pretty, dark-haired girl who is obviously not my mother. They wear gold paper crowns.

"Prom King and Queen," he says.

"Who's he with?"

"Julie Thompson. Made head cheerleader as a junior. All the guys had crushes on her, but guess who won out?" He gives me a sad grin. "Your dad sure got the ladies. Oh, and in case you were wondering, he didn't meet your mother until after high school. Many hearts were broken when your father married your mother. Let's see . . ." He turns a couple of pages. "Ah. There she is." He tilts the book toward me so I can see the photo better. "Have you ever seen a more beautiful couple?"

I don't say anything, but the truth is, I haven't. Mom and Dad are standing in the living room of this house, dressed like they're about to go out dancing or to a fancy dinner. Back then, Mom had a fuller face framed by long, extravagant ringlets of honey-colored hair. A green satin gown sets off her coloring.

"That's the dress!" There's no mistaking it. It's the dress Mom threw on the pile of clothes to give away because she would "never wear it again."

"What?" Uncle Pat says, but he's already flipping backwards through the book, showing me photos of Dad as a younger teenager. There he is at the wheel of Grandpa's boat, one leg cocked in front of the other like his version of how a boat captain should stand.

"That was taken right before Steve's first trip to Alaska. Look at that grin. Already acting like he's the boss." Pat chuckles. "Those were some heady times, those first few seasons in Alaska with Dad. Start out a boy, come back a man."

"Dad said it's like the Wild West."

"Yeah, in some ways it is. I can tell you this much, you either love it or you hate it. Your dad loved it."

"More than Annisport?"

"Well, now, I wouldn't say that. We were always more than happy to get home."

Pat flips back through the book to a picture of Dad as a boy, standing next to a king salmon that's as big as he is. He's staring up at its hooked mouth, his own mouth hanging open. There are pictures of Christmases past, as well as birthday parties; in each one, Dad, the cutest and most photogenic, is always the focus. I begin to see what Uncle Pat means about him getting the best of everything.

Grandma Grace and Grandpa Bill are almost unrecognizable as the young parents of three boys. Grandpa's potbelly is missing and Grandma, holding baby Alex in her arms, sits up slim and straight. Her smooth face could even be described as pretty.

We've gotten to the front of the book, and I ask Uncle Pat if we can look at the pictures in the back half. He tells me those are mostly of Uncle Alex—that he and Dad had moved out by then—but agrees. As he quickly goes through the pages, I think I recognize Mom and Dad in another photo. I reach out my hand to stop Uncle Pat's turning and make him go back. Mom and Dad are sitting on our couch. She's holding me and I'm crying.

"Not a very nice picture of me," I say.

Uncle Pat's laugh sounds odd, forced. "No." He turns the

last page and closes the book. "Now, maybe you can tell me something." He runs his fingers over the embossed "Memories" on the cover of the photo album. "I was just talking to your mother. She's pretty dead set against a funeral. Do you know why?"

His question takes me by surprise. I want to say, "Because she thinks he might be alive," but something holds me back, so I just say, "Um."

"*Dead set* was a poor choice of words. I'm sorry. Why's your mom so *against* a funeral?"

"Ida?" Mom calls outside the door, relieving me of the need to answer.

My uncle coughs. "In here."

She walks in giving him the stink-eye, like maybe she overheard our conversation. Her open mouth twitches. I know that twitch.

"Ida and I were looking at some old photos," he says. I wonder if he's trying to sound casual, because Mom's mad as all get-out.

"Dinner is ready," she says coldly. As we're walking to the dining room, I hear pieces of their hushed argument behind me. Uncle Pat apologizes, though for what, I'm not sure.

WITHOUT Dad, I expected Christmas to be a half-hearted affair, but the size of this holiday spread tells me otherwise. I don't remember there ever being so much food on the table. The women—particularly Grandma Grace, who did most of the cooking—seem to be trying extra hard to fill the void. There are the usual dishes of spaghetti, sauerkraut, and pork

shank, but more of it, as well as mountains of mashed potatoes, yams, string beans, and Jell-O salad. Even with the lot
of us, I don't know how we can possibly eat it all. Then
Grandma Grace, skin shiny with sweat, places the largest
turkey I've ever seen on the table. We *ooh* and *aah* and clap.
Uncle Pat, who has the job of carving, says once the hubbub
dies down, "Good Lord! Should we invite the neighbors?"
Everybody laughs and Grandma Grace beams, flashing the
crowned tooth that has been a source of fascination for each
new grandkid to come along. We call it her Gold Fang.

In this merry chorus, Mom's scowl stands out like a sour
note. She's not even trying to hide it. For once I'm happy to
be at the kids' table, where I can pretend not to notice the
building storm. I only wish Dena could be here with me, but
she's finally graduated to the adult table. Poor Dena.

When everyone is settled, Grandpa Bill says grace.

"Dear Father, we thank you for this day, this feast, and
everyone at this table. We thank you for the gift of your Son
and for family and friends and the love and comfort they
bring. Although we mourn the loss of Steve, our dear son,
brother, husband, and father, we know that he is with You in
heaven. We ask that you help those who struggle to accept
his passing."

I steal another glance at Mom and am startled when our
eyes meet. Hers are narrowed into slits. Even from here, I can
see the muscles in her jaw tightening. I can't watch. *Please*, I
tell her with my thoughts, *don't make a scene. You can explode
all you want when we get home.*

"Heavenly Father, help us treasure each other this day
and all the days to come. In Jesus's name, amen."

A shuffling sound amid the murmurs of "amen" draws my attention back to Mom. She's standing, hands braced against the edge of the table. Oh, oh, here it comes. Guess she didn't get my message.

"You expect me to say amen to that? What's wrong with you people?"

"Now, Christine," Grandma says. "We—"

She whips around to face her mother-in-law. "You planned this. Don't think I don't know what you're doing. You get us over here and then you start in."

"Christine." Uncle Pat holds his palms out like stop signs.

"I'm not finished!" Mom's cheeks are flushed. "I know where I stand with this family. I know you tried to talk Steve out of marrying me." My relatives are stunned silent. Uncle Pat slowly shakes his head. Aunt Janet has her hand over her mouth. Across from me at the kids' table, Danielle's mouth hangs open, while Dougie purses his thick lips together, suppressing a giggle.

"Nineteen years," Mom is saying. "That's how long I've been pretending to be a part of this family. Well, no more! You can go ahead and have your funeral. I won't be attending!" She throws her red Christmas napkin on the table. Her chair scrapes the floor as she backs away. She walks over to me. "Ida, we're leaving." She takes me under the arm.

"I don't want to go." Her hand drops. I replant myself firmly on my folding chair.

Mom exhales loudly. In the stunned silence, every sound of her exit is amplified—the clomp of her heels, the creak of the closet door, the clang of the hanger as she yanks her coat free. I dare to glance over as she opens the front door. Her coat is draped over her arm, and her slip peeks out beneath the hem of her dress. It's not too late. I could get up, run after her. But I can't move. The door closes behind her, and I hear someone at the adult table, I'm not sure who, mutter, "Merry Christmas."

CHAPTER 11

Compass
*A navigational tool that shows the
direction of the vessel in relation to
the Earth's poles*

Uncle Pat gives me a ride home. We pass houses lined with lights of every color, twinkling and blinking shrubs and snowmen and reindeer, nativities glowing golden under bright white stars of Bethlehem. It's beautiful, and I want it all to go away.

"Christmas can be a cruel holiday," Uncle Pat says, reading my silence. "You're expected to be merry, but . . ."

I nod. He doesn't have to finish his sentence.

"Well, today . . . I know it was hard to watch, but she probably needed to get all that off her chest. I think it's been bubbling for some time."

"Nineteen years."

"Yes, well," he says, slowing down to take a turn, "I think this had to happen. Unfortunate that it had to be on Christmas, but . . . suffice to say, your mom's very fragile right now."

Fragile makes me think of a china figurine. Should I be careful with Mom because she's easily breakable? Or because she could explode at any moment? She seems to me both fragile and dangerous, and it kind of irks me that *I* have to wear the kid gloves when she's the one who spoiled Christmas. Though, who am I kidding? Christmas was already doomed.

"You can and will get through this," Uncle Pat continues. "Both of you will. Because you're strong, and maybe a bit stubborn, eh?" He reaches over and gives my arm a bump with his fist. "In some ways, you remind me of my brother."

He pulls up in front of our house. The porch light is on. So is my mother's light upstairs. Pat reaches behind his seat and pulls out the shopping bag with our presents as I get out of the car. Mom's are still wrapped. As he leans over the seat and hands me the bag, he looks at our house. "You'll be fine," he says. "But know that our home is always open to you if you need it, okay?"

"Okay. Thanks."

I shut the door and watch him drive away before opening the gate to our walkway. The front door is unlocked, which I think must be a good sign. Mom isn't so mad at me that she'll make me dig around for the hidden key. I deposit the bag of gifts next to our fake tree and head upstairs, past the light peeking around Mom's closed door, and into my room. I'll talk to her tomorrow, after we've both had a night to sleep on things.

WHEN my nightstand clock says noon, I force myself out of bed, throw on a robe, and go downstairs. Time to face the music, as Dad would say. But the house is quiet—too quiet. I check out front. The car is still in the driveway. Maybe she took a walk. I go back upstairs. The door to her bedroom is still closed, and, though it's daytime, I can see the faint yellow light of a lamp leaking around the seams. She's always up before me. Do I check on her? Uncle Pat would say I should, but I don't want to. At some point, she has to come down to eat. I'll talk with her then.

I go back downstairs, pour myself a bowl of cereal, and turn on the TV. Then I sort through my presents: a book of Bible verses from Grandma, fuzzy pink slippers from my younger cousins, a sweater-set from my aunts and uncles that looks way too big, and a manicure set from Dena with three different colors of nail polish: pearl pink, fire-engine red, and tropical coral. I open the box, take out the pearl pink, and prepare to do my nails while I watch TV.

The pickings are pretty slim the day after Christmas. I turn through a soap opera and *Jeopardy!* before finally settling on a *Bewitched* rerun. I suck at applying polish. It spills over my cuticles, then I rough up my right middle finger nail when I change the channel before my polish has completely dried. I redo the nail and spread my fingers to dry as I watch *Treasure Isle.* Then come two reruns of *The Fugitive.*

I tighten the cap of the polish bottle and put it back in its box. My nails look like a monkey did them, but at least I didn't make a mess anywhere else.

When it's time for *The Newlywed Game* and Mom still hasn't emerged, I start to worry that something awful has happened. What if she's taken an overdose of sleeping pills, like Marilyn Monroe? I don't even know if Mom uses sleeping pills. But she wouldn't do that, would she? Now I'm scared to go up to her room.

If our roles were reversed and I was the one who wouldn't come out, Mom would probably try to entice me with something to eat. She's not as interested in food as I am, but she might appreciate it if I fixed her a lunch. She missed yesterday's feast, so who knows when she ate last.

I go into the kitchen and get out the bread and the fixings for a turkey sandwich. We don't have any lettuce or tomatoes, so I just make it with extra slices of meat, figuring she could use the protein. The coffee pot sits idle on the back burner. She probably wants a cup of coffee most of all, but I don't know how to make it, so I just pour a glass of milk and get three Oreos for desert, taking one for myself. I cut the sandwich into four triangles and arrange them around the bottom of a plate like teeth. The three Oreos make two eyes and a nose. I giggle at what looks like a bulldog. I set the plate and the glass of milk on a TV tray and consider cutting a flower from outside and putting it in a bud vase, like they do in the movies, but nothing is blooming this time of year.

I somehow manage to get the tray up the stairs without slopping the milk, but now I have a choice. Do I take it in her room? Or leave it outside? *Stop being such a baby, Ida. Take it in.* So I do, knocking twice first.

She's in bed, as I suspected. And though she's obviously alive, her eyes are ringed with puffy red bags and her hair is messy and stuck to her head on one side, showing white scalp. She smiles weakly at me and props herself higher on her pillows.

"I made you some lunch," I say, setting the tray down over her lap.

"Thank you."

Okay, she's not mad, but I don't know if I should stay in the room or leave. She probably doesn't want me to watch her eat. I turn to leave.

"Wait," she says. "I need to talk to you."

I turn around. She pats her bed. When I sit down, she asks me how I got home last night.

"Uncle Pat drove me."

She nods then looks down at her plate. "It's a face. Is it supposed to be the Abominable Snowman?"

"Yep, you got it."

Mom picks up a wedge of sandwich only to set it down on the plate again. "Hey, I'm sorry about yesterday. I guess I overreacted. It was silly."

Silly sounds like an understatement, but I don't tell her that. "Yeah, you were pretty mad."

"Well, I hope *you* can forgive me at least." She waits. I don't dare look up. I don't want to see the need in her eyes.

"Grandma gets to me, too," I say finally. "I mean, she didn't get the nickname Graceless for nothing."

Mom laughs, a bit too loudly. "Moliere said that the best reply to unseemly behavior is patience and moderation. I showed neither, and now I hope for the same."

I'm not sure what she means. She seems to be talking in riddles. Then I remember something from yesterday, something Mom said in anger. "Were Grandma and Grandpa really against Dad marrying you?"

She purses her lips together and looks up at the ceiling.

"Well, let's put it this way. I think they would have preferred your father marry a nice, Slavic girl who was prepared to be the wife of a fisherman."

"And that wasn't you."

She snorts. "That wasn't me."

"But Dad didn't feel that way, did he? I mean, he must have loved you a lot to go against his parents."

Mom turns serious. She lowers her head as if to work out a kink in her neck, but it isn't a kink, because when she looks up, her eyes are filled with tears. She shakes her head, sniffs, and wipes her tears with her fingers. I reach for the napkin on her tray and hand it to her.

"Thank you. You did your nails."

"Yeah, not very well."

She smiles as she blots her eyes and wipes her hands. Then she gamely picks up a piece of sandwich and takes a bite. "Here help me eat this," she says. "Take a cookie."

I end up eating more of Mom's lunch than she does, but it seems to do something. She gets out of bed, takes a long bath and comes out in her robe. She makes us a late dinner of hamburger and beans over rice, then we sit down together to watch the CBS Thursday night movie. It's called *The Pleasure of His Company* and stars Fred Astaire and Debbie Reynolds, so I'm expecting a romantic comedy, with maybe some singing and dancing. I'm not expecting a story that's eerily familiar. Fred Astaire plays this globetrotting guy who comes back for his daughter's wedding after being gone for most of her life. He's really kind of a jerk, the way he worms his way back into the family and interferes with their plans.

"Everyone loves a charmer," Mom says, getting up and tightening the belt to her robe. "I'm going to bed."

"You're not going to watch the end?"

"No, I've seen enough."

She goes upstairs. When I hear the door to her room shut, I hope it's just for the night. I watch the rest of the movie because I want to see how it ends. Fred Astaire doesn't stop the wedding or break up his former wife's marriage, but he does take off with the family cook. Everyone's happy. If only real life were like that. I turn off the TV, thinking the only similarity between Fred Astaire and my dad is a tendency towards big gifts. I finger the locket of the necklace he gave me. Was his generosity just "guilt talking," like Mom says? I'd like to think he didn't fake anything, including his disappearance, but does that mean I'm wishing him dead? My mind goes through those same old loops. They hurt, those loops.

I wake up to another quiet house, but this time Mom really is gone. The car is missing, and in the kitchen, next to the box of Cheerios on the counter, is a hastily scribbled note:

I've gone into town to play grown-up. Love, Mom.

I'm not sure what "playing grown-up" means, but it sounds positive. Still, I decide it's best to lie low and not go over to see Dena, which is what I normally do during Christmas break. In Mom's state, she shouldn't come home to an empty house. I'm sure of that.

Since I overdosed on TV yesterday, I go to my box of books from Nana and pick out a new one. *Jane Eyre*, Mom's favorite. I'm afraid it's going to be boring, with endlessly long descriptions, like some old books, but after a few pages, I'm hooked. The bully cousin, the mean aunt, the "red room," the school where Jane is starved and punished and sees her best friend die of typhoid . . . Jeez, when is she going to get a break?

I'm so absorbed in her troubles, I don't even notice Mom is home until the front door opens, blasting me with cold air.

"Brrr. It almost feels like snow out there." She's wearing a dress under her coat. No wonder she's cold. She hangs her coat in the closet and glances at my book. "Oh, *Jane Eyre*. I couldn't put that one down."

"Yeah, me neither." I want to keep reading, but I mark my place and set the book down on the coffee table, covering half of Vancouver Island. Mom kicks off her boots and sits down next to me on the sofa, curling her legs under her.

"I've been pounding the pavement," she says. I picture a road worker with one of those loud drills that breaks up concrete, but she's obviously not dressed for that.

"I'm trying to find work. I went to three different places today. None of them are hiring right now, with Christmas being over, but at least they'll have my information on file if something opens up."

"Wow, that's great, Mom." My voice comes out sounding flat, almost sarcastic, despite my shock. This isn't the woman who just recently spent a day and a half in bed.

She smoothes her skirt over her knees. "I just decided I had to do something to feel better about myself."

"That's great. Good luck."

She gives me a smirk and I quickly add, "With finding a job, I mean."

CHAPTER 12

Aweigh
*Position of an anchor just clear of
the bottom*

I never thought I'd be so happy for Christmas break to end
and school to begin. After two weeks that seemed like a
month locked in a cave, it's a relief to be back among my
friends, following the same schedule they are, doing the same
things they're doing. It's much better thinking about things
that don't involve my mother, like the events that led to
World War I.

When I see Dena at lunch, she asks me if I'm doing okay
and if my mom's still mad.

"No, more like embarrassed," I tell her.

She must sense that I don't want to talk about it, because
she changes the subject. She's over Andrew, her first crush of
the year, and has moved on to Paul, this boy in her algebra
class who's helping her with the trickier equations.

"Yeah, I bet."

She takes a bite of her apple and gives me a wink. "What about you?" she asks with her mouth full. "Still stuck on David Mackey?"

"Not after he stood me up."

She swallows. "Stood you up? You mean you made a date?"

"Not the kind you're thinking of." I tell her about meeting David in the library to talk about my dad and our plans to meet again the next day. I tell her how I'd lost sleep the night before and agonized over what to wear, all for nothing. "He never showed, and I know he was in school."

"How rude," she says, taking another bite of her apple.

"He probably just forgot, but still."

"You haven't talked to him since?"

"No, but I've seen him around, and I'm pretty sure he's seen me."

"Forget about him," Dena says. "What about that Filipino guy in your English class? He's kinda cute."

"Sam?

She nods.

"He's nice, but he's just a friend "

Dena raises one perfectly penciled eyebrow.

"Honestly, Dena. There's nothing there." I don't say what I'm really thinking, that Sam and I simply don't match—a wiry Filipino boy with a tall, kinda chubby white girl? It's one thing meeting him in the library, quite another to be boyfriend and girlfriend. Besides, Mom would probably have a cow, given her view of canneries and the seasonal Filipino workers who fill them.

I wonder if her opinion has softened now that she's looking for a job. If she has trouble landing one, maybe she'll be more understanding of the people forced to work the slime line.

I never get the chance to find out. On Thursday afternoon, a woman calls our home asking for Mrs. Petrovich. I think it's probably a solicitor, but I tell her to hold on and get Mom to come to the phone. When the brief call is over, Mom screams and jumps up and down like a kid.

"What?" I ask, though I have a pretty good idea.

"That was the manager of Fine Lines Women's Boutique. One of their saleswomen has decided to take an indefinite bereavement leave. She asked if I could start next Monday." She squeals again.

"I guess you said *yes.*"

"Honestly I would have said yes if she'd asked me to come down to the shop this minute. God, I hope I didn't sound too excited. The woman I'm filling in for just found out that her son is missing in action, poor thing. I know how she feels."

The job, even if it is only temporary, has Mom flitting around the house like a hummingbird. One minute she's replacing mothballs in the coat closet and the next she's laying out possible outfits for her first day. I'm asked to pick which one would make the best impression on her clientele, which brings to mind old ladies shopping for girdles and sensible shoes. I point to a chocolate brown pantsuit paired with a paisley scarf because it looks comfortable.

"No," Mom says, pinching her chin. "Think I'll go with the red sweater and gray skirt."

"Yeah, you're probably right. That pantsuit's way too modern for Fine Lines."

"What do you mean? They sell classics that never go out of style."

"If you say so."

She sighs, but it's the light-hearted sigh of a woman with plans. "We need new drapes for the living room. The carpets need cleaning. And wouldn't it be nice to have a complete set of matching dishes?"

"I guess," I say, but she's not really listening. She knows the things she wants to replace never bothered me.

As keyed up as she is, this sure beats a mother who won't get out of bed. Monday morning, she's out the door before me, even though her day starts an hour later than mine. When she gets home at five thirty, her back is sore from standing and her feet are killing her, but she's alive with stories about her day—the husband shopping for a gift for his wife, the big-hipped lady she managed to steer away from bold prints, the woman who needed a blouse to go with an awful green tweed skirt.

"I found her three blouses and another, more suitable skirt. She took them all." Mom beams. She asks me how school was, if I've done my homework, and what I've eaten. The last question lets her gauge how quickly she has to get dinner on. Today it's Chef Boyardee, which is fine by me. I could eat Beefaroni every night.

We establish a new routine. She's out the door when I am, dressed to the nines in skirts and dresses accessorized with scarves, belts, bead necklaces, and big plastic bracelets that make an attractive clinking sound when she walks. She doesn't get home until five thirty or sometimes six, which means I'm home alone for at least two hours every afternoon. I let myself in with the hidden key, fix myself a snack, and watch TV. I've seen every episode of *Gilligan's Island* at least twice. If I can't stomach watching another repeat, I'll do homework or read. I raced through *Jane Eyre*, and now I'm reading *The Secret Garden*. Both books are about houses that hide secrets. Another sign?

Maybe this house holds a clue to that thing I don't know about Dad. Maybe he left something behind that will explain the part of him I never knew, the part that loved risky fishing, Native folktales, and Alaskan prostitutes.

CHAPTER 13

Scuttlebutt
A water-filled barrel sailors used to drink from

I don't know what I'm looking for, but Dad's workshop seems like a good place to start. So after I do my homework, I count to three and run down the basement stairs, as if diving into a cold lake or ripping off a Band-Aid. If I'm fast and fearless, no ghost or fear of ghosts can get the better of me.

I'm hit with the familiar smell of glues and resins as I open the door and head to Dad's filing cabinet. With its eighty drawers full of knickknacks, this was my favorite thing in the world when I was younger. The few times I was allowed to be in his workshop with him, I begged to explore the things he called fillers: buttons, shells, ceramic shards, sea glass, map fragments, rope, and other things he used to add spots of color and context to his table tops, trays and coasters. If he was feeling generous, he would play a game of Concentration with me, making me guess what was inside a drawer

before opening it. If I guessed right, I'd get to open three
more. The big, flat drawers were easy to remember. They
held things like maps and old game boards. But the little
drawers were easily confused. I'd get buttons mixed up with
coins mixed up with bottle caps until I got to know the contents of his cabinet as well as he did.

I reach for a random middle drawer. This will be . . .
marbles. I pull the handle, and immediately realize my error.
The drawer is too light. It holds puzzle pieces, grouped in
plastic bags according to size, from big wooden kid puzzles to
those maddeningly hard five-thousand-piece jigsaws in
blending shades of blue, green, and brown. I close the drawer,
releasing a puff of dust. When Dad spread his epoxy, he did
everything in his power to prevent dust from marring the
sticky, glass-like surface. Now that he's not around to clean,
the dust has returned to settle over everything.

My favorite drawer is three rows down, right middle column. I open it to find it still filled with the little toys you'd
find at the five-and-dime, or at the dentist's office as a reward
for your pain—rhinestone rings, spinning tops, whistles,
jacks. It took all my willpower not to rifle through that stuff
when I was younger, and I don't do it now.

The last drawer I try is a wide, flat one at the bottom of
the cabinet. It appears to be empty, but when I try to push it
closed, it gets stuck on something. I reach my hand in and
touch the corner of what feels like an envelope. It takes some
tugging. When I finally pry it loose, it's an envelope all right,
but empty. I shut the drawer and leave the envelope on the
worktable. It was mailed to us marked "DO NOT BEND!" in
red, probably because it held someone's precious mementoes,

maybe old letters or photographs, maybe keepsakes from a wedding or a birth.

For all the sentimental projects he did for others, Dad wasn't one to save things for himself. A quick glance around his workshop reveals nothing of *his*, like a photo of me or Mom or a paperweight with my first baby shoe. The only thing he ever made for us was the map coffee table, and that was just so we'd have a handy reference when we wanted to know where he was.

The absence of personal things makes me wonder if he wanted it that way. In the event of his death, maybe he thought it would be easier for us if he left no meaningful objects behind. I'm glad I have the one picture of him, but where did all those departure and arrival pictures go? I do the multiplying in my head: nineteen years times two equals thirty-eight, and that's assuming we only took one photo each time. Surely Mom didn't throw them away during her cleaning binge.

Maybe I'm searching in the wrong place. Maybe I should try their bedroom, which of course is Mom's room now.

And she's at work.

The smell of Tabu warns me that I'm entering her space. It's orderly, intimate—forbidden. The clothes in her closet hang according to item and color, lights to darks. Pants and skirts take up the bottom rod, while shirts, blouses, and jackets fill out the top. Her shoes are all perfectly paired on a rack on the floor. I'm afraid to touch anything for fear that she will immediately spot something amiss. Before I go through anything, I memorize exactly how it's all arranged.

There's a big cardboard box on a back shelf labeled

"Green Giant Corn." I pull it down. It's surprisingly light for its size. I set it down on the neatly made bed, telling myself to remember to smooth the dimples out of bedspread when I'm done. I undo the box's overlapped flaps to find . . . baby clothes. There's the pale blue polka dot dress Mom made for me when I was four. I remember being very excited about it, particularly the pink flower appliqué she sewed on last. On the fireplace mantel is a framed studio photo of me in that dress. It's the only time I remember wearing it. In the picture, its sheer blue fabric is fluffy as a cloud. Out of the box, it's flat as a pressed flower. I run my fingers over the girly appliqué and set it aside.

The rest of the baby clothes include some things I remember, some I don't. There's a tiger costume I recognize from another photograph, some pajamas with feet, and a pair of swim pants with rows of ruffles over the bottom. I also find a pair of impossibly tiny baby shoes, along with some yellow booties that Nana probably knitted. Underneath it all is a blue book, the *Better Homes & Gardens Baby Book*. I pick it up and it falls open to the middle pages, where Mom has pasted photos and written in my information. My birth certificate is displayed in a border of pink stars opposite a page, titled "Identification." There's a stamp of my newborn foot at the top and a section for "Distinguishing Marks" in the middle. The bottom third of the page is devoted to "Baby's First Snapshots." There's only one photo: I'm asleep next to my mother, who looks very tired, but happy, propped up in her hospital bed. The only part of me that's visible in the blanket is my red and blotchy face. I'm not very cute. I wonder if Dad thought the same thing as he took the picture, and then I remember that Dad probably wasn't there. By late May, he was already fishing.

I put the book and clothes back in the order I found them in, fold the flaps closed, and put the box back on the shelf where I found it. I smooth the dimples out of the bedspread and move on to Mom's dresser. In the top drawer are the predictable underthings, including an unopened box of day-of-the-week panties, as bright and shiny as jewels. A gift from Dad? I'm intrigued by which colors go with which days. Saturdays are black with red stitching, like the devil, while Sundays are white with pink, like an angel.

The lower shelves contain sweaters and knit pants and tops that don't wrinkle—all very orderly and expected. As I go to pull out the bottom drawer, I'm thinking this is a waste of time—and then it doesn't budge. I have to give it a good yank to finally open it, and when I do, it nearly falls off its tracks and onto the floor, spilling the top layer of what has to be hundreds of loose photographs, cards, and letters. They appear to have been dumped in there with no thought other than to store them out of the way. The mess is so unlike my mother that I decide she won't notice if I take anything.

I go through the letters first, because there are far fewer of them and they hold the greatest potential reward. The first one I open is to Mom from her sister, Corrine. It's mostly an update on all the people Mom left behind in Butte, Montana, along with Corrine's complaints about how bored she is and how lucky Mom is to have finally gotten out. Anticipating more of the same, I find all the letters from Aunt Corrine—identifiable by her cheerful return-address sticker in the left-hand corner—and put them aside without reading them.

There are also letters and cards from Nana and Grandpa Mack, some with yellowed newspaper articles, including two wedding announcements and an obituary for people in Butte I've never heard of.

What I want to find is a letter from Dad, but there isn't one, not even a Christmas or birthday card. I guess he wasn't ever one to write—but then, why would he need to if they were living in the same town and dating or already married? Come to think of it, he never sent so much as a single post-card from Alaska. He always called, and things were always going well. Maybe he didn't want to alarm us—or run up long-distance charges—with all the gory details.

I move on to the photographs, starting with the color photographs because they're more recent and there are fewer of them. It's a mishmash of Christmases, birthdays, and—could it be? Yes, there's Dad in his red sweater on the deck of the *Lady Rose*. He's younger in this picture. The date on the side is May 2, 1961. So that's one departure picture. Where are all the others? I dig down deeper in the drawer, but all I find are early black-and-white pictures of me. It's a miracle I didn't go blind from all the flashbulbs. No wonder I look like such a surprised and angry baby.

The toddler photos are more flattering because I'm usu-ally focused on something other than the camera. Also, I have hair by that time, lots of it. Mom says my curls were so pretty that she didn't want to cut them. There's one picture of me, at about three years old, standing in the backyard, naked ex-cept for a pair of Dad's black shoes, which look like freighters on my feet. The sun shines on my white body and my mass of black ringlets. I was a lot cuter then.

Toward the bottom of the pile, I come across another baby picture that's oddly familiar, and then it dawns on me why. It's almost exactly like the one of Mom and Dad that I saw in Uncle Pat's photo album, except I'm not crying in this one; I'm staring straight at the camera with my mouth hanging open. Another flattering shot of me. It was taken at my grandparents' house. There's Grandma Grace's shadow box hanging on the wall with all her figurines. When was this taken? The date stamp says March 24, 1949. That's odd. Someone must have made a mistake. I was born in 1952.

I set the photo down and shove the drawer closed. I'm getting nowhere looking around this house. It makes sense. Why would my parents leave clues to some shameful secret just lying around? I know Mom wouldn't. And Dad, well, his real home was a place I'll never see again. The Lady Rose is either resting on the bottom of the ocean or has been changed so it looks nothing like the original. Maybe it's been painted a different color, with a new name to go with his new life. Either way, I'm out of luck.

CHAPTER 14

Strike

Any hit by a fish taking a lure or bait

Dena pops her gum and curls her pointer finger, motioning us to huddle. Loud as the lunchroom is, I don't know why she thinks she has to whisper to a whole table full of girls, but I lean in with the others.

"Veronica and Charlie broke up," she says.

"What?" asks Kathleen, who's sitting on the end.

"I said, Veronica and Charlie broke up," she repeats in a louder voice. "You know what that means, don't you? The two most popular people at this school are without dates for the Valentine's Tolo."

"What's a tolo?" I ask.

Dena rolls her eyes. "Okay, for the benefit of all you young'uns, a tolo is a dance where the girl invites the guy. And Veronica and Charlie are now wild cards, provided they don't get back together before Valentine's Day. And I'd say the odds of that are zero to nil."

"Zero and nil mean the same thing," Gerry says.

"Why, what happened?" Sophie leans in farther until her nose is inches from Dena's ear.

"Charlie was cheating on her. Some girl at the junior college."

Sophie's eyes widen behind her glasses. "Wow, how do you know that?"

Dena stops chewing her gum long enough to draw a finger across her mouth. "My lips are sealed. I just thought some of you might like to know Charlie's available. But you better move fast. The dance is just two weeks away."

"Heck, I'm going to ask him right now." Gerry makes a move like she's getting up, prompting an eruption of laughter. I love Gerry.

News delivered, Dena leans back, takes her gum out of her mouth, and rolls it in the edge of her lunch sack. "I'm thinking of asking Paul."

I vaguely remember her telling me about the boy in her algebra class. "You should. It sounds like he likes you."

She takes out her sandwich. "I don't know. I'm kind of scared."

"Since when have you been scared of anything?"

Gerry snorts at that.

"What if he says *no?*" Dena pouts.

"What if he says *yes?*"

"Okay, if you're so brave, why don't you ask Sam?" Dena points her sandwich at me.

I roll my eyes to show her how ridiculous she's being. "I already told you, we're just friends."

WALKING to the library, I catch my reflection in a glass display case and suck in my stomach. I wonder what Sam's answer would be if I *did* ask him? Maybe he'd turn me down flat. Maybe he thinks I'm big and ugly. But then why would he go to the trouble of returning my photo? Why would he invite me to the library to share his newspaper? For that matter, why do I keep coming here to see him?

Nothing has changed between us, yet I get a touch of the jitters when I see him sitting at our customary table, his face hidden behind the front page.

My "hi" comes out sounding too high.

"Hi." He glances at me then goes back to his paper. "The Vietcong attacked the US Embassy in Saigon, but we got them all." He turns back to page one to show me the headline. EMBASSY SECURED. SUICIDE RAID WIPED OUT.

"That's good, right?" And here I was, worried about a stupid dance.

"Good we got them. But scary they got in."

The bell rings. He folds the paper and grabs his books, and we walk to English together. I want to say something reassuring, but he knows so much more about what's going on than I do, I'm afraid whatever I say will sound dumb. To me, it's just a war in a far-off place that's killing our boys, nothing reassuring about it.

My thoughts return to the dance. Do I even want to go? I've been to dances before. Everyone stands around. It's really awkward. I try to picture me and Sam arm in arm, but even my imagination can't make our pairing graceful. We're mismatched. About all we have in common appearance-wise is our dark hair. Dad would tell me those superficial things don't matter—that it's what's inside that counts. I'm not sure what Mom would say.

Or Sam, for that matter. He's so polite, I'm sure he'd reject me in the nicest possible way, but I'd be so embarrassed I'd probably start avoiding him, which would mean no more talking to him. And I *do* like talking to him. At least I have time to think about it. I doubt any other girl will ask him. He's cute, but he's not a hot commodity like the newly eligible Charlie Hanson or even David Mackey, who's probably been asked already—not that I care.

DENA chickens out on asking Paul, while Gerry and Sophie never get around to asking anybody, so they all ask me to ask Sam to be our shared date, which is much easier than asking him to be *my* date.

I present it as a sort of charity mission on his part. Actually, I don't have to try too hard. He just needs convincing that I'm serious.

Deciding to go as a group solves several problems in addition to the obvious one. My mother can't say no if I'm just going with friends. In fact, she thinks it's a brilliant idea and even helps us find four dresses at Fine Lines that teenagers would actually wear.

We all pile into Dena's car—going together has also solved our transportation problems—to pick up Sam. He lives in a basement apartment in a former boarding house kitty-corner from the canneries. We walk down a moldy concrete stairwell.

There is no bell, so I knock loudly on the weathered door.

A lady who looks more like Sam's sister than his mother opens it. She throws up her arms and says something that sounds like, "Oh." I imagine what a sight we must be—four girls in pastel dresses with big, hair-sprayed 'dos, rather like a girl singing group or a bowl of after-dinner mints. We all file into her small living room.

"Wow!" Sam's eyes widen as if he's really seeing a famous singing group. "You're all so beautiful."

"Aww, so are you!" Dena says—then, realizing her mistake, adds, "Handsome, I mean." He's wearing a tie, navy blue slacks, and a brown tweed sports coat that's a bit big on him. His hair is greased and combed back.

"Four girl!" his mom says. With her accent, it sounds like *poor gull.* She leans in to ask Sam a question, and I distinctly hear her say my name. Sam introduces us, calling Dena "Dinah," and stopping at Sophie, whose name he can't remember.

"Picture?" Sam's mom holds up a Brownie camera and motions for us to stand together.

"Wait." I open the little white box I'm carrying and take out Sam's boutonniere, a pink rose to go with my dress. Sam is *my* friend, after all. In my attempt to pin it on his lapel without sticking him, I end up sticking myself. I suck on the end of my stuck finger and shake it.

Sam's mom poses us for about a zillion pictures, including some of just Sam and me. I'm thinking we probably won't make it to the dance at all, and then she gets to the last exposure on her roll of film. As we're leaving, she reaches out and pats my shoulder. "Happy I meet you!" she says, bringing her hand to her throat.

We're forty-five minutes late to the dance, not because of the pictures but because Dena planned it that way.

"Only dorks show up on time," she says.

The gym has been transformed into a ballroom with the help of low light and a professional DJ, a giant of a man with a growly voice and a small, pointy beard. Even though we're late and the song "Cry Like a Baby" is definitely something you can dance to, we don't dance. We stand. We sit. We walk around and try to talk to other people who are standing and walking around, but the music is too loud to really hear each other. To have an actual conversation, you have to go to the restroom. I hesitate to leave Sam alone, but I'm dying to talk girl stuff and make sure my beehive is still standing up straight.

I needn't have worried. Sometimes having thick, naturally frizzy hair is an advantage. My beehive is stiff as a Brillo pad. Sophie's, meanwhile, is leaning dangerously to one side, and no amount of bobby pins and hairspray can get it right. In frustration, she rips out all the reinforcements and lets her hair flop like one of Nana's cakes. We all stare at her sad reflection in the mirror and decide there's only one thing left to do.

"Ouch!" She winces, eyes tearing, as the three of us work together with wetted combs to get through the rat's nest one tangle at a time.

"Sam's such a cutie, I just want to hug him!" Dena wiggles her tongue at me.

"He's obviously sweet on Ida," Gerry adds with a wink in my direction.

I blush.

"Ooh, and Ida's sweet on him! She's turning red," Dena says to my reflection in the mirror.

"Stop it, you guys."

Once Sophie's hair is combed out and my regular skin tone returns, we all head back out to find Sam holding up the wall near the restrooms. Now I feel more responsible for him than ever. If he's bored and miserable, he might stop liking me. I don't want him to stop liking me, now that I realize I like him.

Thank God for Aretha Franklin. "Respect" comes on. Gerry squeals, "I *love* this song!" and pulls Sam out into the throng of couples dancing. He has no choice. Neither do we. When she sees Dena, Sophie, and me standing with the spectators she runs over and corrals us in, too. My movements are awkward and jerky at first, but pretty soon I forget myself and just go with the music. Gerry is in heaven, and the rest of us, even Sam, can't stop grinning. The five of us dance to the next three songs.

Then the DJ puts on a slow one, and everyone stops.

I'm turning to go back into the margins when Dena pushes Sam and me together and leaves with Gerry and Sophie before we can object. The song is "My Special Angel." Sam shrugs and reaches out one arm and then the other, taking me in a loose embrace with his hands light on my back. We rock back and forth, taking tiny steps in what can hardly be called a dance. With my hair, I'm at least three inches taller than he is.

The song ends and we pull apart. We turn to join the others, who are sitting somewhere along the dark outer edge of the gym. I don't notice what's happening at first because I'm walking ahead of him, but there's no mistaking that word.

"Hey, Chink!"

I turn around. Three guys have blocked Sam's way. I recognize one of them, a thick kid with blond hair, from that afternoon in the woods. I stand beside Sam.

"We have a score to settle," says the blond boy. "Lose the dogs and meet us outside?" Dogs? Then it dawns on me that he's talking about me, Dena, Sophie, and Gerry.

"We're a whole lot more attractive than your dates," I say, giving him and his cronies my best stink-eye. I take Sam's arm.

"So now you're letting your girlfriend fight for you?" the boy shouts above the music, which has started up again. "She *is* a lot bigger than you are."

Sam's body stiffens next to mine. "Don't take the bait!" I say into his ear. As I try to pull him away, the blond boy gets in one last dig.

"Must be nice having a bodyguard," he says. "But who's on top? Girl like that could crush you like a bug."

Sam springs. The kid's face registers shock as they both go down.

"Sam!" My shout is lost in the growing commotion as everyone starts to react to the fray in their midst.

Sam and the boy roll on the floor, punching and clawing at each other. Sam's smaller but a better fighter, getting in two sharp jabs for every sloppy punch the other boy throws. I'm desperate to stop them, but my reflexes twitch uselessly as I watch Sam land blow after blow. Around me, some kids have caught on and made way, shouting "Fight! Fight!" as if this is some featured entertainment.

"Stop!" My scream pierces through the chaos just as the

music ends. Everyone stops talking and turns toward me. While Sam is distracted, his opponent clocks him under the jaw and he falls backwards.

The lights come on. "Get back," growls a low voice. The crowd parts to make way for someone big.

"Break it up." With one hand, the DJ grabs the blond boy by the neck of his jacket as you would a kitten by its scruff. He's still flailing and kicking, leaking blood from his nose. It leaves bright red drops on the polished gymnasium floor. His skin is all blotchy red and he's bleeding from his lip as well. His shirt is torn. Sam rolls over on his side, rubs his jaw with his hand. His knuckles are raw and bleeding. I hope his jaw is okay. I want to go over to him, but I remember what the other boy said about me being a bodyguard and I hold myself back. Sam slowly gets up on his knees. His hair, once neatly combed back, falls over his sweaty forehead as he reaches over to retrieve something small and pink off the floor—his rose boutonniere. It's all crushed and hardly worth saving, but he slips it into his pocket.

"What's going on here?" Mr. Balducci, the assistant prin-cipal, pushes his way through the crowd of kids.

"These two got into a scuffle," the DJ says. He's still got his grip on the other boy, even though he's stopped thrashing.

One of the boy's friends comes forward. "He jumped my friend!" The friend points at Sam.

"You guys started it!" I yell.

"Okay, you, you, you, and you—come with me," Mr. Balducci says pointing at me last. "Oh, and Mr. DJ," he says to the big man, "thank you. Now, can you put on something slow and soothing?"

I take Sam's hand, sticky with blood, and squeeze it very gently to let him know I'm with him as the five of us leave the gym with Mr. Balducci. We're halfway down the hall to his office when I hear over the speakers the first chords of Steppenwolf's "Born to be Wild."

Somehow I don't think that's the "slow and soothing" Mr. Balducci had in mind.

ON the drive home, we all offer to help Sam explain to his Mom what happened, but he says no, she'll understand. His father was the one who taught him to fight.

"With him gone, I am the man of the house. He taught me how to fight with my whole body, arms and legs. Sticks, too. But I sometimes wish I didn't learn because now I'm like a magnet. Everyone wants to prove he is better."

"Have you ever tried just walking away?" Sophie asks.

"That's the problem. I can't."

CHAPTER 15

Spring
A species of salmon, also called
Chinook and King

Sam gets a two-week suspension from school. When Mom finds out, she's appalled, but not for the right reasons. She doesn't care that the other boy called him a bad name, or that Sam stood up for me. All that matters to her is that I was with a boy who was disciplined for fighting, and she wants me to "nip this relationship in the bud."

Of course, I'm ignoring her.

Sam and I meet outside the fence by the football field after school. I give him his homework assignments so he doesn't fall too far behind. Then, because the buses have all left, he walks me home. He doesn't come in the house, though. Even with my mom working, he thinks it's too risky.

I like walking with Sam, even though the crocuses are blooming and the trees are starting to bud. Spring is the leaving season. It's never been easy for me; this year, though, I'm wondering how I will survive it. Right about now, Dad would be growing antsy. Even with the declining runs, he always enjoyed the preparations, being busy with a purpose. Making tables and coasters couldn't compare. This year, I'll see all the fishermen, including my uncles, getting ready for the season and know my father won't be among them.

To make matters worse, I'll be saying good-bye to the two people who could help me through the long summer ahead: Dena and Sam are both going to Alaska to process fish—Dena to Wrangell, which sounds like it should be in Wyoming, and Sam to Petersburg, which sounds like it should be in Russia. Sam will be working at Nagoon Seafoods, another weird name. His mom knows a foreman up there who has agreed to take him on even though he's not eighteen yet.

"But there are canneries *here*," I tell him as we take a shortcut through Causland Park.

"But the overtime is up north."

I know without him having to explain that he'll do much better in Alaska. Our canneries are closing, one by one. A few years ago one burned down and everyone figured it was done intentionally, to get the insurance money.

The old photographs that decorate the walls of the post office show the good old days, when huge warehouse floors were shin-deep with salmon and the waterfront was lined with processing plants. Today, Cannery Row reminds me of a comb with half its teeth missing. The fishing fleet still goes out every spring, but they're not necessarily staying in Puget Sound. Most are continuing up the coast to Alaska.

"I'll be back by the third week in August," Sam says, as if

this is a consolation. Late August is too late to have any summer together. I know it and he knows it.

"That's when the fishing boats return," I say. "I used to go down to the dock to wait for them and log the arrivals."

He gives me a quizzical look.

"It was a way to mark the time until my dad came home."

I kick at the gravel path with my scuffed-up loafers. The air smells of daffodils and cherry blossoms, adding to my despair. "I hate the time of year everybody loves the most. Spring and summer are just seasons to get through."

"Well, I'll be scooping fish guts for hours and thinking about you."

He stops and pulls me into a hug, then awkwardly lets go. We haven't graduated to kissing, and now I wonder if we ever will. He'll be up there with older, prettier girls—girls like Dena, but without her loyalty.

She's still pestering me to find a way to go with her. If only. I keep reminding her that I'm underage, with an overprotective mother who just lost a husband.

"Alaska may as well be on Mars," I tell her. "But I'll ask, just to make you happy."

"YOU can't be serious." Mom stands at the stove opening a can of bean-with-bacon soup.

"But Dena says you can earn, like, two grand in one summer, and I thought, with money being tight, this would be a way to pay for college." There, I've dropped the magic c-word.

She slaps the bottom of the soup can over the pot to release the suction. The soup plops out, can-shaped.

"You're too young," she says, finality in her voice. "I'm pretty sure they have child labor laws, even in Alaska."

"But I'm almost sixteen. Sixteen-year-olds can work. All of my friends are getting summer jobs." This is a bit of a stretch. I actually only know of three—Dena, Sam, and Gerry. Sophie's going to some pre-college enrichment camp for smart kids.

Mom fills the empty can with milk and pours it over the blob of soup. "So get a summer job around here. You don't have to go to Alaska."

"But I want to go with Dena." As soon as the words are out of my mouth, I know I'm sunk. I have no reason to believe Mom's opinions of my cousin have softened any since that Halloween party. And it's not like Dena's had opportunities to get in Mom's good graces given what happened over Christmas. The relatives have pretty much left her alone. Maybe they're waiting for an apology. They should know better. Mom may have told me she was sorry, but she would never admit that to the in-laws. She's way too proud.

"When you're eighteen, we'll talk," she says as the soup begins to bubble.

"But—"

"No."

WITH nothing better to do, I go back to searching her room. Her nightstand yields nothing—a half-empty bottle of Ponds cold cream, one of those black eye-mask thingies ladies wear to sleep at night, and an advice book on grief that she never cracked open—I can tell by the unwrinkled spine. The nightstand on Dad's side is empty.

Once again, I pull out the bottom drawer of her dresser. On top is the pile of letters from Aunt Corrine I set aside. I look at the return-address stickers.

Oh . . . my . . . God. How could I be so dense?

I shove the drawer closed, run out of Mom's room and down two flights of stairs to Dad's workshop. That envelope. I never checked to see if it had a return address.

It's sitting right where I left it, on top of Dad's worktable. I pick it up and turn it over. Sure enough, it was mailed from Alaska: P.O. Box 977 in Ketchikan, to be exact. I stare at the handwriting in black ink. No name or business, just the post office box in Ketchikan. Isn't that where The Salty Dog is? I reach inside the envelope, expecting it to be empty, but this time my fingers touch a piece of paper. It's a handwritten note in the same black ballpoint pen: *My favorite photo of you and Miss Red. Love T.*

I stare at the note, trying to make sense of it. Did Dad have his picture taken with a lady named Miss Red when he was in Alaska? The note makes it sound like there's more than one photo of him and her, like she was a good friend. With the *Miss* in front of it, it sounds like something old-fashioned. I'm picturing Miss Kitty on *Gunsmoke*.

Could T stand for Two-Bit, the ex-prostitute who was friends with Dad? She signed the note *Love*. And Miss Red? That's got to be a nickname, because it sure sounds cheeky. I don't want to think what I'm thinking, but I can't help suspecting that Dad was up to more than fishing in Alaska.

Of course, I could be wrong. T could stand for countless names, and Miss Red may not be what I think either. Heck, she could be a red dog that hangs out at The Salty Dog. She could be anyone or anything.

It takes me the better part of two hours, but I finally end up with a letter that doesn't sound stupid. I copy the final version in my best handwriting onto a sheet of stationery:

Dear T,

My name is Ida Petrovich. My father, Stephen James Petrovich, was lost last summer. The Coast Guard thinks he drowned in a fishing accident. You may already know this because he was in Alaska and his disappearance was on the news.

While going through his things the other day, I found an envelope with a note from you in it. The note says, "My favorite photo of you and Miss Red! Love, T." I'm sorry to say that I couldn't find the photo.

Anyway, I'm writing you because I'm trying to find out more about my dad and the time he spent in Alaska. I've heard that he liked to go to a bar called The Salty Dog and share stories, including Native Alaskan legends from a book he carried around. Do you know the book? Any information you can provide would be greatly appreciated.

Sincerely,
Ida Petrovich

PS. Here's a recent photo of me. Everyone says I look a lot like my father.

I fold the letter around one of the snapshots Sam's mother took of us before the tolo. With my hair, dress, and makeup, I look to be in my twenties. I seal it all in an envelope and address the back, double-checking to make sure that I have it written down clearly and correctly. I also write my return address in block letters, now that I know how important that is. I lick not one but two stamps, thinking that it might need the extra postage because it's going all the way to Alaska. For the same reason, I bypass the dark green mailbox in our neighborhood and walk the eight blocks to the post office on Main Street, where I take my place in line behind about a dozen people with packages.

When it's finally my turn, the lady behind the counter waves me away. "Oh, honey, you didn't need to wait in line. You can drop your letter in one of the boxes out front."

I blush at my mistake. "Thank you. I'll do that."

Outside, I stand in front of the mailbox and say a prayer. It's hard to let the envelope go, but I do. Watching it disappear into the slot, it feels a lot like I'm fishing and I've just cast my line.

CHAPTER 16

Leader

*A length of wire or other material
tied between the end of the line and
the hook*

With each passing day, I imagine my letter moving along on its journey, first traveling in the belly of a jet to Alaska, then by mail truck to the Ketchikan post office. I imagine that T or someone working for her comes daily to get the mail from Box 977 and takes it to a small corner office in a quaint house. The house will have lots of red velvet furnishings, since it used to be a bordello, but T's office will be strictly business, with a sensible desk and telephone and typewriter, maybe a stained coffee cup with a saying on it like "World's Best Boss." I picture her as a no-nonsense businesswoman—in a pantsuit, since it's still winter in Alaska and too chilly for skirts. She'll have her hair pulled back from her handsome face with a long print scarf that matches her suit. She'll be sipping her coffee and going through the mail, and my letter will stand out because it's handwritten and from Washington State. She will be surprised. Of that I have no doubt.

Maybe she's hiding Dad or knows where he is. I hope my letter will trigger her conscience and she'll write back immediately, filling me in on everything—including who she is and how she came to know my father. But that's wishful thinking.

A week goes by. Dena orders her cap and gown. Sam's back in school. I hear over the intercom, "Will all eighteen-year-old Lumberjack men please report to the office to register for the draft," and I realize that Sam will have to register next year if this stupid war doesn't end. Given what the boys are facing, I've no right to complain, but I'm still depressed. The highlight of my day is checking the mail, and all we ever get is bills.

As March winds down, I start to lose hope.

Then, on April 1, it finally arrives, and it's no April Fool's joke. In my shaking hands is an envelope with the all-important "AK" scrawled in a hasty hand in the return address. I sit down at the kitchen table and tear it open, nearly ripping the enclosed letter in half.

Dear Ms. Petrovich,

Thank you for your letter. But I have to say it was a surprise. I didn't know Steve had any children.

First let me say that we were deeply saddened to hear of his death. I'm sure I don't need to tell you this, but he was one of a kind, and his loss has been keenly felt here.

You say you want to find out more about your dad and the time he spent in Alaska. Just how much do you know? If you can write back and tell me that, I can attempt to fill in some blanks.

Better yet, would you consider making a trip up here? To see Alaska is to believe it. Letters just can't do it justice. Consider this an invitation to visit as my guest. We're at Deermount Avenue and Totem Street in Ketchikan (big light green house).

Sincerely,
Trinity "T" Lukin

PS. I can tell you the book he carried around because I gave it to him. It's Aleut Tales and Myths, *collected by Roger J. Swanson.*

It's a letter that raises more questions than it answers. Her name is Trinity, not Two-Bit, and she didn't even know about me, which means Dad never told her, which makes me think that maybe Trinity was more than a friend. You wouldn't tell your girlfriend about the wife and kid you left behind. She does talk about Dad's death as if it's a given, but that could be a cover. She could still be living with him in secret. But then, why would she invite me up there? Unless she doesn't want me to suspect anything. Or maybe, just maybe, Dad told her how much he misses me. Maybe Trinity is trying to get me up there to see him, but she couldn't say that in a letter that others might read. I notice she didn't invite Mom to come up.

Do I show the letter to Mom, see if she knows anything?

I'm not sure what would be worse: her saying, "Oh, yeah, Trinity Lukin," which would mean she knew and they both didn't tell me, or Dad not telling either one of us. He was obviously doing something up there other than fishing, because his loss has been "keenly felt." By whom? Is this why he was always so anxious to leave each spring?

I refold the letter and tuck it into the ripped envelope, meticulously matching the torn edges to each other so it appears whole again. Pressing it against my stomach, I walk across the kitchen, through the dining room, up the stairs, and into my room. I sit in front of my mirror and stare at my face, the face that looks like Dad's. Trinity never mentioned the photo of Dad with Miss Red. And there's still the question of Two-Bit. Do I write her another letter? I'd love to take her up on her offer to visit, but I can't go by myself, and I can't go with Mom. What if Dad were to answer the door? That would be awkward. Ugh! I need to figure something out, but first let me just stick my head outside and scream.

I'VE just started watching *The Secret Storm* when it's interrupted by one of those annoying special news reports that cause you to miss half your program. Walter Cronkite is always serious, but this time he looks really serious. In a voice fighting to stay level, he says that Dr. Martin Luther King, Jr., has been shot in Memphis, Tennessee.

The news is a jolt to my heart.

"Why would someone want to kill someone who was trying to do good?" I ask Mom when she gets home.

"Well, not everyone agreed he was doing good, but this is

madness." She hangs her coat in the closet, shuts the door, and sits down to watch the news, which has moved on to tell all about King's life and his contributions to the Civil Rights Movement. "Sometimes I think the whole country has flipped its lid."

IN school the next day, Mrs. Holland somberly tells us that she's postponing the lesson she had planned on the atomic bomb. Instead we talk about prejudice and civil disobedience. The latter prompts the bozo in front of me to say that Dr. King "was kind of asking for it," which really gets people going. As the debate rages, Mrs. Holland writes a quotation on the blackboard: "Misunderstanding arising from ignorance breeds fear, and fear remains the greatest enemy of peace." The quote isn't from Dr. King but from some guy named Lester B. Pearson. She tells us that our homework tonight is to think about what it means.

I turn the quote around in my head as I walk to the lunchroom. As often happens, my thoughts roll back to Dad. Ignorance means not knowing, and they still don't really know that he drowned. Maybe his death was just a huge misunderstanding and now everyone, including Mom, is too afraid to talk about it. Maybe he's . . . what? The same question always leads to the same conclusion: either he left us and started a new life, or he really did die. I hate both answers, but most of all, I hate that I may never know which is true.

One of our school's three black students, a girl named Imogen, is walking the other way, reminding me about Dr. King, but she's past me before I can express my sympathy. I'm prepared to share my thoughts on Dr. King's shooting with anyone who will listen, so I'm surprised to find that, outside of class, no one's really talking about it. When I bring it up at lunch, Dena, Gerry, and Sophie agree that it's terrible and sad, but they're much more concerned about finals and graduation.

After lunch, I head to the library. I know Sam will talk about it. Sure enough, he's reading the paper. REV. KING IS SLAIN IN MEMPHIS, JOHNSON URGES CALM reads the headline across the front page. Underneath are photos of Dr. King and the Memphis hotel where he was shot. I say hello to Sam and sit down across from him. When our eyes meet, his are wet with tears.

"Are you just now finding out?"

"I heard someone say he was killed," he says. "I had to see if it was true." He folds the paper up and sets it down on the table between us. I wonder how he could have missed the news on TV then remember that his family doesn't have one.

"I'm sorry." I try to recall some of the better comments made in Mrs. Holland's class. "All he wanted was equality for the Negroes."

"Dr. King wanted equality for everybody, not just Negroes."

"I know, I was just . . ." I stop, not wanting to say something stupid. Then I remember Mrs. Holland's homework assignment. I open my binder to my notes and show him the quote about ignorance and fear being the greatest enemies of peace. "I mean, why ignorance and fear? Why not anger and violence?"

He lets out a long breath. "You need to experience it to

understand. Have you ever had someone cross the street because they don't want to pass by you?"

"No."

"I have. Strangers make slanty eyes at me. I have been called *chink* and *gook* and *Charlie,* even *spic*, because they just don't know. And you saw what happened at the tolo. People are scared of people who are different. You're white. You can't begin to understand."

I know what he's saying, but the words sting. "I can't help being white." I say it so loudly that Mrs. McDaniel whips her head around and holds a finger to her lips. I lower my voice to a hiss. "Just like you can't help being Filipino."

I pick up my books and stomp out before Sam can have the last word. Then I ignore him in English class, which isn't hard because we spend the whole hour reading and working on our book reports.

As soon as the bell rings, I'm out the door.

"Ida. Stop. I need to talk to you."

I turn around.

Sam runs up to me. "I'm sorry if I was rude. I'm mad, but not at you." He sucks in his breath. "I've been thinking about your fear quote."

"You have?"

"Yeah. You know how I said that people are afraid of those who are different?"

I nod.

"Well, most of the kids at this school seem a little afraid to get to know me. And, um, maybe I've been a little afraid to get to know them, too. They just see me as Filipino or whatever, and I just see them as white." He looks down at the floor and shakes his head. "Ugh, I'm not explaining this."

"You're doing fine."

He looks up and meets my eyes. "You came over to me. You weren't afraid."

"You had all the Poe books."

He laughs. "And now we're friends. Uh, we *are* friends, aren't we?"

"Yes," I say nodding. "Yes, of course, we are." I want to hug him right there in the hall, but I'm not quite *that* brave.

MRS. Holland said we only had to think about the quote, but I'm feeling so inspired I write pages in my notebook, adding stuff and crossing out stuff until I get a paragraph that says exactly what I want:

Fear remains the greatest enemy of peace because it prevents people from getting to know each other for who they really are. When we're afraid, we don't reach out, we don't question, we don't try to understand. We don't make friends. It takes courage to really get to know people who we think of as different, but we must. Otherwise, the misunderstandings and lies will become our truth, and we will be forever divided.

I read the paragraph to Mom, and she's actually impressed.

"You're brilliant when you want to be," she says.

CHAPTER 17

Passage
A journey from one place to another by ship

The month I"ve been dreading has arrived. June should be a happy time. School's letting out. The world's in bloom. The days are long and people are getting married, though no one I know. The harbor is quiet now that most of the fishing boats have left for the season. Main Street is dead too, but Mom's excited about the cute summer clothes they're getting in at Fine Lines.

She buys me a green and turquoise dress, calling it an early birthday present. In three weeks, I'll be sixteen. Now that Dad won't be coming home for my traditional make-up birthday, I wonder if we will celebrate my real one.

I wear my new dress to Dena's high school graduation ceremony, which everyone in the family attends but Mom. I give a Dena-like cheer as my cousin gets her diploma. I also cheer on Sophie and Gerry, and even David Mackey.

It will be my turn in only two years, but right now that

seems impossibly far off. What I wouldn't give to be going with them, any of them, anywhere but here. Sophie's Smart Camp? Sign me up.

But any hope I have of convincing Mom to let me do anything vanishes when Bobby Kennedy is assassinated. She comes into my room that night to tell me the news.

"What's this world coming to? First Dr. King. Now Bobby Kennedy. God, that poor family, and Ethel with all those kids."

I'm half asleep, so it takes me a while to absorb what just happened. "Who shot him?" I prop myself up with my pillows. "Why?"

"They don't know yet, or at least they're not saying." She clamps her hand down on my leg, covered in blankets. "Look, I want you close to home this summer, and no staying out 'til all hours. Eleven o'clock is plenty late."

"Eleven? That's—"

"Final," she says. "There are just too many crazies in this world with guns."

"But other parents are letting their kids go places. I bet Dena's still going to Alaska."

"Dena isn't my concern."

I don't bother to point out that I stand a much greater chance of dying from boredom than being shot. It's pointless trying to reason with her when she gets like this. Her mind is double-locked and dead-bolted. Arguing with her would only make her mad—and add another padlock. But I'm just as stubborn. The harder her line, the more determined I am to cross it. If she were more flexible, I might be willing to spend my summer in Annisport, babysitting my younger cousins

and watching reruns of *Dark Shadows.* But now I will do everything in my power to bust out of this prison.

When Sam said that I wasn't afraid, it was probably the
nicest compliment I'd ever received. Maybe it's even true.
Dad used to say that still waters run deep. Quiet people can
surprise you. Take Rosa Parks. If she can refuse to give up
her seat on the bus and get arrested, I can look for a way out
of here. I can go to Alaska. I can try to solve the riddle that is
my dad.

IT'S such an incredible coincidence, it has to be a sign from
the fate gods. David Mackey, who I watched graduate, is
walking toward the school as Sam and I are leaving.

"Hi, Ida," he says breezily, as if he never stood me up, but
I don't really care about that now.

"What are you doing here? I thought you'd be halfway to
Alaska by now."

"No." He bounces a full backpack on his shoulder. "I have
a bunch of books to return. Mrs. McDaniel sent us a bill for
$53."

"Ouch." I turn to Sam and ask him if he can leave David
and me alone for a minute.

"Sure." He walks halfway through a courtyard bordered
with cherry trees then turns, unsure if he should wait. Finally,
he sits on a bench next to the scattered remains of someone's
lunch.

I'm conscious of Sam watching us as I ask David why he
never showed up that day. Laying on a little guilt might make
him more willing to do what I'm about to ask him.

He tilts his head to the side, brow wrinkling.

"We were supposed to meet again, in the library? To talk about my dad?"

"We were?"

"Yeah, I thought so."

"Jeez, I'm sorry."

"It's okay. I found out some stuff on my own." I like being able to say that.

His eyebrows pop. "You did?"

"Yep."

"Well, that's great."

"Yeah, I'm going up to Alaska to see this woman who knew Dad really well." Okay, a bit of a stretch, but I've got an idea. I just need David's help and the courage to carry it out.

"The only problem is you have to be eighteen to travel without a guardian on an Alaska State Ferry, and my mom can't go."

His blue eyes narrow on mine. "So you need some fake ID."

"Yeah. And I need it, um, kind of fast?"

PART TWO

CHAPTER 18

True North
*The direction of the geographical
North Pole*

I can't believe I really did it. I'm on a ferry to Alaska, and no one knows—not my mother, who wouldn't have let me go, and not Dena, who left for Alaska last week, or Sam, who left soon after. Okay, David knows. But he's on his own boat to Alaska, so he's not going to tell anyone. This morning, I left a note for Mom telling her I'd call her in a few days. I couldn't be specific because I wasn't sure how long it would take me to get to Ketchikan.

All the money I had in savings bought me a one-way ticket, with enough left over to get back, plus $16.42 for expenses. Knowing I'll have to stretch every cent, I've stuffed my backpack with sandwiches and oranges. In the flowered canvas suitcase I've had since I was six, I've packed a week's worth of clothes and my warmest sweater, along with a few books, a pen and notepad, and the photo of me and Dad.

Today, my birthday, I got up at 6:00 a.m., snuck out of the house, and took the Green Island Empire bus to Seattle. Then I hailed a yellow cab to the ferry dock, bought my ticket, and fell in with the foot passengers boarding this big blue boat flying the Alaska state flag—also blue, with eight yellow stars, the Big Dipper and Polaris, the North Star. I've asked myself what the hell I was doing about a hundred times. Now it's too late to turn back. The ferry is slowly churning away from the dock, leaving the Seattle waterfront on a more-than-two-day voyage to Southeast Alaska.

We will be taking the same general route my dad took, up the Inside Passage between Vancouver Island and British Columbia, past the Queen Charlotte Islands, through the Dixon Entrance, across the "A–B line" that divides Canada from the United States, and into the Alexander Archipelago, a group of more than a thousand islands that, I know from Dad, are actually the tops of submerged mountains.

Dad's last known location was near the Dixon Entrance. I wonder if I'll feel something as we pass through it?

The ferry picks up speed. I'm sweating but my hands are cold. Clasped in my lap, fingers interlaced like they're praying, they seem to belong to someone else. The view outside is gray-blue-green. Water-sky-land.

Trinity's letter, which I've read and reread, is in my backpack. I never would have guessed that name behind the T. From church, I know about the Father, Son, and Holy Spirit that make up one God, but I didn't know, until I looked it up in the World Book, that Trinity was also the name of the world's first atomic bomb test. I hope that's not a sign of how our meeting will go.

I get out my pen and notepad and start writing down
questions for her, including, "Is my dad really dead?" When
I'm done, I check the clock on the ferry's observation deck.
It's after five. Mom will be closing up the shop about now. In
less than half an hour she'll be home, unless she stops at
Tradewell first. The thought of her coming home with a
birthday cake makes me feel bad. The long hand of the ferry
clock ticks off the minutes.

Five. Ten. Fifteen . . . Thirty.

Of course, nothing happens. The clock keeps on ticking.
The ferry stays its course. But in a small house in Annisport,
I've just triggered a mother quake. *I'm okay, Mom.* I chant this
in my head over and over, trying to convince myself while
I'm at it.

Around eight o'clock, the public areas of the ferry empty
of the moms and dads and kids and couples who've paid for
sleeping cabins. Without their happy noises I'm suddenly
aware of all the non-human sounds: the metallic clinks and
clanks, the low drone of the engine, and the sleep-inducing
background music that's even worse than the crap on Mom's
favorite radio station. Sitting in this family-sized booth, staring at the window-turned-mirror at my pale reflection, it's
easy to imagine myself as someone else. A runaway. I guess
that's what I am.

I stare into my own eyes until they start to creep me out
and I have to turn away. Reaching for my suitcase, I get out
my copy of *Aleut Tales and Myths.* I had to special-order it
from the bookstore, which ate into my travel money, but I
figured it was a small price to pay for a better understanding
of Dad's time in Alaska.

I open it to the first story, titled "The Woman Who Became a Bear," and start to read:

On the banks of a river there lived a man and his wife and children. One day the man told his wife that he was sick and about to die. He asked her to leave his body on the ground, uncovered, next to his boat and bow and arrows. The next morning she found him dead. She left his body, as he'd requested. For three days, it stayed there as she and her children sat and wept. But on the fourth day, it vanished. Not one sign of the body or boat could be seen.

I read the last two sentences again and remember the Coast Guard's words after their failed search. A queasiness bubbles in my gut.

Not many days after this, a little bird came to the house and sang, "Your husband lives. He is with another woman at the mouth of the river." Hearing this sad news, the woman felt very bitter toward her husband, and she wept a great deal.

I can see Mom crying over Dad. I can even see her traveling to the place where he's living with a new wife. But I can't see her killing the new wife by holding her face in boiling water. Nor can I see her turning herself into a bear and ripping Dad to pieces.

It's just a story, a fable with a lesson. You're supposed to learn from it, not take it literally. Still, the similarities are spooky. A fisherman fakes his death so he can live with another woman. Is that why Mom said he might still be alive? Why she didn't want a funeral? My brain goes through the old loops again. If he's alive, then he went somewhere else. If he went somewhere else, then he left us. If he left us, then he must not love us.

My stomach lurches. The sign to the ladies' room buzzes

in and out of focus as I rush toward it, ducking into a stall just in time to heave up the PB&J and orange I had for dinner. I throw up a couple more times, until nothing comes out. Then I wipe my mouth with toilet paper and flush. I leave the stall feeling better but shaky. Standing at the sink, I splash cold water on my face, pull the towel roll down to a fresh spot, and pat myself dry.

I wish I'd thought to ask Mom about Dad's stories. No doubt she heard some of them. Or did she? Maybe, like me, Mom only got the nice tales about Raven bringing light. Maybe Dad saved the not-so-nice ones for his pals at The Salty Dog. Why did Trinity give him that book with that story? Which I've just left in my booth, along with my suitcase, backpack, and all the money I have left.

I rush out of the restroom, heart pounding, but my stuff is right where I left it. I glance at the clock. It's only ten thirty, though it feels like the middle of the night. Without a cabin, I will be sleeping on this exposed, vinyl-covered bench, next to an aisle people use as a thoroughfare. Better get used to it.

My suitcase serves as a pillow and my coat a blanket. I sleep fitfully with scattered dreams.

THE gray light of morning brings the ferry's janitors, then families with young children, followed by families with older children. Finally the couples and groups of friends in their late teens and twenties emerge, carrying Styrofoam cups of coffee.

The second day drags on much longer than the first,

though the scenery is beautiful. I stare out the window at emerald green islands reflected in sun-dimpled waters. Fish jump here and there. Seagulls glide by. We pass a rock covered with sea lions. I walk around the deck to take in the sights on both sides, but feel stupid carrying my luggage around, so I head back to my booth, which I staked out with my coat.

For breakfast, I eat another sandwich but no orange. The citric acid combined with my nerves probably had more to do with my stomach upset than the bear-woman story did. In the light of day, my reaction seems silly, so silly I pick up the book again and read more folktales, including a couple more about trust and betrayal that end with violent revenge, an eye for an eye. Have the Aleuts never heard of forgiveness? Sheesh! I prefer the stories without beheadings, drownings, poisonings, and death, the stories that playfully explain nature, like why frogs sing and why the stars don't come out on cloudy nights. The Raven stories are okay, too, but even they're meaner than they have to be. Apparently, our hero was not above pooping on people to make a point.

"Must be a good book." The voice is male, maybe twenties. I don't look up to check. The big grimy backpack and the sharp smell of tobacco and sour milk tell me all I want to know. I feel his eyes wander over me. I continue to read without reading.

"I'm just trying to be friendly here."

Yeah, and I'm just trying to read. That's what Dena would say, but I only think it.

"I'm going to Alaska, see if I can get on one a' dem salmon boats. Can make a year's salary in a few months. He sounds like he's trying to convince me to go with him. "Gonna take that money and get me a place in Tucson. I like the desert." He chuckles. "That's ironical, ain't it? Desert-lovin' man going fishing." He pauses and the seat squeaks as he changes positions. "Hey, you sure got pretty hair." He leans forward, releasing a waft of stink. Still looking down, I get a fix on the handle of the suitcase at my feet, a strap sticking out from the backpack at my side.

One. Two. Three.

I grab my things and bolt once again to the ladies' room, spilling my book in the aisle. I don't stop to pick it up.

"Hey!" he yells after me. Safely out of reach, I glance back at a big, oafish guy holding up my book. Maybe he was just trying to be friendly, but a Mom-ism lodges in my brain: "A woman alone always has to be on her guard." I duck into the restroom, where two kids in PJs are brushing their teeth. A toilet flushes and a woman with her hair in pincurls walks out.

"I'm sorry," I say, panting. "There's this guy . . ." I tilt my head toward the door and catch a fleeting glimpse of my scared self in the mirror. Her children stare, toothpaste dribbling down their chins. "He's kind of weird. I don't want to go back to my seat."

The mom turns to her children and reminds them to spit. Then she looks at me and her children again, as if adding up the numbers.

"You're by yourself?" she asks.

I nod.

"Come back with us. You can't spend the night in here."

She introduces herself as Fran, short for Franny. They're headed for Juneau, and she gives me the empty bunk in their four-berth cabin. I return the favor by playing endless games of Old Maid, Crazy Eights, and Go Fish with her kids—Bobby, who is five, and Jane, who's seven. When they tire of cards, I get out my pen and notebook so we can play tic-tac-toe, hangman, and connect-the-dots.

Later that evening, after I help Fran get them to sleep, she thanks me and tells me I'm really good with children.

I shrug.

"No, seriously, you should work with kids, be a teacher or counselor or something." With her plain, no-nonsense face and muscular arms, Fran seems capable of handling a whole cafeteria full of children. I decide she knows what she's talking about, and that she can be trusted.

"My dad loved kids," I say.

She tilts her head. "Loved?"

"He, um, was lost last summer. Fishing accident, they think."

"Oh!" She presses a hand to her lips. "I'm sorry. How awful for you."

"It's okay." I mean that it's okay she asked, but I'm too tired to clarify things.

Fran doesn't probe, though she does get that pained expression of sympathy I've seen so many times now. Like a mother, she tells me, "Good night and sleep tight."

Dad would add, "and don't let the bedbugs bite," so I do too, which makes Fran giggle. I roll over on my side, nuzzling into the luxury of an actual pillow. If, during the night, we cross the same waters that might have swallowed the *Lady Rose*, I am too comatose to notice.

OUR first stop in Alaska is a town called Metlakatla. Next is Ketchikan, "Salmon Capitol of the World," and my destination. I'm in the dining area with Fran and her kids, eating the breakfast of pancakes and sausages she bought for me. All around us, people move, haul luggage, drag children, make plans. Ketchikan must be a popular spot. My stomach flutters with nerves. I have all my stuff with me, minus the book I dropped. I went back for it, but it was gone. It really bummed me out until I told myself that the Native myths were meant to be shared. That weird, smelly man looked like he could use a morality tale or two.

In fifteen minutes, we'll be docked in Ketchikan, possibly a long stone's throw from Trinity's big green house and where Dad may be living. Just the thought makes my heart do a tap dance. I really should be saying my good-byes to Fran and her family, but I can't seem to breathe, let alone move. I have Trinity's letter with her address. It wouldn't be hard to find, and I have money for a cab, but suddenly the idea of showing up on her doorstep unannounced seems crazy. And what if, miracle of miracles, Dad answers the door? Will I say, "Hi, it's me, the daughter you abandoned"?

"Isn't Ketchikan your stop?" Fran asks me. "Bobby, that's enough syrup."

"Um, no, not really," I stutter. "I mean, I'll be going there eventually, but first I'm, uh, visiting my cousin in Petersburg." As I say it, relief fills my lungs and I can breathe again. Sam's in Petersburg. I'll go see him at Nagoon Seafood Packers. Maybe I can even get a job there. I wanted to work this summer. This is my chance to earn some money. And I'll be with Sam. What could be better? I can always see Trinity, and maybe Dad, once I work up the courage.

"I must have misunderstood," Fran says, eyeing me uncertainly. "Then you'll be getting off one stop before us."

"Yeah, I guess so."

Bobby bounces in his chair, bumping into his sister.

"Stop it, Bobby!" Jane turns to me. "I wish you could come with us to Juneau."

"So do I. It's going to be tough saying good-bye to you guys."

AND it is. While Fran waves, the kids lean over the ferry railing blowing me kisses like I'm going off to a new world where nothing is familiar. It kind of feels that way. Petersburg looks like it's trying to be someplace in Europe. There's even a Viking ship in the center of town, though I don't think it's real. There are also green tree-covered hills, snow-capped peaks, colorful houses on stilts, and a big white building with red shutters painted in flower designs. It's all very pretty and quaint, but nothing says Nagoon or Nagoon Seafood Processors. Somehow I thought I'd spot the cannery as soon as I got here. I thought the town would be built around it. That's clearly not the case.

An uneasiness seeps into my gut as I walk into a white building with a rainbow-shaped sign; "Scandia House, Fine Lodging." I ask the lady behind the counter if she can direct me to Nagoon Seafood Packers.

"Well, the fastest way is by seaplane."

"Seaplane?" I try to make sense of the words "sea" and "plane" together, and I draw a blank. "You mean I can't walk there?"

"Nagoon Island? Not unless you can walk on water." She bends down behind the counter and brings out a map, spreading it in front of me. "You can walk to the seaplane dock from here." With fast swipes of her pen, she draws an X where we are and an X where the dock is and a line between the two.

"How much does it cost? The seaplane?"

"We had some schedules." She checks behind the counter, digging through a pile of loose paperwork. She frowns. "Must be out. But Chet can help you. He runs the office over there."

"Okay, thank you." I take the map and head for the door, glancing up at the back of the rainbow sign advertising lodging I can't afford. I sure hope I can find Nagoon and Sam before I have to spend the night on the streets of Petersburg.

As I reach the door, the woman calls out after me, "You know, if you don't mind waiting a bit, I could probably get Karl to run you over there in his boat."

I want to collapse in relief. "I don't mind waiting."

Thank you, God.

I introduce myself, holding out my hand so she can shake it.

"Kate," she says, taking my hand. Her grip is firm. She glances at my suitcase. "Figured you were far from home, thought maybe you could use a break."

She has me put my stuff behind the counter. "I'm from Annisport. I took the ferry."

She whistles. "The scenic route. Most cannery workers from the lower forty-eight fly up."

KARL, who I learn is Kate's son, doesn't say anything as he takes my suitcase, my backpack, and then me on board. He's clearly doing his mom a favor, but I'm so relieved I don't care if he resents me. The ride over is windy and beautiful. Karl points out a sea lion on a red buoy and a big white glacier bisecting blue mountains. When we get to Nagoon and the cannery, it looks much more like the Alaska I imagined than Petersburg. The cluster of white buildings with red roofs is the only sign of civilization in a landscape of forested islands, water, and mountains. I feel very small in this wilderness. Karl seems at home, though. He drives the boat with the assurance of someone who knows these waters like city people know their stretches of concrete.

Just when I think we're about to ram the dock, he cuts the motor and we drift up and nudge it. He ties up, jumps out, and then helps me out, taking my stuff and lending me his hand. My legs wobble—the wooden dock feels more liquid than solid—but I recover enough to tell him thank you.

"No sweat," he says over the rumble of the engine. Then he's off in a belch of blue exhaust.

CHAPTER 19

H & G

A fish processing term meaning "headed and gutted"

Up close the cannery resembles an army camp, or at least my impression of an army camp from watching *Hogan's Heroes*. Most of its barracks-style buildings have seen better days. The paint is peeling and the red roofs have been patched over. What passes for a road through the cannery site has potholes the size of Volkswagens. Seeing no one, a panicky voice inside me wonders if this place has just been abandoned and I'm the last to know. Then I hear a faint thumping and follow the sound to a group of guys behind a house playing basketball. I'll ask them where I can find the owner. There's got to be an owner, right?

"You mean the manager?" asks a tall guy with sweaty blond hair. He directs me to a small house with a sign out front that says "Administration." I knock on a plain wood door.

"Come in," calls a female voice.

I enter a small room with a big desk. Behind it, a pixie of a girl with short red hair and spider-like eyelashes is thumbing through a magazine. "Can I help you?" she asks, turning a page.

"I—I heard you may need cannery workers?" This is a lie. I've heard nothing.

She looks at me for the first time. "We've hired our crew already. You're too late." She goes back to her magazine like I've already left.

Oh, crap. Now what do I do?

My feet are rooted to the floor. I have no way of getting off the island. I let out a whoosh of air. "Okay."

Pixie Girl sighs. "Wait." She turns around in her chair. "Daaad?" My heart jumps. "My dad'll be out in a minute."

"Okay." My voice sounds girlish, more like twelve than eighteen. This girl's dad is going to see right through me and call my mother. I'll be on the next ferry out of here. I hear a door open, approaching footsteps. This is either the smartest or the stupidest thing I've ever done.

A short, potbellied man whose freckled skin is redder than his daughter's hair emerges and tells me to come on back. I stand up, willing my legs not to shake, and follow him into a small, cluttered office. He plops into the chair behind his desk and asks me for some picture ID to show that I'm a US citizen. Trying to appear calm, I struggle a bit with the zipper on the front pocket of my backpack, get out my coin purse, and produce the fake driver's license David's friend made for me. I present it to him with what I hope is a steady hand, praying to God he can't tell a forgery from the real thing. He gives the card a cursory glance and asks me if I'm prepared to work sixteen to eighteen hours a day at a job that's both physically and mentally exhausting.

I nod.

His chair creaks as he leans back and gives me the once-over.

"So, where you from, Susan?"

The name from my fake ID stops me a second. I swallow and say, "Seattle."

For what seems like an hour, he just stares at me, saying nothing. He leans forward again, and the chair creaks so loudly, I fear it might break. "How'd you get here?" he asks, finally.

"Boat."

"Okay." He pauses. "Well, you timed it right. We just had a girl quit. Do you have a way home if you can't hack the job?"

"Yes." A half-lie.

He squeezes his hand into a fist, cracking his knuckles. "You seem sturdy enough. We'll start you in the slime house. Pay is $1.65 an hour, $2.55 for overtime. It's not much, but we provide meals and housing, such as it is." He fishes through a drawer in his desk, removes a form, and hands it to me. "Fill this out. Annie!" he yells. I flinch.

His daughter appears at the doorway. "This is Susan Stone. I'm putting her at the washing station to start. Get her gear, go over some safety stuff, and have her bunk with Jody."

It's so easy; too easy. "You mean I've got a job?"

"Yep."

The form is an application, which seems a bit backwards, but I fill in the blanks, giving my fake name and fake hometown but my real address and telephone number. Lying gets easier the more you do it. I hand it to Annie, who's forced once again away from her magazine. She leaves my application on the desk, gets up, and grabs a jacket off a hook on the wall. "You can leave that here for now," she says, looking askance at my girly suitcase.

We walk to the main cannery building. A small room in back is filled with rain gear. Each worker gets a pair of bib overall pants, a hooded jacket, boots, and two sets of gloves—a woolen pair and a rubber pair to go over them. The outfit comes in green or yellow. I choose green.

My safety lesson consists of learning where the First Aid box is located. I'm to raise my hand, like I'm in school, if I'm hurt or need a supervisor. Hand signals are used instead of words because the noise of the machines makes it too loud to talk.

"Don't wear anything loose and dangly, like scarves or jewelry," she warns.

I don't tell her about the locket hiding under my clothes, the locket I won't remove for any reason, even showering. It's part of me, even if the man who gave it had divided attentions.

"Oh, and do you have something to hold back your hair?" Annie looks at my frizzy mane like she'd like to take scissors to it. "We had a girl last year got her hair caught in the conveyor belt. Ripped out a quarter-sized chunk of her scalp." She holds her thumb and pointer finger about an inch apart to show me just how bad the wound was. "If you don't have a stocking cap or a bandana, you can maybe find a baseball cap at the general store. Otherwise, you're going to have to wear a company-issue hairnet." She scrunches up her nose as if she wouldn't be caught dead in a company-issue hairnet, which seems an odd thing to be vain about considering everything else that's unattractive about this job.

On the way to the women's bunkhouse, she points out "the mess," which I learn is another word for cafeteria, and tells me that her full name is Annie Murphy but everyone calls her Murf. "You're here long enough, you get a nickname. This your first time canning in Alaska?"

"Both," I tell her. "First time canning. First time in Alaska."

"We have lots of newbies this year. You're lucky to get Jody as a roommate. She started with us last summer. She's nice and can teach you all you need to know."

The women's bunkhouse is at the end of the road. Beyond the roadblock, a narrow trail continues through the trees. I'm about to ask Murf where it goes, but she is explaining that the women's showers are in a separate building behind the bunkhouse. "In some ways, the guys have it better, but your dorm is nicer."

"Nicer" is a long white building, barracks-style like all the rest. We walk into a big common area furnished with a ratty orange sofa, a mix of plush and hardback chairs, and a Formica table. My room is toward the back of the common area, on the right. With its two sets of built-in wooden bunk beds, it could sleep four, but my only roommate is stretched out on one of the lower bunks.

"Susan, meet Jody. Jody, meet Susan," Murf says.

Jody slides her legs around to the side of her bunk and stands. She's about a head shorter than I am but strong and wiry, like she'd lap me running around our school track. Her red T-shirt is faded to almost pink, and her blue jeans are faded to almost white. She wears her long black hair in a ponytail hanging through the back of her red baseball cap, also faded. She reaches out a dark-skinned arm and shakes my hand, jiggling, as she does, a bunch of macramé-bead bracelets dangling from her wrist. Her skin is callused, her grip firm.

"Welcome to Can-a-lot." Her low voice seems to belong to a much bigger person.

"Jody can show you around and explain what you'll be doing," Murf says to me.

"What *will* she be doing?" Jody asks.

"Slime House, washing station."

Jody smiles. "Lucky you."

Murf leaves, Jody puts on a coat, and we exchange what I've come to learn are the usual cannery introductions. Like Murf, she asks where I'm from and if I've canned before. Unlike Murf, she wants to know what I plan to do with the money.

Jody is a local girl and envious of the fact that I come from the "big city." She assures me that I'll get the hang of canning in no time. The challenge is how long you can stand it. The work is so tiring and monotonous that making it back for a second summer qualifies you as a veteran. It's the opportunity to earn a grand or two in overtime pay that attracts so many students from the outside.

"Next month, if we're lucky, we'll get a solid block of twelve- to sixteen-hour days." She seems excited by this prospect, and since I'm supposedly here for the money, I have to agree.

"If we're lucky," I echo.

"Hey, time and a half. Got to make enough to get me out of this hellhole." Jody reaches into her coat pocket, pulls out a pack of cigarettes, offers me one.

"No thanks. I don't smoke."

"Good for you." She lights one, takes a drag and blows the smoke out her nose.

As Jody and I walk towards the cannery, she points out the main buildings along the way. Administration, post office/ general store, mess, the men's bunkhouse, where the same four guys are playing basketball, and the Filipino bunkhouse and mess, both older buildings with peeling paint.

"I don't know why there's a separate house and mess for Filipinos." She shrugs. "Maybe because they're mostly old timers and don't want to be around us kids. But they have some young ones, too."

I want to ask her about Sam but think better of it. She might guess that he's the reason I'm here.

Jody begins my tour of the cannery building on the dock, where salmon are unloaded from the boats into huge bins, each the size of my bedroom. From there, the fish travel by conveyor belt into what she calls the blood and guts of the operation. I learn why so many canneries are built on pilings. The gurry—a gray waste of fish heads, tails, fins and guts—all gets dumped through holes in the floor directly into the water.

"The seagulls have a field day," she says. "Of course, everything's quiet now. Fish'll start in about a week, kinda slow at first so you can get used to it, then the fun begins. The chink'll be spitting 'em out a mile a minute."

"Chink?"

"I'll show you."

She takes me to a squat machine that feeds the fish through a wheel-like guillotine. "This replaced the Chinese workers who used to do the butchering by hand. That's why they call it the Iron Chink."

I remember the slur used against Sam even though he's not Chinese. "That's kind of—"

"Rude?"

"Yeah."

"I've heard worse," Jody says. "I'm Indian. Tlingit, Eagle moiety, Killer Whale Clan, Moon House."

"Wow." I could never remember all that, so I don't even try. "That's a lot to be."

She laughs and breathes out smoke from her cigarette. "It's how we identify ourselves. A house is just an extended family. Of course, white people don't refer to us that way. They just call us Indians or Natives, if they're being polite. Drunks or bums if they're not." She waves her cigarette around. "Anyhoo, *way* more than you wanted to know. On with the tour."

We come to a long platform with a conveyor belt running between two troughs. A couple dozen rubber hoses hang from an overhead pipe.

"Here's where you'll be working," she says. "Normally, water would be running nonstop so you can hose out any blood and guts left in the fish."

So much for washing being an okay job. "What will you be doing?"

She grins. "I got a dry job this year. Cooking cans."

She takes me to the can-making, cooking, and storage

wing, which is attached on land to the cannery building like the smaller leg of an upside-down L. This is where the packed cans are sealed and cooked and stacked on crates bound for points across the globe. As we walk through the plant, I learn that dry and warm jobs are better than wet and cold jobs, and being a washer is about as wet and cold as you can get. The only possible exception to the dry-wet rule is the job of feeding the Iron Chink. Though the work is bloody, gross, and potentially dangerous since fingers can be lost, it carries a measure of respect because everyone down the slime line depends on how well you do your job. If the fish come out cleanly cut and gutted the slimers have a much easier time of it.

"The egg sacs are saved and processed separately for the Japanese," Jody is saying. "Roe's a special food to them. Speaking of which, I'm hungry. You hungry?"

"Um, sure."

We leave the cannery building. I'm just about to ask Jody if there is a public pay phone I can use—I still need to call my mother—when we're both distracted by a group of guys moving big wooden crates into the area where the finished cans are stored. They look like the Filipino cannery workers back home, and my breath catches, searching for Sam. Several of the younger ones say hi to Jody and give me the once-over. But only one recognizes me.

"Ida?"

I turn around. I might have looked right past him if he hadn't noticed me first. His upper lip is shadowed with the start of a mustache, and his hair is now so long, it's in his eyes.

"Sam?" I want to run up and hug him, but not with all these people around.

"What are you doing here?" His eyes are bloodshot, like he hasn't been sleeping.

"I'm working here, or will be." I'm proud of my job, no matter how gross.

Jody clears her throat loudly.

"Oh, sorry. Sam, this is my roommate, Jody. Jody, this is Sam, a friend from school."

"Small world," she says. "Why did you call her Ida?"

Before Sam can answer, I jump in. "Oh, that's a nickname. Susan's my real name." Sam gives me a look like, *What the hell?*

"I think I'll let you two catch up." Jody says. "See ya later, Ida-Sue." She gives me a wink and walks off in the direction of the mess, leaving me to squirm under Sam's gaze.

"What was that all about?" Sam's brows are knit in confusion.

I lean over and whisper in his ear. "Susan Stone is the name on my fake ID."

"You came here on your own?" He studies me like he's not sure who I am anymore.

"Well, isn't that what *you* did?"

He shakes his head. "I had an uncle waiting for me. My mom arranged it. Your mom—"

"Doesn't know," I say firmly.

"You're kidding, right?" He's looking genuinely panicked now.

I bite my lower lip and shake my head.

Sam's jaw falls open. "You mean you just ran away?" He says it so loud, I cringe.

"Sorry." He leans forward, his voice quiet. "Your mom, your family, they must be so worried."

"I left her a note. I said I would call her."

My skin prickles like I've been slapped. After all those hours on the ferry, spending almost half my money, risking everything, I actually make it up here and even get a job. Yet all Sam can do is make me feel like a schmuck.

CHAPTER 20

Above Board
On or above the deck, not hiding anything

M y pocket weighed down with change, I pull open the folding door of an ancient phone booth and try to read the worn and cigarette-burned directions for making a long-distance call. A dozen quarters later, I hear a mysterious series of clicks, followed by a faint ringing, and then, finally, my mother's "hello" through what sounds like a tunnel of candy wrappers.

"Mom?"

"Ida?" Her voice is a crackly shriek.

"Yes, it's me."

"... God ... where ... you?"

"Mom, I can't really hear you. I just want you to know I'm okay." I say the words loud and slow into a receiver that smells of brine and cigarettes.

"Wha ..."

"I said I'm fine. I got a job."

". . .ere . . . you?"

"I can't tell you that."

The connection continues to pop and hiss. "In . . . ska?"

So she's guessed I'm in Alaska. No surprise, there.

"Mom, I can't—"

The operator cuts in, telling me to deposit another twenty-five cents. I sigh and insert another quarter into the slot.

"Please don't worry about me. I love you." I wait for her reply, but there's only static. "Mom? Are you there?"

Click. Dial tone. I've lost her. It wasn't much of a conversation, but at least now she knows I'm alive.

I go into the general store, where everything costs about three times more than normal. Turning through a rack of postcards, I pick out one of an Aleut girl. On the back it says, *Colorful citizen of the 49th state in Native attire, Caribou Skin Parka trimmed in fur and beadwork.* The girl is smiling into the wind with her right arm raised as if waving to someone far away. So what if it reveals my general location. Mom still doesn't know *where* in Alaska, and it's a really big state.

I pay for the postcard and a can of spray-on bug repellent for the Alaska-sized mosquitoes. I better get paid soon, because I'm running out of cash.

As I walk back to the women's bunkhouse, I hear music. It's a happy, simple tune that's vaguely familiar. Eventually, it dawns on me. The Beatles. "Hello, Goodbye." Someone has set up a record player on the porch just outside the main door. After the Beatles, another 45 drops down from the stack and the needle lands on a wolf howl and Sam the Sham & The Pharaohs singing about Little Red Riding Hood.

Pop-pop-pop-pop-pop-hsss.

Someone down the beach is lighting firecrackers. The competing noise oddly complements the song. "Oooh yeah!" yells one of the guys setting them off. So much has happened the last few days that I forgot all about the Fourth of July. The celebration, such as it is, seems out of place until I realize that we're still in the United States.

The record player has been turned on as loud as it will go. Fuzzy base notes vibrate through the soles of my sneakers as I walk into the bunkhouse. The ratty couch and both chairs have been claimed by couples. The guys sit with their arms draped around their girlfriends or with their girlfriends on their laps. They're passing around a bottle that's half gone and taking turns sucking on something that looks like a small cigarette but smells like a slash burn of forest waste. I recognize one of the basketball players from earlier, the tall blond guy who told me where to find the office.

The girls are my housemates, but Jody isn't among them. There's Pandora, who appears to be a real live hippie, or at least dresses the part. She's from Eugene, Oregon. Jill is a petite blonde from Spokane with pink-frosted lips. And Valerie, who's as tall as I am, is studying to be a large-animal vet. All are cannery newbies. I remember to introduce myself as Susan from Seattle, which Joshua, a small, elfish guy with no permanent address, keeps repeating because he likes the S sounds.

"Susan of Seattle slaughters salmon by the seashore." He bounces to the beat of it. "Susan of Seattle, you're a tongue *tweezer*."

"That sounds painful," says a girl to my right. I catch a

flash of boob and underarm hair as her tank-topped torso swoops in for a pack of cigarettes on the table.

Joshua topples forward laughing. "Twister. I mean twister."

"You're stoned, Josh." The girl lights her cigarette, introduces herself to me as Marlene, and asks if I'd like some of the bottle that's going around, only a quarter full now.

"No, thanks," I tell her, hating how dainty that sounds. I don't want them to think I'm a snob, or worse, a goody two-shoes, but my Halloween party experience kind of soured me on drinking.

A rush of air hits my back. "Bear!" the couples yell in unison.

I whip around, coming face to hairy neck with a big, ponytailed man. He slides around me and plunks a case of beer on the rickety table, which tilts so much I fear the weight will collapse it. "Fish tomorrow," he announces, ripping open the top of the box and grabbing a can. Soon there's a rush of bodies and hands grabbing for beers. The box empties in seconds.

"About time," Marlene says, popping open her can.

"For the fish or the beer?" Bear asks.

"Both."

"Load of pinks." He takes a long, gulping drink then belches, rather like a bear, if a bear were to get hold of some beer.

I think back on that Aleut story about the wife who turned into a bear, and a strange thought occurs to me. If every person in this room were to magically transform into his or her spirit animal, we would all see each other's true natures, our weaknesses as well as our strengths. Wolf and rabbit, beaver and loon, otter and frog. What would my animal be? Something noble, like an eagle? Or lowly, like a snail? Dad said there were no good or bad totems, that they're all respected, which strikes me as empty talk coming from someone who could change to suit his whims. He was like Raven, the trickster, turning from father and husband to fisherman, storyteller . . . and beloved friend of prostitutes? How did he keep all those roles straight? Yet one more question to ask Trinity, if I dare.

I make my way to what is now my room. Opening the door, I expect to see Jody stretched out on her bunk, but all I find is her open backpack. Maybe she escaped for some peace and quiet. The music changes to the Rolling Stones, the beat thrumming through the thin wall.

I only left Annisport a few days ago, but it seems like years. Amazing how so much can change in the space of a week. I'm in a new state with a new job. I could start a new life, become a new person. Isn't that what lured Dad to Alaska in the summer and made him retreat to his basement in the winter? It wasn't just the fish he caught or the tables he crafted. He needed to escape.

I get the photo of us out of my suitcase and stare at his happy face. What else was that smile hiding? I put it back, get out my pen, and sit down at a small table in the corner opposite our bunks. I take out the postcard of the Aleut girl and begin to write.

Dear Mom,
Sorry our call was cut short. I am safe in Alaska
(obviously from this postcard). I have a job and am
making new friends. I'm doing well. Please trust me. I'm

*not a child anymore. I promise to be careful and come
home. I will call again very soon.*

Love,
Ida

In the space that's left, I draw a raven in flight.

THE party ends. A cannery foreman finally comes by to
break it up. The fish rumor is true, but it will be a short day.
I hear all this through the wall.

I'm in bed, trying to fall asleep, when Jody walks in. I sit
up, bumping my head on the empty bunk above me. I rub
the spot on my head. These bunks weren't made for big
girls like me.

"Where did you go?" I ask her.

"Who are you, my mother?"

"No, I just . . ." I mumble, thinking of the one I left worrying.

"Mind if I turn on the light?" she asks.

"Go ahead. I couldn't sleep because of the party. Now I
just can't sleep." I squint in the sudden light as Jody takes off
her jacket.

"Get used to it," she says. "Partying is how people here
pass the time."

"But not you?"

"Nope." She slips off her boots, flips off the light, and
slides into her sleeping bag still wearing her clothes. Just
when I think she's done talking, her words come floating
through the dark. "Drinking makes it too hard to get up in

the morning. Once the fish start, all you newbies will be too tired to party. 'Night, Ida-Sue."

I tell her good night back. In minutes, her breathing takes on the heavy rhythm of sleep. I wish I could drop off that easily, but I've never done well with strange beds in strange places. Nerves aside, I'm beginning to understand the thrill my dad felt coming here. Alaska is freedom, fear, and guilt, all rolled into one.

CHAPTER 21

Blood line
A line of blood located along the backbone of a fish that's removed in processing

We get to sleep in, but the start of the day still comes way too soon for most of the girls in our bunkhouse. Pandora looks like the walking dead, her hands shaking as she cradles a mug of coffee to her lips. The bunkhouse common room smells like pickled cigarettes from all the beer cans serving as ashtrays. It's enough to make me gag, and I don't have a hangover, though I had a rotten night of trying to get to sleep, capped off by a weird dream.

I was on a ferryboat in wildly swaying seas, like an amusement park ride where the centrifugal force keeps you from falling. Suddenly the ferry turned into a dinghy. Waves swamped my boat. As I sank under water, I was surrounded by fish. Big green ones, small orange ones, giant blue ones. They were beautiful and frightening at the same time. I tried to swim away, but I couldn't. As panic set in, someone gave me a push. My arms and legs started working again. It got lighter and lighter. Finally, my face broke the surface, and I gasped for air. I didn't see who helped me, but I somehow knew it was Dad.

The aching haunt of the dream is obliterated soon enough. Cannery work is every bit as bad as Mom made it out to be. First there's the smell, which starts out tolerable, like our waterfront on a warm day, then hits you like a rogue wave. The fish are fresh. You can tell, I'm told, by their shiny eyes. But the cumulative effect of so many fish at once is overwhelming. Their butchered bodies release a thick, sickening stench, like life turned inside out. I don't have the luxury of dwelling on it, though, because I'm too busy trying to keep up with the flow of carcasses Sam is sending our way. Turns out he has the all-important job of fish inspector, which sounds more impressive than it is. Standing behind the Iron Chink, he picks up each cut and gutted fish and turns it first to one side, then the other. If it's clean, it goes directly to us. If it still has parts of its head, tail, and fins attached, it goes to the cutters. Using wickedly sharp knives, they chop off the unwanted bits—and sometimes more. Rubber gloves are no protection against a fine blade.

Washers don't use knives; we use spoons connected to jet hoses. We don't risk losing a digit if we screw up, which is good because scraping and spraying out fish innards is a finger-numbing job. My first attempt slips from my grip and plops down hard in front of me, splashing bloody water. One of the first things I learn is to keep my mouth closed.

The worst part of my job, however, isn't the blood and

guts, or even the smell. On my first day, it's the cold that pains me most. The fish are half-frozen, the water slightly less so. Though I'm dressed like a fisherman in full rain gear, with wool gloves under my rubber ones, the cold spreads from my numb fingers up my arms and down my spine, making me even clumsier than usual. I usually fumble my fish while my supervisor is looking. Luckily, I'm not the only one. The belt stops and starts a lot that afternoon because of glitches and mishaps along the line. Each time I think about quitting, just walking away, but then there's Sam, a stalwart at his station, and I tell myself to get to the next break.

At long last, we get the signal to quit. Gloved hands mime slicing throats, with a motion to pass it along. The belt stops for the day. Human sounds replace the clank and clatter of machines. The talk is reassuringly ordinary, full of misery shared, as my coworkers go about satisfying their most urgent needs, whether it's a cigarette, something to eat, or just a warm place to sit down. I seek out Sam and we fall in with the others, boots sloshing through the blood on the floor. Moving from standing on sore feet, I wobble.

Sam's there to catch me. His hand stays protectively pressed against the small of my back as we head for the nearest door. This is the Sam I know, not the moody, distant boy I saw when I first got here. He could just be taking pity on me, but I like it.

We get outside, and Sam withdraws his hand. The air is fresh and light. Then I remember that it's four in the afternoon. I've only worked five hours.

"God, if this was a short day, I don't know how I'm going to make it through a long one."

"No kidding," Sam says. "I will be turning fish in my sleep."

"I can't feel my fingers."

"Here." He stops me. He removes his gloves and then mine. Taking my right hand in both of his, he starts to rub. It takes a while for the warmth to creep back into my hands, but Sam keeps at it until our temperatures match.

"Hey." Jody runs up to us, dressed like summer in cutoffs and a T-shirt, skin shiny with sweat, cigarette wafting from her fingers. "Sorry to interrupt."

"You're not," I say, though I'm pretty sure my blush betrays me. "Sam was just warming my hands."

"Uh-huh." She smirks. "You could try working in the cookhouse. Man, it's hot in there."

"Too bad we can't switch back and forth," I say. "Slime for a while, cook for a while, slime for a while . . ."

"Like going from sweat lodge to snow and back," Jody says. "Could even be therapeutic." A mosquito the size of a horsefly lands on her arm. She slaps it and wipes the remains on her cutoffs. "You guys headed to the mess? I'm starving."

"Actually, I need to go back to my bunkhouse." Sam kicks the ground with the toe of his boot.

I don't want him to leave. "Come eat with us. You can shower later."

"I can't. I mean we have our own kitchen." He looks beyond us toward the mess hall then down at his jacket, sprinkled in fish scales.

"Why?" I ask. "Is Filipino food better?"

His snicker has an edge to it. "We eat a lot of rice and soup."

"I think I'd rather have a hamburger," I say.

"So would I."

"Then come with us." I grab his arm.

"You don't understand. We *can't* go to your mess. It's for whites."

"I guess they overlooked me," Jody says with a snort.

Confused, I release my grip on Sam's arm. This sounds like what they're fighting in the South, but I didn't expect it up here. "You mean it's . . . What's that word? Segregated? And people accept it?"

"It's just how the canneries were set up, probably starting with the Chinese," Sam says.

"But it's screwed." Jody expels a mouthful of smoke.

Sam leans in, waving us closer. "Don't tell anyone, but there's talk of something big, a court case. We're gathering evidence."

"Can we help?" Jody asks.

"Yeah," I say, "we can be your spies."

Sam shakes his head. "Thanks, but you're not even supposed to know about it. The *manongs*—elders—don't want us making trouble."

"If no one makes trouble, nothing will change," I say.

"I know." Sam's jaw clenches. "Go get your dinner. I'll see you later." He turns around before we can object and walks away.

Jody and I slink into our mess, too hungry to fight the unfairness of it all. I try not to enjoy my cheeseburger, French fries, cookies, and chocolate milk too awfully much, but I'm so relieved to be done for the day that I can't resist making a toast to surviving.

Jody just stares at me and my raised milk carton like I'm the weirdest person she's ever seen.

"You're supposed to hold up yours, too," I explain.

She looks confused, but imitates my move. I touch my carton to hers and say, "Cheers."

"What a weird custom."

"You're supposed to do it with wine or champagne," I tell her.

"That'll be the day."

I laugh, even though I'm not sure if she's being funny. I'm learning that, with Jody, it's sometimes hard to tell.

NO one throws a party to celebrate our first day of canning. Everyone's too tired. Jill, the small blonde from Spokane, does us all the huge favor of throwing away the beer-can ashtrays, so the common room smells less like a tavern. After some groaning about sore muscles, we all hit our bunks early even though the sun's still up.

"Is Sam your boyfriend?" Jody asks.

I hesitate, because I don't really have an answer. "I don't know."

"What do you mean, you don't know?"

"We haven't, uh . . . You know."

"Had sex?"

"Jeez, Jody!" I'm glad we're both in our bunks with the light off so she can't see me turn red. "I was going to say that we haven't talked about going steady."

Her pillow muffles her laugher.

"What's so funny?"

"*Going steady*. You are *such* an innocent!"

"Well, we *haven't*," I whine, blushing deeper.

"It's okay. To be innocent, I mean. Wish I still was."

Jody likes a boy named Connor who drives a forklift in the warehouse. We both agree that driving a forklift has to be about the coolest cannery job, short of foreman.

"He's even Native," she says, "though I'm not sure if he's Tlingit. Could be Haida or Aleut. Whatever he is, he's choice."

I milk her for details. Turns out, their one and only interaction consisted of a smile (hers) followed by a nod (his).

"I think you should try words next time," I tease.

We talk and giggle until we drop off.

CHAPTER 22

By-Catch

The unwanted marine creatures caught during commercial fishing

We can't work because there's no fish, and we can't go outside because it's coming down in buckets.

"Pretty typical," Jody says. "Three days without rain here is a drought."

So we join Jill and Marlene in playing penny-ante poker on the tippy table, until Jody can't take it anymore and props up the short leg with an old issue of *16* magazine. Pandora is sitting on the floor doing some weird exercise she calls yoga and complaining about Jody's smoke, so Jody goes out on the porch to finish her cigarette. Meanwhile, Valerie is sprawled on the couch reading a book called *Black Like Me*, even though she's not black.

"That's kind of the point," she says. "The author darkened his skin to look black. Then he traveled through the South and wrote about all the prejudice. White people would give him this hate stare."

I remember Sam telling me I would never know what it was like to be feared or hated based solely on how I look. "Can I borrow that book when you're done?"

"Sure," Valerie says. "But I need it back. It's a library book."

"Okay, never mind."

Maybe it's not shyness holding Sam back. Maybe he can't consider going steady with me because I'm white. Isn't that prejudice in reverse? I know he likes me. But does he like me enough to actually call me his girlfriend? I wish I could see him, but the rain is determined to ruin any chance of that. It hammers our roof like an overlong drum solo, and I'm getting mighty tired of it.

When we've had enough of poker, Jody gets out her twine and beads and shows me how to make a friendship bracelet. Macramé is like braiding, but more intricate. She knows all these fancy knots, so the bracelet she makes me is much cooler than the one I make her. But she praises my effort and adds it to the collection on her wrist. I never wear jewelry, so I can't stop fiddling with this novelty on my arm, pulling it, shaking it, turning the beads between my fingers.

I don't notice that the rain has stopped until Jody looks up at the ceiling and sucks in her breath.

"Want to take a walk?" she asks me.

"God, yes."

We throw on our jackets. Jody lights a cigarette, and we head out under a bruised sky that shines milky white where the sun is straining to break through. *If the sun comes out, that means Sam wants me to be his girlfriend. Oh, it's trying so hard. Come on, sun.*

The puddles reflect the clouds. We thread our way through them, heading for the cannery exit. The complex is on a thin lip of land between forest and water, so there really aren't many places to walk without getting wet or dripped on.

Of course, Jody has other ideas. As we come to a giant puddle, she gives me a shove, making me step in it. My left sneaker soaks through, but I get back at her with a muddy kick. Before long, we're both jumping in the puddle and giggling hysterically. Jody drops her cigarette in the mud. "Damn." Her face is covered in brown spots like she has some dreaded pox, and I know I must look just as bad.

"We could drop in and see what the Filipinos are cooking up," she says.

"I'm not hungry."

"I'm not talking about eating, silly."

I have no idea what she's getting at.

"The protest, lawsuit, whatever you want to call it?"

"Oh, yeah." I swipe at some of the mud on my face; I'm pretty sure I've just made it worse. "But Sam said we weren't supposed to know about that." My pulse speeds up just saying his name.

"Come on, I've never seen the Filipino bunkhouse."

"It's right over there." Next to the cannery itself, the sprawling building is the biggest one here. It's also the most run-down, which is saying something, because all the buildings are run-down.

"I mean the inside," Jody says.

"But we're covered in mud. We'll track it in."

Jody rolls her eyes. "This is Alaska. Besides, Sam won't mind."

As she says it, the sky cracks open and a wondrous silver sun shines through, drenching us in *happy*. Sam does want me as a girlfriend! I must be grinning like an idiot, because Jody just looks at me and cracks up.

Then she dashes up to the door of the Filipino bunk-house and knocks before I can stop her.

No one answers.

I grab her sleeve. "Come on, let's go clean up. We can come back later," I plead, but my heart is doing a tap dance in my throat, waiting for that door to open.

She knocks again. No answer. My pulse slows, sinks back into my chest. As we turn to leave, an older man opens the door. He takes in our muddy pants and jackets and our spotted faces.

"We've, uh, been out walking," Jody says, holding a snicker behind pursed lips. "Is Sam here?"

"Sam?" he asks with a heavy accent.

"Sam Tap . . . o . . . soak," I say.

Way, way too eager.

The man goes off to check, closing the door and leaving me with my galloping heart. So much time passes, I wonder if he decided to ignore us. Now that I'm not jumping madly in mud puddles or exalting the Sun God, my warmth is fading fast.

Finally, finally, Sam opens the door. His hair sticks out at odd angles like he just got up, and he's wearing a big flannel shirt over long-underwear bottoms. He's also barefoot. An electric thrill shoots through me. I've never seen his feet before.

"What are you doing here?" Not a warm welcome, but not a cold one, either.

"It was Ida-Sue's idea." Jody looks at me.

"Was not!" I yelp.

"Could we, uh, borrow a towel or something?" Jody starts taking off her muddy jacket.

Sam watches her take off her shoes. "Uh, sure, I'll give you mine."

I've been at the cannery long enough to know that this is a generous offer. It's probably Sam's only towel. He'll have to wash it after we're through, and clean towels, not to mention clothes, are a luxury around here. Still, I follow Jody's lead, piling my jacket and shoes on the porch before going inside to wipe myself down with the towel *that has touched Sam's body.*

God, get a hold of yourself, girl.

"We're watching the old men play mahjong," he says when we emerge from their communal bathroom, still damp but more presentable. "It's a Chinese game, kind of like American rummy."

We walk into a room at the end of a hall that's foggy with cigarette smoke. A single hanging light bulb casts dramatic shadows on the men sitting at small, square table. With magician-like moves, they assemble green and white plastic blocks into rows, the meaning of which is lost on me. The blocks have patterns on them, look like hard candy, and make a pleasing percussion when they click together. I'm so mesmerized, I don't realize I'm blocking someone's view until I get a tap on the shoulder.

"Oh, sorry." I step out of the man's way, only to stand in front of someone else. Then I notice the room is lined with spectators slumped in folding chairs. Jody and I are the only girls in a gathering of young Filipino men watching older Filipino men gamble. She bites her lip. I shrug and shake my head. Then I hear my name, my real name. Sam waves us over. A couple of guys switch seats so Jody and I can sit next to him. Jody makes sure I'm sitting next to Sam.

He leans over to whisper, as if his normal voice, already so soft, would disturb the concentration of the men in the middle of the room. "That's my uncle." He points out a small, bespectacled man at the table. "The *manongs* play every night, sometimes 'til one or two in the morning. If my uncle wins, I'll get to share the pot."

"So you gamble on the gamblers," Jody says.

"Yep."

That would explain why Sam's eyes are so bloodshot. He isn't getting any sleep.

"Mahjong!" yells a man in a green hat. A chorus of *aahs* and *oohs* greet this news. Sam's uncle says something I don't understand, but the meaning is clear enough. He lost.

"Damn!" Sam slaps his thigh. "The winner had a secret kong."

"A what?"

"A kong is four of the same suit." Sam goes on to explain what you need to win in mahjong, something about pongs and chows, three-of-a-kinds and straights, but I can't focus on what he's saying because he's leaning so close, his breath is warming my neck.

Jody looks supremely bored, sucking on a cigarette and playing with her bracelets. When the winnings are doled out, so is the booze. I can't see what they're passing around, but it's clear and hard. Rum? Vodka? Lighter fluid? Has no one in

Alaska heard of cups? I watch the bottle go from person to person. Some use one hand to tip it up to their mouth. Some use two. The more fussy drinkers use their sleeves or shirt-tails to wipe off the lip before taking a swig. Jody has stopped playing with her bracelets. She sits up in her chair, eyes on the bottle like she plans to attack it. When it finally comes to her, I realize I've got it all wrong. She doesn't attack. She bolts, out of her chair and through the door we came in. Even the mahjong players notice.

The man who tried to hand her the bottle looks surprised and a little hurt, as if he's responsible for her reaction. Then he shrugs and passes the bottle over to me.

"Is she okay?" Sam asks.

"I don't know."

It's rum. I hold the bottle, wondering what to do. Should I run after Jody? Or take a drink? The thought of swapping spit with so many people kind of grosses me out, and I really don't want to get sick again. Sam's waiting for me to drink or pass. I drink. The liquor burns going down, making me cough like the rookie I am. A couple of the guys snicker, and, though they mean no offense, I give them the stink-eye. I'm not mad at them, though. I'm mad at myself—for having no willpower, for staying with Sam, for being the worst friend ever. I should have followed Jody out. I could still leave, go find her, ask if she's okay, but I can't move. I'm waiting for the weight of Sam's arm on my shoulders.

Like at the Halloween party, a pleasant numbness takes over. I like this part, but not the getting sick. I'll stop before that happens. Meanwhile, I'm enjoying the relaxation. I could take a nap on Sam's chest. Then he'd have to put his arm around me. Fortunately, I don't have to be so forward, because it eventually happens. Sam's arm moves from the back of my chair onto my shoulders. I chart his progress as his hold gets tighter and tighter still, until his fingers reach under my sleeve and softly caress my upper arm. I never knew an arm caress could give me the chills. Soon, I'm slouched in my chair, leaning back into him. His body is so solid and warm I could live there.

He takes me back to his bunk, but it's anything but romantic. His cot is one of thirty lined up on either side of a long barracks room, just like I've seen in war movies. We're not alone, either. About half a dozen guys are stretched out reading or sleeping. Pig-like snores come from the man two beds over. The room is so cold and drafty that I start to sober up against my will. Sam shows me the cracks in the walls where they've stuck cardboard to block the wind from whistling through.

I shiver. He sits across from me on the bed and takes my hands. With his skin flushed from the rum, the white scar in his eyebrow is more noticeable.

"I'm glad we got some time alone."

I glance over at the snoring man.

"Okay, almost alone," he says. "Why are you here, Ida? It's not to work, is it?"

I try to think through the gauze in my head. "Not really."

Sam already knows about my dad, but he doesn't know what brought me north. So I force my brain to focus, telling him about the note that led to Trinity and my plans to visit her.

"But before I go to see her," I say, "I wanted to talk to you."

"Me? Why?"

"Because I thought you'd understand. You still have a dad, but he's gone, a lot. He has this other life in Vietnam. You're always worrying, always wondering. Well, what if your dad supposedly died but they never found him? Sorry, I hope that doesn't happen, but what if it did, and you found out you maybe didn't know him like you thought you did?"

I pause, and Sam motions for me to go on.

"See, after my father was presumed drowned by the Coast Guard, my mom acted really weird about it, like more angry than sad. She even threw out all his stuff. Right there in front of me. Then I heard her tell my grandma that she's not sure he's *even dead*, like maybe he ran off on purpose, and now this thing with Trinity." I stop, willing myself not to choke on the words I'm about to say. "I love my dad, love him more than anything. But maybe—maybe he was just a jerk. A jerk to my mother. A jerk to me."

I swallow.

"So." Sam tilts his head. "You came all the way up here to find out if your dad was with another lady?"

"No. I mean yes, but it's more than that. I want the truth." I pull my posture up straight, like Mom has always told me to.

But Sam's not buying it. I brace for the question I see forming behind his bloodshot eyes.

"Okay," he says, "so what if you find out your dad was a jerk?"

"Then at least I'll know. It's better than not knowing." A draft comes through the wall and I clench my teeth.

"Is it? Will it change anything?"

It won't change the fact that my dad is gone. My mom

and I will still be alone and possibly more bitter than ever, knowing that he was, at best, sharing his love, or, at worst, taking it elsewhere. The truth could really hurt, but not knowing hurts too. Maybe I need the truth so I can put it to rest, like my mom says. Accepting my father for who he was, accepting what I can't change. Accepting *is* change.

"Yes," I say. "Yes, I think it will."

He leans forward. "Ida, I know what you are saying. But even if your dad did something bad, he was still your dad. He still loved you. I mean, you can't fake that."

"I suppose." My lame response tells me I'm tired. I love being with Sam, in spite of his testing questions, but if we aren't going to make out, I want to go back to my bunk, crawl into my sleeping bag, and let dreams do with my problems what they will.

"Hey, it's late." I let go of his hands. "I should let you get to sleep." I grimace. "Heard a rumor of fish tomorrow."

"Good . . . I think." Sam frowns. "I still don't know why you wanted to work at a cannery."

"Blame my mom. All my life she's been telling how awful it is, like it's the worst job on the planet, and you know what?"

"What?"

"She was right."

Sam's perfect lips curl up into a smirk.

It's after ten o'clock. As he walks me back to my bunk-house, everything, even the mosquitoes buzzing around us, gives off the golden glow of a sun that hardly sets. *Raven stealing the sun.* I giggle at the thought of Dad flapping his arms like wings.

"What?" Sam asks.

"Just remembering something."

When we get to the door of the women's bunkhouse, we both stop.

"Well . . ." He stands there awkwardly.

"Deep subject," I say, repeating a joke I heard at school.

He swoops in so fast our teeth click together. I grab him by the shoulders before he can swoop out again, and, finally, I get the kiss I've been waiting for. His lips taste rummy and his clothes smell of fish, but all I want to do is take him in.

I float into my room, lips and teeth reverberating with the smash of Sam's mouth. I want to jump up and down, but that would wake Jody, who's curled in her sleeping bag.

Oh yeah. I've been a horrible friend. I saw her run out of that room like someone who was about to puke, and I didn't even care enough to run after her. As quietly as I can, I take off my pants, mud-caked and stiff at the bottoms, and set them on top of my dirty clothes pile in the corner. Then I open my sleeping bag and bump my head. I hear the crackle of the plastic mattress on Jody's bunk, but she doesn't wake up.

CHAPTER 23

When you share a small space on a remote island, it becomes painfully obvious when your friend is trying to avoid you. Ever since that afternoon at the Filipino bunkhouse, Jody has been giving me the cold shoulder. She doesn't come over to eat with me, preferring her can-cooking friends. She doesn't hang out in our room or in the common area. I don't know where she goes, but the only time I've seen her the past couple of days has been during work breaks, smoking with the other smokers, or at night, when she's asleep—or pretending to be.

During one of our breaks, we actually made eye contact. She was standing outside the can-making wing talking to another girl. She saw me, flicked her ashes on the ground, then slowly and deliberately turned around. Stung, I just stood there, waiting for her to glance back at me. She didn't. I walked on, deciding that if she's going to be a bitch, I can be a bitch right back. I don't need her. I've got Sam, and a growing number of friends at the Filipino bunkhouse.

To them, I'm Sam's daring *puti* girlfriend, Susan. It's pronounced *pootee*, which sounds kind of dirty, but it just means "white" in Tagalog. I earned the "daring" label after I started stealing food from the white mess for them. Fruit is a favorite. They can't get enough of it. Problem is, I'm only one person with so many pockets. I can't make repeated trips to the mess. The cook, Roz, is a stern woman who could be George Washington's sister. I feel her eyes burning through my back when I leave with an extra apple or two or three. She doesn't care if you take your food out, but she doesn't like it if you take more than your share. This makes stealing more challenging, as well as exciting. It's become a kind of game. How much food can I hide in my pockets and under my coat without her becoming suspicious? I once managed to squirrel away four extra sandwiches, six cookies, and three milks while she was in back taking a smoke break.

The guys at Sam's bunkhouse loved that one. They crowded around me, their eyes following my every move as I unloaded my booty on the table in their kitchen. I thought they might fight over who got what, but order prevailed when a tall guy in glasses came in with a big knife and some Dixie cups to portion out the food and milk. It was all gone in about three seconds. They then bombarded me with special food requests for next time, and the tall guy—who, I learned, is a law student named Rafael—had to step in again. He told them that while I was obviously very good at what I did, I was neither a waitress nor a modern-day Robin Hood. The thought of myself in a short green tunic and leotard made me blush, but I felt myself stand a little taller and suck in my stomach.

I have less to suck in, too. I can tell. Mom would approve of my losing weight, but she wouldn't approve of how I'm doing it, and she'd be horrified to know that I'm stealing food, even if it is to right a wrong. I think Dad would be pleased, though. He had a thing for underdogs, not to mention risk and adventure. I'm beginning to understand why he loved coming up here so much. Trinity was right. You do need to see and experience Alaska to believe it.

Being the center of attention at the Filipino bunkhouse takes some getting used to. I kind of like it, but I'd be just as happy basking in Sam's private glow. I don't need the admiration of his friends too. I've noticed that Sam doesn't correct them when they refer to me as his girlfriend, but he hasn't used that word himself. He doesn't really have to. He's made it pretty clear that he thinks of me as more than a friend. We spend all our free time together, walking on the beach, drinking in the gambling room, and kissing until we're gasping. I know the salty taste of his lips and the Ivory soap and fish smell of his skin. I know each and every callus on his hands and the ropy strength of his arms. I get a tingle that rips right through me every time I even *think* of those things. Mom would call it infatuation. I call it love, although we haven't used that word either.

Alaska has been our test. We've seen each other at our absolute worst. Tired and cranky with bloodshot eyes, rat's nest hair, and filthy clothes. He's even held my hair back while I've puked my guts out. Turns out I'm a cheap drunk, but he's not much better. One night, while walking me back to my bunk, he slipped and fell into one of the car-sized potholes. We both laughed so hard, we doubled over, and Sam fell down *again*.

I usually get back to the room after Jody has gone to bed. I try not to wake her, not that she'd say anything if I did. Sam says I should talk to her. He thinks she's waiting for me to make the first move. But I have my doubts. She seems content to avoid me, taking her cue from her other dry-job friends. They aren't separated like the Filipinos are, but they always claim the same tables in the mess hall, and the wet-job people claim theirs. It's just like high school, but without the unifying force of Dena. I wonder how she's doing in Wrangell? She's probably found some way to make her oilskins look stylish. God, I miss her.

Of course, she would approve of my food capers. Heck, she'd be right there with Rafael, leading the charge. I'm not quite that involved, but Rafael and his friends certainly trust me enough to talk about their plans in front of me. I've heard all about the lawsuit and their efforts to gather evidence from canneries throughout Alaska. He and this other guy, Carlos, take notes as I go through the meals and food choices offered in the "white" mess, and they've asked me to describe in detail our bunkhouse and other "accommodations."

TONIGHT, we're sitting in the gambling room watching another game of mahjong after a ten-hour shift when I remember to tell Rafael about our cafeteria's storage room. I describe the floor-to-ceiling shelves filled with boxes of dried and canned goods, like beans, tomatoes, peaches, pears, and, my favorite, fruit cocktail.

"How do you know this?" he asks. "Did you work in the mess?"

"No," I say. "Roz, the cook, leaves the door open so any-one can see what's in there. I guess it's easier for her going in and out so much."

Rafael's eyes flash in the dim light. "Does she leave it open when she takes her smoke breaks?"

"Probably."

"Can you check on that and report back?"

"Sure."

Rafael slaps me on the shoulder. "Guys," he says, leaning back in his chair, "I'm thinking of a little raid—or maybe a big raid, depending on what Susan here finds out."

It doesn't take a sleuth to track Roz's habits. If one of us wants something that's run out in the buffet line, we know to go in back of the building, where she'll be sitting on an old milk jug, puffing away. She'll get up, usually with a grunt, and waddle back into the kitchen or storeroom for whatever it is we need. And she never bothers to shut the door if she's going out for a quick cigarette.

I've timed her breaks. They're anywhere from five min-utes to fifteen. And the best time to steal from the mess is just before it closes in the evening, at nine o'clock. By then most everyone has hit the sack to rest up for the next long workday, and Roz is hanging out in back because there's no one to attend to in front.

"IT'S not stealing," Carlos corrects me. We're sitting in the woods behind the Filipino bunkhouse, laying the ground-work for our raid, which I guess isn't really a "raid," since, as Carlos says next, "We have a right to this food."

I couldn't agree more. What I *do* have a problem with is their choice of Sam and me for the actual "not stealing" part. If we're caught, they reason, we won't get into that much trouble because Sam's young and I'm white.

"But you're not going to get caught," Carlos says. "Roz's attention will be on us, not you guys."

"But how will we know when to go in?" Sam asks.

Carlos grins. "Oh, you'll know."

FINALLY, what Rafael calls the white man's "night of reckoning" arrives. Sam and I hide between the metal smith shop and laundry shed waiting for Carlos's group to light the first M-80. We wait so long that Sam and I start to wonder if the plan has been called off.

Finally, we see Carlos creeping soundlessly around the side of the building.

One. Two. Three. BOOM! It sounds like the dock exploding.

About a minute later comes another *BOOM*—this one farther away, but still incredibly loud.

"Okay, let's go." Sam nudges my elbow and we run through the front door to the mess, which is, fortunately, empty. I lead the way to the storeroom behind the buffet counter and through the kitchen.

"LOOK at all this stuff!" Sam's eyes bug out. I have to remind him to stop gawking and start grabbing.

Emboldened by another loud concussion, we each take a big box of quart-sized canned fruit and hobble as fast as we can out of there, handing off to Rafael's group, which is strung like a bucket brigade through the trees, leading to the back door of the Filipino mess. Sam and I make two more trips before we hear the fourth M-80, our signal to get the hell out of there.

As we run back to the bunkhouse, I'm afraid of running into Roz or a cannery foreman, or really *anyone*, but we reach the cover of trees without anyone seeing us. By the time we reach safe haven, my legs and arms are shaking—those boxes weigh a ton—but I've never had so much energy. So I jump. Up and down. Up and down. Sam lets out a hoot and joins in. We are a pair of human pogo sticks, electric with joy.

"I feel like Raven!" I yell. "He's always tricking people and stealing their food!"

"Raven?" Sam stops jumping, so I do too.

I pause to catch my breath. "A Native mythological hero. He created the world, among other things."

"Oh, okay. We have Amihan, a bird who flew between the sea and the sky and rescued the first humans from a bamboo plant."

"Same sort of deal, except Raven's kind of a jerk."

Sam laughs. "Well, depending on the story, Amihan either started the fight between the sea and sky gods or stopped it."

A thrashing sound makes us both turn around just as Carlos and one of his cronies charge through the trees and almost run us over. Flushed and out of breath, they grab Sam and me in a group hug, and the four of us dance around in a circle.

"Roz tried to chase us down, but we were too fast." Carlos bends down with his hands on his knees. Seeing the boxes of canned peaches and fruit cocktail on the ground, he walks over and tears open the plastic covering. "Whooo-eee! Who has a can opener?"

News of the pantry theft spreads through the plant. A lot of people heard the explosions, but no one can pin the blame on us. No one, that is, except Jody. I'm getting into my bunk, expecting the usual wall of silence from her half of the room, when she rolls over, surprising me.

"Hey, Ida-Sue . . . or should I call you *Can* Ballou? You ever see that movie, *Cat Ballou*, with Jane Fonda and Lee Marvin?"

"Funniest Western ever," I respond, relieved to hear her voice again. "That scene where he's showing his sharp-shooting and misses the barn? God!"

"Or when he sings 'Happy Birthday' at the wake?" she snorts. "Even *I* had to laugh at that."

"Yeah, that was funny, but what about the drunken horse? I thought my dad was going to split a gut."

In the shadows, Jody's face is just a dim half-moon, but I can tell she's grinning. "So that *was* you, you and Sam, stealing that fruit," she says. "Maybe I should call you Bonnie and Clyde."

"You can call us whatever you want. I'm just glad you're talking to me again."

"Yeah, I've been thinking about that." She gets out of her sleeping bag and sits up on the edge of her cot.

"So what have you decided?"

"That we should talk."

I sit up on my cot, careful not to bump my head, and turn towards her. "Okay."

"I don't want to ruin your fun, Ida-Sue, but the truth is I

can't be around you if you're going to drink. See, for me, drinking isn't funny." She grins. "Well, unless it's Lee Marvin."

"Is that why you left the Filipino bunkhouse in such a hurry?"

She's silent for so long, I fear I've just reminded her why she should stay mad at me.

"I won't be in the same room with a bottle."

Her revelation has so much gravity behind it, I'm afraid to ask why. So I pick a safer question. "How can you stand to work here?"

"It's hard. Soon as I can, I'm getting out of Alaska. I just need to save some money. That's why I'm here, to work. I swear some people just come to party. Last summer, I had a roommate who got drunk every day. I finally had to ask Murf to move me. She's the only other person here who knows."

"That you hate drinking?"

"Correction. I *love* drinking. That's the problem. Alcoholism runs in the family. It runs in a lot of Indian families, but mine's been destroyed by it. Both my parents, my grandfather, and my uncle Frank are . . ."

She pauses, like it's hard for her to force the word out, so I jump in. "Alcoholics?"

She shakes her head. "Dead. My mom and dad in a car accident. My grandfather froze to death. He passed out in the snow. Uncle Frank took the direct route. Alcohol poisoning."

"Jesus."

"Once I start drinking, I can't stop. I keep going until I black out. I've lost whole days of my life. I once woke up in a strange place with a man I didn't know. That's when I knew I'd end up dead too." Jody lets out a ragged breath. "So now I don't take any chances. People start drinking, I'm gone."

"Wow." This time someone else's tragedy is the conversation stopper, and I'm reminded what it's like to be on the other side, the lost-for-words, afraid-to-say-the-wrong-thing side. "Wow, I'm sorry."

"You don't need to apologize. You didn't know. You and Sam are away from home for the first time. You probably want to bust loose a little. But if you plan on getting blitzed every chance you get, one of us is going to have to—"

"No . . . I mean, we can stay roommates. I didn't come here to party. I didn't even really come here to earn money, although I could use it."

Jody looks at me like I've just sprouted a second nose.

"As long as we're being honest with each other, I may as well tell you the truth. Promise not to tell anyone?"

"So long as you haven't killed anyone, okay, cross my heart, hope to die, and all that," she says, leaning in.

"I haven't killed anyone, but I may have broken the law."

Jody raises her eyebrows.

"I suppose you could say I ran away from home." I swallow hard before I spill it. "I'm only sixteen. Ida isn't a nickname, it's my real name. Sue is just the name on my fake ID."

"Yeah, I figured it was something like that."

"I didn't really come up here to get a canning job."

Jody eyes me with suspicion. "So what are you doing on Nagoon?"

"Okay, I came to Nagoon mostly to see Sam. But there's this lady, this, um, friend of my dad's I'm going to go see in Ketchikan."

Jody looks more confused than ever, but I'm too tired to go into it. Maybe later. "It's complicated."

"That's okay. You don't have to explain." She leans back and rubs the palms of her hands on her sleeping bag.

"Thanks." I reach over and pat one of her knees. "In any case, you don't have to worry about me getting drunk every night."

She grins. "Then you won't have to worry about me, either."

CHAPTER 24

Anchor Watch
*A crewman assigned to watch the
ship while anchored to make sure it's
not drifting*

Every part of me wants to sleep—my muscles, my bones, my *hair*. But I made a pact with Jody. Coming to this beach party was her idea. She heard that Connor, the hunky Native forklift driver, would be here. "This may be my last chance," she said.

When I told her there would be a keg, she noted that it would be outdoors, so it technically wouldn't violate her alcohol rule.

She asked me to keep an eye on her, though. If she so much as touches a beer, I'm supposed to tackle her to the ground. I agreed to the first part, the watching, but even that isn't easy with all these people holding white Styrofoam cups. The keg is under someone's hooded rain jacket so that, from far away, it looks like a very small, very still person standing under the trees—with many tall friends.

There must be more than sixty people here, mostly slimers, newbies, and second-year vets like Jody. The real veterans, the *manongs* and other "lifers," don't mix with us. According to Sam, they weren't amused by the canned-fruit caper. Even I can sense the resentment in their flat expressions. They know we don't really need these jobs. We can leave after our Great Alaskan Adventure.

That doesn't mean we don't work hard, though. It's late July, the peak of the run, and we're putting in twelve- to fourteen-hour days. Jody says that's light. The long days used to be longer, before the earthquake in '64, before they started seeing drop-offs in the numbers of fish. Still, it's more than enough work for me. When I close my eyes, I see running water and the pale orange cavities of fish. A spastic jerk of my head jolts me back to reality, our bonfire on the beach, mesmerizing in its shapes and colors. From blue to green, then pink to orange. Sam and I sit like stacked chairs, his chest to my back, his knees serving as armrests. The flames pop and sputter, sending up tendrils of smoke.

Jody finally convinced me to try salmon cooked the Indian way. Mounted and trussed on sticks, it tastes like no salmon I've ever had. It's crisp and smoky, almost sweet on the outside, and so tender on the inside.

"The Tlingit believed salmon were a tribe of people who lived in the ocean and traveled upstream on invisible canoes," she says, blowing cigarette smoke out her nose. "Pretty trippy, huh?"

"So does that make us cannibals?" Sam asks.

"Yes, it does . . . just kidding! But you *do* have to show the proper respect. My grandmother tells stories about day-long ceremonies to welcome home the first salmon. They would take the bones back to the ocean to make sure the salmon people kept returning. Nowadays, though, we just throw our bones in the garbage like everyone else."

"That's sad." I search for the words to explain why, but Jody's attention is elsewhere. I follow her stare straight to Connor, who's standing at the water's edge, about a hundred yards away from us, skipping rocks. With an effortless side arm and flick of his wrist, they leap over the calm surface of the water before trailing off in countless tiny ripples. Even trying to balance a cup of beer in his non-throwing hand, he's able to skip without fail. And I have to admit, he's easy on the eyes, with no shirt and the fang of some animal swinging from a chain around his neck. Even here, where guys outnumber girls at least three to one, Connor could have his pick.

"Have you two talked yet?" I ask.

Jody sucks on her cigarette, rolls her eyes, and blows the smoke skyward. "Yes, we've talked."

"More than hello?"

"Ye-es."

"Okay, just checking."

To look her best for Connor, Jody took a shower before putting on her cleanest pair of dirty jeans, some makeup, and the necessary bug spray. She even took my advice and ditched her red baseball cap so Connor could see her eyes better.

"Go on, walk up to him. Start a conversation." I nudge her with my foot. "What have you got to lose?"

She presses her lips together. "Oh, just my pride."

Sam's snort makes me turn around. "What's so funny?"

"It's just that guys are the same way about girls. We're scared too."

"I'm not *scared!*" Jody crushes her cigarette on a log and throws the stub in the fire. "Fine. All right. Here goes."

She stands up, brushes the sand off the seat of her pants, and starts toward him. On the way, she picks up a chunk of granite the size of a fist. *That's one way to get your man. Knock him out first.* Of course, she doesn't hit Connor over the head. She waits until he's between throws and hands him the rock. I can't hear what she's saying as Connor turns the chunk around and around in his hands. Then they stop talking. Eyes on the water, Connor plants his feet and squares his shoulders. He swings his arm back and flings that rock so perfectly level that it skips. Twice. So Jody hands him another, bigger rock. It might have skipped, too, but for the fat wake thrown up by some guys in a passing motorboat. The driver turns around and comes back for another pass, pumping his fist in the air as the waves from his boat slap the shore.

"Hey!" Connor yells as the boat roars past a third time, angling toward the beach like it's going to crash our party— literally. The driver, a wild-haired guy with a big red beard, cuts the engine just in time to pull it up before the propeller scrapes bottom. Then he and his friend jump out to pull the boat to shore. Once the boat is secure, the bearded guy reaches under the seat and pulls out a bottle and something else. They survey the beach, fixing on our fire pit gathering.

Bear, who has been watching them, straightens his back. "They're coming over."

Sam and I privately dub the boat's driver Red Beard because he reminds us of a pirate. He even has a dagger holstered in his belt. His friend has a Popeye body with big tattooed muscles. I can see a naked lady on one arm, a skull on the other. His waist is so narrow his jeans hang down, revealing grimy white underwear. They both have that glazed, red-eyed stare that I now recognize as being stoned.

"Hey, I know what this party needs," Red Beard says to his friend so loudly we can hear. With the bottle in one hand, bag in the other, he raises his arms as he enters the light of the fire. His skin glows red, sunburned. His friend sways on his feet, eyes at half-mast.

"You all canners?" Red Beard asks, looking around the circle.

No one says anything. Finally, Valerie answers, "Duh."

Red Beard grins. "Mind if I . . . ?" He plops down, squeezing between her and Pandora, giving them both a squeeze around the shoulders while staring south of their faces. His friend, who volunteers that he goes by Hoggy, finds a cozy spot between Marlene and Jill. If he were a dog, he'd be drooling.

Red Beard takes a swig from the bottle and passes it to Valerie, who surprises me by taking a drink.

"Yeah, that's right." His voice is guttural, his gaze approving. He turns his attention to the brown pouch in his lap, pulling out a pipe and something in a plastic bag that looks like a turd and has a name like a sneeze. "Ha-sheesh," he calls it. He fills his pipe, lights it, and takes a long drag. Still holding the smoke in his mouth, he hands the pipe to Pandora. She takes a dainty puff on it and passes it along.

"Man, you gotta get on a fishing boat next summer," Red Beard says to no one in particular. "That's where the real bread is, not this canning shit. I made four grand last summer, and that's not counting what I spent on entertainment. That peeler bar in Ketchikan." He chuckles to himself. "Man, those chicks was fat and ugly."

"Hey, dude." Bear leans in like he's going to challenge him, but all he does is slice his hand across his throat. The universal cannery signal for stop.

Red Beard's grin goes slack. "What? I walk into the Queen's tea party or something?" His friend laughs, but no one else does. "Sorry, ladies, guy talk." He gives a bow. "Hey, drink up. Take a toke. Let's loosen things up around here." He waves his arms in opposite circles. "Everybody happy, eh?"

Sam and I pass on the bottle and the pipe. I don't want to swap spit with these two. Some of the others don't appear to mind, though, including Jill, who I always thought was so dainty with her pale-frosted lips. Beyond her shoulder, I notice the beach emptying of people. Jody and Connor aren't skipping rocks anymore. I don't know where they are, but if she's with him she's probably okay. After all, he's why we're here.

"Yeah, that mess you got yourselves into," Red Beard is saying, "makes me proud to be Canadian. Any draft dodgers here?"

Sam's muscles tense. I squeeze his knee just in case. These guys aren't worth a fight. But Bear doesn't see it that way. He shoots Red Beard a murderous glare.

Red Beard holds his arms up in surrender. "Hey, it's cool, dude. Didn't mean no offense."

His friend looks at Bear then back at Red Beard then back at Bear again, mouth straining to keep a smile. Red Beard gets his bottle back. He takes a long, sloshy swig, and finishes with an exaggerated "aah."

"Any you slimers been out on the water? Really should see the scenery while you're here. Clarence Strait is real pretty by boat, and I got one right over there."

I'm not sure what he's offering, whether it's the use of his boat or a sightseeing trip with him as a guide. No one takes him up on his offer either way.

He looks around, casting a wary glance at Bear. "No one wants to go for a spin? Nice boat, comfortable seats . . . ?"

I make the mistake of smiling at him. "How 'bout you, sweetheart? Yer boyfriend can come, too. I don't discriminate."

"No thanks," Sam says.

I shake my head.

When it finally sinks in that he isn't going to get a date from any of us, Red Beard says, "Well, okay, have fun canning, eh?" He staggers to his feet. He collects his pipe and he and his friend leave our circle to try their luck down the beach.

"God, I wouldn't be caught dead with that guy," Jill says when they're out of earshot.

Josh does a dead-on impression of Red Beard talking about "peeler bars, aye!" and we all laugh. I look up the beach to see where they're going next, and that's when I spot the friend, Hoggy, talking with Jody. They're just standing there smoking, but it makes me nervous seeing her with him. Red Beard has left them to visit the keg.

"What's wrong?" Sam asks.

"Jody's talking with Hoggy." Sam doesn't know about the secret agreement we have, but I think he senses my worry.

"She can take care of herself," he says.

"I hope so." I watch them until they go their separate ways, Hoggy to join Red Beard, and Jody to join Connor and . . . is that Murf? They're sitting on a log littered with white cups. Jody appears to reach for one, but her hands go to the small of her back in a stretch. Cannery work is hard on the lower back. Mine is stiff too. I decide to give Jody the benefit of the doubt, because I really, really don't want to tackle her.

Murf, on the other hand, is obviously drunk. Leaning back, she almost loses her balance on the log, prompting Connor to reach out an arm to catch her.

Jody's got competition.

The boat stays on the beach. No one's going for a ride with those guys. They're just too weird, and the air is too cold. I'm content in my cozy nest by the fire, curled next to Sam, head resting on his chest, a tired numbness taking hold.

I don't know how long I sleep, but when I wake up, a big, black bird is pecking at the remains of our salmon. "God, that crow is huge!"

"It's not a crow," Sam says.

I've never seen a real live raven before. This bird is magnificent, and just a bit scary with its large, hooked beak and shiny black eyes. As it steals morsels from the still-smoldering fire pit, I can see why ravens have come to symbolize death and the underworld. I can sense the quick intelligence that inspired Edgar Allen Poe and the Native trickster tales. This is no ordinary bird.

"Wow," I say, transfixed. It's almost enough to take my mind off my full bladder. Almost. "I really, really have to pee." There is no public restroom. My choices are the beach, which is way too exposed, or the woods. I start for the latter.

"Hold on," Sam says, slowly getting to his feet. "I'll go too. Don't want you getting dragged off by a bear . . . or pirates."

I roll my eyes. Then I notice that the boat's gone. "They left."

We walk up the beach and into the forest. Under the thick cover of evergreens, it's more like real night. It's probably much later than it appears. No doubt the sun has already set in Annisport. I wonder if Mom is asleep or awake. Maybe she can't sleep because she's too keyed up. I really should call her again. I said in my postcard that I'd call. She probably thinks that, because I haven't, something horrible has happened. She's probably cleaning the grout in the bathroom right now because she can't stop imagining all the terrible possibilities. The guilt weighs on me, making the need to pee even more urgent. Squatting behind a fat tree trunk while Sam stands guard, it takes me an embarrassingly long time to empty my bladder. Meanwhile, Sam's done before I know it.

"Guys have it easy," I say as we walk back to the fire, just embers now. The party has thinned out considerably. Couples are silhouetted in the glow of the coals, against the blues of sky and water. I'm reminded again of those impossibly hard 5,000-piece jigsaw puzzles that are half one color, and you can't tell what's what. I recognize Murf's head poking above a beach log. She looks like a boy. And there's Connor with his arm around her.

Wait a minute. "Where's Jody?"

"What?" Sam asks.

"She's not with them." I scan the beach for her short, muscular body, a head with a ponytail. "Oh my God, Sam. She's not here."

I run over to Murf and Connor, feet slipping over the rocks. "Where's Jody?"

"Christ!" Connor jerks away from Murf mid-kiss. Murf looks up at me, all dreamy. Suddenly I hate her. I hate her for stealing Connor. And I hate Connor for being stolen. I hate them both for making Jody so mad or depressed or both that she took off. Maybe she's drinking. Maybe she's already drunk. Maybe . . .

Up the beach near the water's edge, a glossy black bird hops over a groove in the rocks where a boat once was.

"Do you know where Jody is?" I try to stay calm, but my heart is pumping so hard I'm amazed they can't hear it.

Connor shrugs. "Sorry."

"But she was with you guys!"

Connor's jaw clenches. "You her chaperone or something?"

I spin around, almost running into Sam, who I didn't know was behind me. There's a black blur in my peripheral vision. The raven flying off. Sam's eyes reflect worry and fear, like he doesn't know me, like I've just been body-snatched. Maybe I have. I turn back to Connor and Murf. "I was supposed to keep an eye on her to make sure she didn't drink because, well . . ." I'm about to explain Jody's family history, but stop myself. "Anyway, now I'm really, really scared that she did drink and then left with those guys." I flap my arm toward the spot where the boat was.

Sam puts a hand on my shoulder. I know my fear makes no sense to them. How do I explain the fluttering in my stomach? If only I hadn't been so tired. I'm not tired now. I'm wide awake.

"You know, come to think of it," Connor says, "she said she was going for a walk."

I suspect Connor may be trying to get rid of me, but I ask him where.

"Down the beach, I think."

"Did she go alone?"

"I think so."

"How long ago?"

"I don't know, twenty minutes, half an hour? I wasn't really paying attention."

"Obviously." I glare at Murf.

As Sam and I turn to go, Murf wishes us luck, but with her slurring speech, it sounds like "suck."

CHAPTER 25

Devil Seam
*The seam in the planking of a
wooden ship that's on or below the
waterline and therefore very difficult
to seal in the event of a leak*

The wind kicks up. Sam and I scan the beach for signs of Jody. The sky glows. It's not light but it's not dark, either. Our long shadows stretch across the rocks.

Then I see it. Something white caught by the wind. A Styrofoam cup.

"Well, someone passed this way." I catch it before it blows off again, smell inside.

"What are you doing?" Sam asks.

"Seeing if it smells like beer."

"Does it?"

"Hard to tell." I stuff the litter in the pocket of my jacket. "Jody!"

"Jody!" Sam's voice breaks as he shouts, like he just woke up.

Our nap was much too short. Besides the long day of canning, we've been going for almost twenty hours. Every time my foot slips on the rocky beach, I startle awake. The crunch of our steps echoes in my brain, like we're walking in some gravelly tunnel.

"Sorry to drag you into this," I tell Sam. "I was the one who promised to look after her, not you."

He shrugs. "I couldn't let you go off by yourself."

Sweet, loyal Sam. Sworn to protect, just like his sailor dad. He's standing by me even though he probably wants nothing more than to crawl onto his cot and get a few precious hours of sleep before our shift. I grab his hand and squeeze it. He squeezes back. Jody is his friend too. Together, we'll find her. We have to. I imagine her drunk and despondent over Connor, staggering down the beach alone, a big, fat target for pirates. Red Beard and his friend could have scooped her up and taken her anywhere to do whatever.

"JODY!" I yell, hands cupped around my mouth.

"JODY!" Sam echoes.

"Do you think she went into the woods?" I ask.

"If she did, we'll never find her in there," Sam says.

"Better stick to the beach, I guess."

"Yeah, although we're running out of beach."

Up ahead, our path narrows against a steep rock bluff, then disappears completely where the rocks form a point jutting into the water. After some hemming and hawing, we agree to go to the point and then turn around. We don't want to get trapped by the tide. Unlike the bluff at home, this one isn't climbable, even by daredevils. The vertical drop is broken by slim shelves and trees hanging on by exposed roots.

The trees that have fallen litter the base of the cliff as drift-wood.

Sam gets to the point before I do. By the time I catch up, he's halfway up the barrier. He makes the climbing look easy, but I know the seaweed-topped rocks are slick and the barnacles on the edges would be sharp and unforgiving if I fell. Up close, the tiny, volcano-shaped creatures release a chorus of wet clicking sounds. I'm standing there staring into their grasping mouths, or whatever they are, when Sam appears above me and asks what kind of cigarette Jody smokes.

"I'm not sure. Why?"

"I found this." He holds up a stub with blue lettering on the smashed white end, next to the brown filter. I make out three letters: i-n-s.

"Winstons," Sam says. "My uncle smokes them."

"Are the packages white with red?"

"Yep, that's right."

As if on cue, we both yell, "JO-DY!" We yell it three times together, and then we wait, but the only response we get is the lap of waves and the crackling suckle of sea life.

"A lot of people smoke Winstons," Sam says.

"I know. If only Jody wore lipstick." I picture Jill's signature frosted pink. "Then we'd know for sure."

"So, what do you want to do?" He stands up from his crouch.

I measure the danger of climbing around the point against what we stand to gain. Even if the stub was Jody's, she may have simply stopped here, like us, had her smoke, and headed back. She wouldn't try to get over these rocks drunk, would she? But then, alcohol makes you do stupid stuff. I know this now. She could be nearby, within earshot even, but unconscious or too hurt to speak. If that's true, I'd never forgive myself for abandoning her.

"I think we need to get to the top of this barrier and see what's on the other side."

"Okay," Sam agrees. "But we better hurry." He hoists himself over the top like there's nothing to it. "Watch your step."

My method is to crab-crawl, planting my feet carefully and using my hands to brace myself. I crunch on barnacles for traction, trying to avoid, as much as possible, the green stuff. I have a couple of near falls, but I eventually get to the top to find Sam already on the other side, standing in a shady pocket of beach surrounded on all sides by more bluff.

"Dead end!" Sam yells, as if it isn't obvious.

It may be a trick of the light, but the water on this side of the island is the most gorgeous, glowing blue color I've ever seen. Looking out, the otherworldly blue is dotted with the dark, green lumps of the islands nearby. Beyond them, the Alaska mainland seems to stretch forever.

Sam climbs back up to meet me. "It's pretty, isn't it?"

"Yeah. I've never seen water that blue. It's like a kid colored it."

"Aquamarine," Sam says. "That's the Crayola crayon name. I used to draw a lot. Crayons were the one art supply my mom could afford."

I remember the doodles all over Sam's Pee-Chee. "I'd like to see some of your drawings."

"Sure." He looks down at his shoes. "I've never shown them to anyone, but I'd show you."

I lean in for a kiss, but he stops me short. "We need to get

out of here," he says. I follow his gaze towards the bluff behind us. "See where the wall goes from dark to light? That's
the high-water mark."

"Okay. Say no more. We'll go back."

With the tide coming in, the point is no longer a point,
but we can still get over it. I think of all those happy barnacles, safe in their tidal beds as I try to retrace my steps. Going
down is a lot scarier than coming up, but Sam hopscotches
ahead of me like he was born to it.

"What are you, part crustacean?"

I glance over at him, not where I'm stepping. That's all it
takes. My feet slide out from under me. Hips. Then head.
White light, stars, a whole blinking constellation in a black
sky. How did the sky get so black? A voice, low and guttural,
almost purring, then three sharp calls. The blackness takes
the shape of a head, hunched on wide shoulders, two shiny
eyes, a long pointed beak, and a ruffled neck. Raven. He
stands on the rock above, looking down at me. He bows and
the tip of his beak touches my cheek, and I fear he plans to
peck my eyes out. But his head turns to regard me with one
eye, and it isn't hungry or mean. It's protective—and so shiny,
I can see my reflection.

"Dad?"

"Ida."

He turns again, cocks his head. Wings with ends like fingers form a dark tent that folds me in. I feel my head being
lifted, the fingers making a pillow.

"Ida?"

The shiny black becomes slick yellow, the smell of fish
and plastic. A rain slicker, folded into a pillow, is placed under

my head, and above it is the face I've come to know so well, the smooth brown skin, scarred eyebrow, and eyes full of concern.

Sam. I'm lying on the rocks. He fills my view.

"Ida, can you hear me?" He's shouting but the words sound far away.

My head slides up and down on the slick surface of his jacket.

"We have to move you. Can you roll, just roll onto one side?" His hands slide under my shoulder. My body moves under Sam's push, but it's so disconnected. "Come on," he urges. "That's it."

Waves crash against the rocks behind me, spraying droplets of saltwater on my face as I roll onto my stomach. The back of my head doesn't hurt. It's just cold, like the wind's blowing right through to my brain. I don't realize I'm whimpering until Sam tries to comfort me.

"It's okay. I'm going to help you." His hands are on my back. "Can you prop yourself up on your arms?"

I try to do what he says, raising myself into a kind of girl push-up, but it kills my tailbone.

"You okay?"

"Yeah," I say through gritted teeth.

"Okay. I'm going to guide your feet, one at a time." Sam pulls my right foot loose. My balance shifts, and for one heart-stopping second, I'm falling, but he's there to brace me. I need to trust him. While he positions my feet, I hold on with my hands. Red fingered, white knuckled, they look like starfish clinging to life.

"You're doing great," Sam says, his voice straining with the effort of bracing me.

"Ugh!"

"Okay, here comes a kind of big drop. You can do it."

I scream as my foot goes down, down, down . . . and finally finds a landing. My rain gear slides over the barnacles. If not for that layer of plastic, my skin would be scraped raw like a keelhauled sailor's.

"Not much farther now," Sam says. "About three or four more steps."

The last one is a doozy. First Sam lets go. Then I do. We land in a heap on hard sand, but at least it's sand. Sam mostly breaks my fall.

"Are you okay?" I roll off of him.

"Yeah."

We take a few minutes to lie there, flat on our backs. Then the sickness bubbles up.

"We did it, Ida . . . Ida?"

I roll over just in time to throw up all that good salmon I ate earlier.

Sam puts his arm around my shoulders and helps me sit up, head between my knees. "Just rest here a minute." His hand makes slow circles on my back.

"God, I love you." It just comes out.

Sam's hand stops mid circle.

"Sorry," I say. It's an all-purpose apology for dragging him into my crazy life and now this. With each pass, the waves inch closer. They've already swallowed half of the rock outcropping. The little alcove of sand we're on is getting smaller and smaller.

"It's okay." Sam reaches over and lifts my chin so I'm looking into his face. "I love you too."

Time stops. We sit and stare at each other. My head hurts, but my stomach feels better. We're both exhausted. He's got chapped lips, his hair is sticking up strangely, and his eyes are bloodshot. I can tell by the way they're burning that my eyes are no better, and I'm pretty sure we both stink, but none of that matters as he pulls me close and kisses my forehead.

"What are we going to do, Ida?"

I think he's talking about the future and my mother's prohibition against my seeing him, but when he grimaces at the incoming tide, I realize he has more immediate concerns. He lets go of me and stands up. "Are you okay walking?"

"I think so."

"How about swimming? We have to get around this bluff. If we hurry, we'll just be wading."

Fighting another dizzy spell, I grab Sam's hand and let him haul me up. That's when I notice he's in shirtsleeves. "Your jacket?"

"Up there." He points at the rocks we just came down. "I'm not going back for it."

Together, we walk into the waves.

"Jeez! It's freezing! Isn't it summer?"

"In *Alaska*," Sam reminds me.

"Screw Alaska!" My scream bounces off the bluff.

To get around a pile of driftwood, we have to go deeper, up past our waists. Sam doesn't see the wave. It crashes into us. I'm under. Cold. Gasping, I gag on saltwater. Oh, God. Oh, God. It's so cold, so, so cold. *Calm down, Ida. Just calm down.* The waves keep coming. I'm stuck on something. My hood is snagged on a piece of driftwood. I yank it free, losing my balance. I can't feel my feet. I only know I'm standing because my head is above water. Sam. Where's Sam? He was right next to me.

"S-S-Sam!" I'm shivering so badly, my yell is more like a croak. His yellow jacket should be easy to spot, but then I remember he's not wearing it.

"Sam!" I force my legs to move, one in front of the other, bracing for the waves when they come. I don't want to get knocked down again. I'm already too cold. Am I making progress? I can't tell. The bluff doesn't seem to be getting any shorter. I'm tired, so tired. Keep moving. Damn these waves. If they get any stronger and I get any weaker, I'm going into that driftwood. I really don't want to be trapped in a bunch of dead trees or impaled on a sharp root. I have to move out and forward, but I can't feel my legs. My brain is telling them to move, but they just feel like dead weights. Maybe if I use my arms. Okay, I'm swimming now, but I don't know if I'm swimming in the right direction. I can't really see anything but water. Waves wash over my face, burning as the water goes up my nose and into my eyes. My head keeps slipping under. God, is this really happening? Am I about to drown? And where's Sam?

Dad, is that you? I can hear his voice, gentle and warm like a purr. Don't let me die.

Hahaha-ch-ch-ch. It's getting louder. *CH-CH-CH-CH.*

"Ida-Sue!"

I must be hallucinating. That sounds like Jody.

THERE'S the chug-chug-chug of a motor and the smell of gasoline. Two guys, one with a big red beard, haul me out of the water. Jody wraps me in a blanket. Sam's already in the boat, shivering like crazy even though he's wrapped in a sleeping bag. The man with the red beard is at the wheel, talking about a yellow jacket drifting in the tide. Sam's icy fingers find my icy fingers. Relief, of course, but also *gratitude*. For Sam and Jody, for the men I thought were pirates, for all the people who care what happens to me. I don't deserve them.

I'm lifted onto the dock and then into a waiting seaplane. A woman onboard feeds me something warm through a straw and says something about core temperature. She places some padding on the back of my head and yells something to the pilot but her words are lost to me. I'm lifted, rolled, pushed, sky above, then ceiling tiles, then bright light divided into squares and triangles. People talking at me and about me like I'm not there. A prick in the bend of my arm.

I wake up in a white room under white sheets with something beeping.

"You're awake," says a woman dealing with whatever it was that was just beeping. She's all in white, too, except for her pearl-pink glasses.

For a second, I'm afraid I'm in Heaven or some weird weigh station. "Where am I?"

She turns to face me. "You don't know? Why, you're in the hospital, dear. St. Joe's Hospital in Ketchikan, Alaska."

CHAPTER 26

Becalmed
*Unable to move due to lack of wind;
said of a sailing vessel*

A young doctor whose hands smell of iodine shines a light in my eyes. He asks me to watch his pen as he moves it up and down and side to side. With the same pen, he touches the soles of my feet and asks me if I can feel it. I can, along with my hurting head and back, sore neck, bruised right elbow, and scraped hands. I'm one aching mess.

A man wheels me to another room so another man can take an X-ray of my head. When I see the black-gray image of my skull, I'm fascinated and creeped out at the same time. If Dad drowned, is this what he's been reduced to? A skeleton? Do bones dissolve in saltwater? There could be nothing left of the man who used to swing me over his head for a ride on his shoulders. My tears prompt the nurse to apologize for the pain of the antiseptic scrub she's using to clean my wound. She's already shaved the back of my head, and I didn't cry when I felt my long hair fall away, so why would I cry from a little sting? Still, I'm thankful that the doctor shoots me with a "numbing agent" before he sews me up. Eight stitches.

"When you hit your head, your brain banged against the inside of your skull," he explains. "There's some bruising, but you should be fine. Just no more rock climbing for a while." He pats me on the shoulder.

"What about canning?" I just assume I'll return to Nagoon to finish the season with Jody and Sam. They have to be wondering if I'm okay. I'm aching to see Sam something terrible.

"That would probably be okay, but"—the doctor taps his pen against his clipboard—"I'll have the nurse come in and talk to you."

I don't like the sound of that, but he leaves the room before I can ask him why.

After a while, the nurse comes in carrying a bag with my clothes. "Your mother's on her way."

WHA-AT? My mother? On her way? "But I can't go home!" I know from the nurse's flat expression that my whine is falling on deaf ears.

"You'll have to take that up with your mother," she says.

I don't want to take it up with my mother. I know what she will say. No. Maybe I can get back to Nagoon before she gets to the hospital. But how? I have no money for a seaplane, and I can't call on that hotel lady's son again. Maybe the cannery . . . Oh, who am I kidding? They won't take me back, let alone pick me up, not after all the trouble I've caused. Let's face it, I'm trapped. Mom will get here and she'll be furious. She'll want to take me home—immediately—and this whole trip will have been for nothing. Here I thought I was so cool, working at a cannery, stealing fruit, loving Sam. But I'm just a great big chicken. I should have seen Trinity when I had the chance. Now I won't be able to, even though I'm in the same town as she is. Heck, I could probably walk to her door, but the letter with her address is on Nagoon. What were those street names again? *Deer*-something.

" . . . you ran away."

"What?"

"Your mother," repeats the nurse. "She says you ran away."

"No—it wasn't like that."

She twists her mouth in an I-don't-believe-a-thing-you're-saying frown. "In any case, we're legally required to return you to her custody. You're a minor."

I nod. There's no arguing with the truth. Or the law.

"She was really worried about you," the nurse adds.

Again, I have nothing to say, because I know in my heart that it's true. While I may fall miles short in Mom's eyes, I'm all she's got right now. I've no doubt that she was worried, probably more than worried. Crazed. She probably thought I was close to death and hooked up to one of those machines that shows your heartbeat blipping . . . or is it brain waves?

"Does she know about my accident?" Stupid question. If Mom talked to the nurse, she obviously knows how I got here. The question is, who called her? No one up here knows my last name and where I'm from. No one, that is, except Sam. It would be just like him to call her. After all, it was

Sam who got me to call home after I got to Nagoon. I don't know whether to be touched by his concern or annoyed.

"We assured her that you were going to be fine," the nurse is saying. "In fact, you can get dressed. But I'm afraid you'll have to have to wait where we can keep an eye on you. There's a room to the left of the main entrance for families and children."

Children? I'm picturing a nursery as she hands me some packets of aspirin with some papers, instructions on follow-up care. Then she leaves and draws the curtain surrounding my bed. Apparently, I'm mature enough to get dressed on my own.

As I take off my hospital gown, I feel more naked than I should. My fingers go to my neck, searching for the locket and chain that's always there, except it's not. I shake out my gown. Nothing falls. I paw the bed, the sheet, the blanket. Nothing. Could this day go any worse? I think of running after the nurse to ask if she's seen it, but I fear it's somewhere in the waters off Nagoon. Or on the beach. Or in the bunkhouse. It could be anywhere. When did I take off my shirt last? I can't remember. That familiar ache bubbles in my chest, knocking against my heart. I want to tell my dad I'm sorry even though I know he would shrug off the loss of a mere thing. *It was only a necklace, Ida. You're lucky that's all you lost.* To which I'd say, "But it was the necklace I had to remember you by." *You don't need a necklace to remember me.* Of course, he'd be right.

I pull on my old clothes, which have been cleaned, thank God. They only smell faintly of fish. Once I'm dressed, an orderly escorts me out to the hospital's lobby and into a glassed-in waiting room that's all bright colors, rubber mats, and plastic. A little girl, her blond hair sprouting from poodle barrettes, slides down a pink slide while a little boy climbs up a lime green cube with holes. This, apparently, is where I belong. If you're not an adult, you're a baby. Right.

A woman, who I assume is the mom, looks up from her magazine as I take a seat next to the glass wall. From here, I can watch who comes in and out of the hospital's main entrance or I can read. Next to me is a table with *Highlights* magazines and board books for the kiddos and several issues of *Good Housekeeping* and *Reader's Digest* for the adults. The only current-events magazine is a *Time* with a graphic of a pointed gun next to the headline, THE GUN IN AMERICA. Hmm. No thanks. I think I'd rather read this *Good Housekeeping* article on Julie Andrews. I loved *The Sound of Music*. I pick it up and flip through the pages, which are mostly advertisements, and set it down again. I can't read. I'm too preoccupied by the thought of my mother coming through that entrance. I watch as a man holds the door open for another man exiting on crutches, his right leg in a new, white cast. These people may be sick or injured, but they're all free to come and go as they please. It's a drag being underage.

I force myself to pick up the magazine again. I don't want to see her walk in. The article I turn to is by a lady doctor. "Maybe you're not too fat," it says. Ugh! Aren't there more important things to write about? When I was on Nagoon, I didn't think about my weight. I ate because I was hungry, and my clothes got looser and looser. Just get me through the day; that's all I asked of my body. And it did the job, over and over again. Of course, now it aches something awful, but that will pass. My bruises and wounds will heal. When it comes to surviving, I'll take strong over skinny any day of the week.

So, I guess my trip up here wasn't a total waste. I got strong. I met Jody. I put my relationship with Sam to the test. None of those things would have happened if I'd stayed in Annisport. If only I had a few more days up here.

SHE sees me before I see her.

"Oh, honey!"

I look up to see her tottering through the door on heels that sink into the rubber-mat flooring of the family room. I stand and am immediately enveloped in a fierce, perfume-y hug that makes me wince with pain. "Ow, that kind of hurts," I say, my chin denting her bouffant.

"Sorry!" She releases me and I see a skeletal version of the mother I remember. I know the shock must show on my face because she looks away as if embarrassed. Her makeup can't hide the dark circles around her eyes or fill in the hollows below her cheekbones. Her hair, I notice, has thinned and dulled under all that hairspray. She's stylishly dressed, as always, but her pale green pantsuit hangs on her.

She reaches up to cradle my face in her hands, shocking me with her cold fingers. She turns my head so she can examine the bandage there. "Do you have a headache? How's your neck?" She holds me at arm's length, eyes filling with tears.

"I'm sore, but I'll be okay. Really."

She comes in to hug me again, then remembers. Her hands stroke my arms as she pulls away. "Oh, Ida, I thought I'd lost you." Her voice shakes.

"I'm sorry." I don't know what else to say. The woman sitting nearby is staring at us. We're probably more interesting than her magazine or her kids. They're in a corner playing with some noisy toys, including one that makes animal sounds. "Uh, do you want to go to someplace a little quieter?"

"There's a café nearby," she says. "Are you at all hungry?"

I feel like I could ask her the same question. "Sure."

She holds a finger up, asking me to wait a moment. She sets her purse down on the magazine table, fishes out a tissue, and dabs at her eyes and nose.

THE café has epoxy-topped tables, like the kind dad used to make. These are covered in pennies—boring—but at least they give me something to look at besides Mom's gaunt face. The waitress brings us menus. Mom says all she wants is tea and toast; I order a turkey club sandwich and a Coke. The waitress leaves, and I'm stuck trying to think of something to say. The pile of issues between us has been growing for so long—since Dad first went missing, and maybe even earlier— that I don't know where to start. If I was as bold as Dena, or even Jody, I'd just start talking, but I'm timid old me.

"So, how was your trip up here?"

"I don't like to fly." Mom takes a paper napkin out of the holder and spreads it over her lap.

"You flew?"

She chuckles at the question. "Of course."

The waitress comes with her tea and my Coke. Mom opens a tea packet and drops the bag into the miniature pot of hot water.

"I had to get up here as soon as I heard about your accident." Mom's hand shakes as she pours tea into her cup. When she tries to take a sip, her cup shakes so much I want to reach out and steady it so she doesn't burn herself.

This shaking, when did that start? I'm pretty sure I know *why* it started. Me. I'm the reason she's lost weight and looks like she hasn't slept in days. I'm the reason she got on a plane even though she hates to fly and spent money we don't have to pay my hospital bill. Selfish doesn't even begin to describe how awful I've been.

Less than an hour ago, the only thing I cared about was going to see Trinity, so much so that an escape crossed my mind. I still desperately want to hear what Trinity can tell me, but not if it's going to push my mother over the edge. And she looks perilously close to the edge right now. A meeting with her husband's mistress, and maybe even Dad himself, probably wouldn't be good for her nerves.

The waitress comes with my turkey club and her toast. I'm embarrassed by how big my plate is compared to hers.

"You can have some of my sandwich," I tell her.

"Oh, no thank you."

"I really am sorry, you know, that I worried you," I tell the pennies in the table. "We can go home as soon as you want."

"You *did* put me through hell." She bends down to find my eyes.

"I know, I can see, um . . ."

"It's that obvious?"

I nod.

"My boss, the owner of the shop, is worried about me.

She thinks I've lost two dress sizes, but I'm afraid to check."
She takes a small bite of her toast.

I push the little pot of jam on the table over to her. She
laughs, but it's a weary laugh.

"Why did you run away?" she asks. "I think I know, but I
want to hear it from you."

"Actually, I didn't really run *away*." I search for the words
I couldn't find when I was talking to the nurse. "I ran *to*.
There's a difference."

"O . . . kay," she says, inviting me to explain.

I take a sip of my Coke. Okay, here goes. I just wish I had
Trinity's letter with me so I could show Mom I wasn't acting
on a complete whim. "I needed to find out about Dad. He was
doing something up here besides fishing."

Mom clenches her jaw, but doesn't say anything. I press
on, telling her what I learned in the order I learned them.
The Salty Dog and the Native Alaskan stories. Dad's friendship with an ex-prostitute named Two-Bit. The note I
found from T, who turned out to be Trinity. Our exchange
of letters and the invitation to visit that I chickened out on
at the last minute. I also admit to rummaging through Dad's
workshop, but not her bedroom.

"Well," she says finally. "I knew about the snooping."

"You did?"

She nods. "But that's beside the point, now, isn't it?" Her
mouth becomes a pressed line. "So, you've yet to see this
woman, this Trinity."

"No, I mean, yes. That's correct."

"And what would you hope to gain by seeing her?"

I try to remember the reasons I gave Sam that day in the

Filipino bunkhouse. The conversation itself is a blur because we were drunk, but it helped me figure out why I was up here.

"The truth. About Dad."

Mom closes her eyes. Her eye shadow has melted into two blue lines across her lids. When she opens them and looks at me, I see the pain that's been accumulating there for years: The hard life of being married to a fisherman. The fights with her in-laws. The husband who didn't come home. And now me.

"Without the truth, it's easy to assume the worst," I add.

"Hmm." She gives me this quivering half-smile, like she's going to break down any second. I have to look away before she does.

CHAPTER 27

Tell-tale

A light piece of string, yarn, rope, or plastic attached to the standing rigging to indicate wind direction

A cab deposits us in front of a big green house. Fortunately, Ketchikan is small enough that the cabbies don't really need addresses. We just said we wanted to go to "the center for Native kids," and he took us to the right place.

There's no sign in front. It just looks like a regular house with peeling white trim and a wraparound porch that's slightly droopy in the middle. Mom and I get to the front door to find it propped open with a rock. Do we go in?

"Well, are you going to knock or what?" Mom asks.

My legs shake as my knuckles meet the rough painted wood of the door. What if Dad is in there? I knock once, twice, three times. There are people inside. I can hear them and see their shadows moving, but no one comes to the door. So Mom and I ease our way inside without dislodging the rock, and we find ourselves in what looks like a rec room, with games and tables on a paint-spattered floor.

The walls are covered in posters, mostly of rock 'n' roll bands. Two boys with their long hair in ponytails play an aggressive game of Ping-Pong while three girls sit at a card table sewing a button design onto a big piece of black felt. They strain to talk over the sounds of a boy playing a hand-held drum. An enormous, furry dog ambles over to us for a sniff. I pet his soft head, thankful that we're not as invisible as I feel.

I venture farther into the room, my body buzzing with the anticipation of a sighting. Either I see him. Or he sees me, or Mom, or this somewhat alarming bandage on my head. I'd rather be surprised, so I decide to study the posters on the walls. There's Jimi Hendrix, The Doors, Led Zeppelin, John Wayne, and some guy named Ray Mala who's old-fashioned handsome. The note attached to the poster tells me he was the first Native Alaskan movie star, appearing in a 1933 film called *Eskimo*, billed as "the biggest picture ever made" by MGM. That surprises me, but not as much as the poster that shows how the state of Alaska compares in size to the rest of the United States. Set one inside the other, it spans the entire country, stretching from Florida to California. It's so big you could disappear in it and never be found. Maybe that's exactly what Dad did, because I don't think he's in this house.

"Are you with First Lutheran?" The voice is too young.

I turn around to find the boy with the drum standing in front of Mom.

"No, I'm not," she says.

I step in. "Is Trinity here?"

"She's upstairs." He points to some stairs in the back of the room and returns to his drumming.

"Ladies?" The voice is too deep, but I jump anyway.

It's not Dad but a man with leather-brown skin and tattoos up his arms and neck who says, "Can I help you?"

"Uh, yes, we're here to see Trinity?" I say.

"Right this way." He leads us up the stairs. "Sorry, things are a little crazy around here. Potlatch tomorrow." We walk down a hallway of doors until we get to the last one. He knocks and sticks his head in, then out again. "Go on in," he says.

A woman with long gray hair sits at a messy desk in a room cluttered with clothes and art supplies. Trinity. I hope my shock doesn't show. I expected someone a lot younger. She's dressed like a hippie— peasant blouse, knit vest, and a long cotton skirt that swishes around her legs as she walks around her desk. She greets us in turn, taking our hands in hers with a firm grip. I can't help but stare at her many rings and bracelets, all silver, all with Indian designs.

"*Yakíei yee y·t· xwal geini.* That means, 'It is wonderful to look upon your faces.' You must be Ida." She turns to my mom. "And you the mother."

"Yes," Mom says. "Christine."

"I had a dream you would come, but I didn't think it would be by way of St. Joe's." She chuckles, and I realize she's referring to the hospital.

How did she know?

"Life's a journey with many bends and detours," she says to me. "I'm glad you're okay."

"So am I," Mom says with a tight smile.

"I don't know how much Steve told you." She looks at Mom, then at me.

"Nothing," we say at the same time.

"Okay, well, how about I give you a tour?" She sweeps an arm around the room. "This is my messy office. I founded C-NAY seven years ago this June. C-NAY stands for Center for Native Alaskan Youth. Our mission is to connect Native Alaskan teens to their heritage through the arts—literature, music, dancing, you name it. Steve was one of our most ardent supporters." Trinity bows her head. "We all miss him terribly."

Okay, so Dad's obviously not living here, unless Trinity is lying. But she seems really sincere. If he is still alive somewhere, she's either not aware of it or she should get an Academy Award for best actress.

Mom makes a sound like a soft moan. Is she agreeing? I can't tell. I'm just glad Trinity can't read my thoughts as I try to switch my bordello-mistress assumptions with this reality. She leads us back downstairs. "Things aren't usually this chaotic. Well, I take that back—they are—but this is a bit more than usual. Potlatch tomorrow."

"Yes, the man who showed us in told us," Mom says.

"That's Russ, my program director." She tilts her head for us to follow her. "I'd like to take you to the new long house first. It's only a short walk up the hill from here."

Mom casts a doubtful glance at her shoes but doesn't object. Minutes later, as she minces her way up the steep, narrow road, she has that grim set to her jaw that says she's out to prove herself. I walk next to her, matching her pace, while Trinity strides ahead.

Finally, the road dead-ends in a mossy clearing. A tall totem pole marks a gravel path that leads to a large, rectangular, brown building. The air here smells new, like it was born of rain and cedar trees. Of course, that's what they used. The wood was carved and planked and painted with Native totems in red, black, and white.

"This pole here is what you'd call a family ancestry pole," Trinity says looking up. "It represents the first boys and girls to come to our Center."

When she starts talking about the master carver and the ceremonies they had to make the pole authentic, my thoughts drift. I'm more interested in the totems on the pole. My hand can't resist touching the smooth rounded surfaces of their features. Maybe it's my imagination, but I sense more than finely carved cedar and paint. I sense spirits.

"Some of the kids knew which clans they came from," Trinity is saying. "But those who didn't know chose their totems, or rather the totems chose them. They went on spirit walks and thought about those who came before."

She points to a beaver. "This boy is going to study law so he can come back to help his people. Beavers are said to be creative and very determined, capable of constructing fine arrows. Lawyers are kind of like that, don't you think?"

I shrug. "The only totem I really know is Raven. Dad used to tell me the creation stories."

"Ah, yes." She points toward the top of the pole at a bird figure with a long black beak that looks like a grin between two piercing oval eyes. "There's our Raven. What we're trying to do here," she continues, "is give these young people something they can believe in. They took their time choosing the totem that best represented them. Their totems became a source of pride."

She points to a round, white face that's vaguely feminine.

"Now the girl behind this moon, she had a habit of running off at night. Her grandmother brought her to the center, didn't know what to do. Getting involved in this pole project helped her discover her path. The moon is the earth's guardian at night, but her own nighttime wandering stopped. Her grandmother told me later that she came home too tired to do anything but eat and go to bed." Trinity chuckles. "I still hear from her. She says Jody is doing well. Wants to go to college."

"Jody?"

Mom and Trinity both turn to me, surprised. "You know her?"

"I-I just saw her. We were roommates at the Nagoon cannery."

"It *is* a small world. How is she doing, anyway?"

"Okay. Good. But she still wanders off occasionally."

I shoot Mom a look, telling her I'll explain later, though she already knows about my accident. A wave of sadness passes through me. Red Beard and his friend clearly weren't the ogres I thought they were. I never got the chance to thank them, or Jody, for rescuing me. I didn't even get to say good-bye.

"That girl has an independent streak a mile wide. Something tells me you share that in common." Trinity winks. "I hope you two can stay in touch."

"Yeah, so do I." Then it dawns on me. "She must have known Dad!"

"*Everyone* knew your dad," Trinity says. "He only visited a few times each summer, but the kids had a great time with him, and they all wanted to go out on his boat."

I get a pang of jealousy thinking about him sharing himself with others. Those times on the boat, hearing about Raven and the stars. I thought that magic was for me and me alone.

"So, what did he do when he visited?" Mom asks.

Trinity's expression turns thoughtful as she considers her answer. "He listened. He asked questions. He played Ping-Pong. He talked about fishing. He cared."

She motions for us to follow her into the longhouse. We enter a space that seems large and intimate at the same time. The light is dim, amber-colored, and it takes a few seconds for my eyes to adjust. The sound of a drum draws my attention to a group of dancers in ceremonial dress. A man directing them sees us and waves. Trinity waves back.

"Our dance group is practicing for tomorrow," she says. "This is where the potlatch will be. I wanted to show you this because Steve was absolutely passionate about this project. He helped us raise the money we needed to rebuild after the fire."

"Fire?" Mom asks, suddenly interested.

"Yes, our old longhouse was among the buildings destroyed in a rash of arson fires some years ago."

I want her to tell us more about the fires, but she turns and starts walking toward the man who waved at us. We're introduced to Joe, a master storyteller, who shakes our hands and tells us that Dad was quite the storyteller in his own right.

"Apparently there were some stories he didn't tell us," Mom says, her voice flat.

As we walk back to the green house, which is actually

called that, Trinity explains the importance of stories to Native Alaskans.

"Our myths and teachings build cultural identity and pride, much of which has been lost. Steve, in his way, was doing his part to make sure our stories never die."

Mom stops and shakes a pebble out of her right shoe. "If he was so involved," she says, resuming her mincing walk, "why didn't he tell us about it?"

I hear the challenge in her voice, but I'm glad she asked the question because I want to know, too.

Trinity is silent for so long, I wonder if Mom's tone has offended her. "I really have no idea," she says finally. "He talked a lot about fishing, but never his life outside of it. I got the impression fishing *was* his life."

Mom's burst of laughter takes me by surprise. "Truer than you know," she says. "Truer than you know."

As we approach the back of the green house, kids pass us carrying boxes and bags of food.

"Hi, Jimmy. Did you find your hat?" Trinity asks a plump boy with a buzz cut.

He shakes his head.

"Keep looking." She leads us up the steps to the back porch. "So this potlatch," she says. "It's a memorial for a clan elder. Geraldine Weaver. Maybe you've heard of her?"

Mom and I shake our heads as we thread our way through the busy kitchen. The smell of bread baking makes my stomach growl.

"Anyway, she made it her mission to resurrect the Tlingit language. Not many speak it anymore. When Russell came to my office, I thought he was going to tell me that some representatives from the church were here. They're taking us on as a charity." She frowns. "Ironic. The church once did everything in its power to strip us of our culture."

We return to Trinity's office, which I now notice used to be a nursery. Running along the top of the baby blue walls is a decorative strip of the cat and the fiddle and the cow jumping over the moon. The clothes I saw earlier spill over the sides of big cardboard boxes against the wall. Next to them is an old-fashioned, foot-pump sewing machine like the one Grandma Grace has. The opposite wall is lined with shelves holding bins of what look to be art supplies. They remind me of Dad's hardware filing cabinet, but messier.

Trinity's desk is buried in papers and mail. It's a wonder she found my letter. Mounted above her desk is a large, framed photograph of a bunch of people posing around a totem pole. Dad isn't hard to pick out. He stands at least a head taller than everyone else and is the only non-Indian. He has his arms over the shoulders of the teenagers beside him, a boy and a girl. Jody's in front, wearing her trademark baseball cap, and, off to the side, like a teacher in an elementary school class photo, is a younger Trinity.

"That picture was taken at the pole-raising ceremony," she says. "Somewhere in here, I have a whole bunch of photos from that day." She turns around and scans a bookshelf above her desk and finally pulls out a thick green photo album. "Here it is. We document everything now. I swear we could single-handedly keep Kodak in business." She plops the album down on top of the layer of papers on her desk. "I'm sure Steve is in several of those pictures if you'd care to flip through here."

Trinity sits down at her desk and explains some of the pictures as we flip through the album. My tall father is like a beacon in his red sweater. There he is walking in a procession of people, pulling on a rope, standing in the crowd, posing, smiling. Seeing him in all these pictures feels like spying, even though I'm now convinced he wasn't doing anything shameful here. Saintly is more like it. Was I really going to ask Trinity if she was harboring a man who'd faked his death? That book she gave him with the story of the vengeful she-bear was just an odd coincidence. If all these pictures don't prove Dad had nothing to hide, I don't know what would.

Oh my God, what about *that* photo? T's favorite.

"Who's Miss Red?" I blurt out loudly.

Trinity stops talking. I've interrupted her in about the rudest way possible, but she just looks at me and cocks her head, as if trying to place the name.

"The note I found that you wrote to my Dad. It said, *My favorite photo of you and Miss Red.*"

The answer comes to her, bringing a smile. "Miss Red isn't *who!* It's a *what.* You knew her as the *Lady Rose.*"

"Miss Red" for a boat that was mostly red. I remember what Murf said about nicknames in Alaska. I want to ask Trinity why people and things up here are never called by their real names, but I'm distracted by a nervous tapping next to me, Mom's heels against the hardwood floor.

"Okay, so Miss Red was the boat," she says. "But how do you explain the condoms? I'd find condoms in Steve's pockets."

I want to disappear.

Trinity pauses. I study the grains of wood in the floorboards. My cheeks are on fire.

"We really don't advertise that," Trinity says. "You see, we started making condoms available to our teens several years ago after we saw an alarming rise in teen pregnancies and sexually transmitted diseases. They're going to have sex, whether we like it or not. We want them to protect themselves."

I look up to see Trinity point out the boxes against the wall.

"As you can see, we get plenty of donations of clothing, but we have to appeal for other necessities, like toothpaste, soap, and deodorant. Condoms are no less necessary, but we don't dare ask for them, for obvious reasons. Steve knew that, and he always brought a bunch to replenish our stocks. Heaven knows what the drugstore clerks must have thought."

I laugh at that, but Mom doesn't. She starts to sway on her feet. Before I know it, she's grabbing the edge of Trinity's desk and sinking to the floor.

"Oh, dear," Trinity says just as Mom lands with a thud and rocks back, one hand still reaching for the desk. I really should help, but I'm frozen. Fortunately, Trinity isn't. She rushes over, bends down next to Mom and asks me to find something in the clothing box we can use for a pillow. Thankful for something to do, I grab the softest thing I can find, a hooded winter parka, and hand it to her. She folds it up and eases it under Mom's head.

"Does anything hurt?" she asks her. "Let's take this off." She removes the scarf around my mother's neck. Mom's hand flutters up to hide what the scarf was covering: a patch of red welts that makes me want to scratch just looking at it. But Trinity has the grace not to say anything, and Mom eventually drops her hands and surrenders to her care.

"I'm sorry," Mom says as Trinity helps her sit up. "God, I've made such a mess of things."

Trinity strokes Mom's arm. "You've lost a husband. This must be a lot to take in when you're still so raw. No need to apologize."

"No."

I don't know what she's saying no to. No, she *does* need to apologize? Trinity and I sit Mom down in a chair, then Trinity goes off to get her a glass of water. Why do people always assume you're thirsty when you're upset? I ask Mom if she's okay, even though the answer should be obvious. For several long seconds, she just sits there hugging herself. Then she clears her throat. "That's a hard question to answer right now."

"Okay."

She reaches out to pat my shoulder. "We have a lot to talk about."

I should be glad that Mom's finally admitting there *is* stuff to talk about, but all I feel is nervous relief when Trinity returns with two glasses of water, one for each of us.

"I have an idea," she says. "Why don't the two of you come to the potlatch tomorrow as my guests?"

"I . . . I don't know," Mom sputters, either uncomfortable or embarrassed, I'm not sure which.

"You won't be the only whites there."

"Oh, it's not that," she says, flustered. "It's just, well, we don't know the deceased."

Trinity waves her hand dismissively. "So what. Seems like you could use a party."

I'm confused. "A party? But you said it was a memorial. Isn't that like a funeral?"

"We had the funeral a year ago," Trinity says. "This potlatch is a celebration that marks the end of mourning for friends and family. The dead are released to go on to the spirit world and be reborn."

"Well, that sounds nice," Mom says.

There's a moment of awkwardness where we're all waiting for someone else to speak first. I don't know about the potlatch, but I'm thinking that Trinity is right. A party might be just what we need.

"We'd love to come!" I say, answering for both of us.

CHAPTER 28

Boat-hook
*A pole with a hook on the end used
to reach into the water to catch
buoys or other floating objects*

Mom booked us a room in Ketchikan's oldest hotel, a musty building with creaky stairs and a bathroom at the end of the hall. The innkeeper's desk is just like the ones you see in old movies, with rows of keys hanging on the wall. As we walk past, the clerk stops us and asks if we're "the Petrovich party." There's that word again. It strikes me as funny given it's just the two of us, and Mom's hobbling because she's still woozy and her feet hurt. I nod.

"Something came for you." He reaches down behind the counter and comes out with my backpack and flowered suitcase.

"Oh, wow! Thank you!" I take the bags, which smell of fish. "Thank you so much!"

"You're welcome, Miss." The clerk, an older man, discreetly wipes his hands on the jacket of his uniform and sniffs.

Our room has two twin beds separated by a nightstand with a drawer that holds the Holy Bible, a tablet, and a pen. On the wall over the beds is a painting of a mother bear and her cubs at the banks of a river. Everything, even the painting, is green or gold—gold carpet, green chair, heavy green drapes over the window. I start to pull them open to see our view of the moss-covered building next door.

"Oh, leave those closed," Mom says. She sits on the bed closest to the door, takes off her shoes, and lies down.

With nothing better to do, I dump the contents of my backpack and suitcase on the other bed. Maybe I'll find my necklace. I start tossing all the candy bar wrappers, moldy leftover sandwiches, and orange peels in the room's little plastic-lined trashcan. There's no necklace, but I do find something else. In the outside pocket of my backpack, where I have Trinity's letter and the partial photo of me and Dad, is a small package wrapped in a magazine centerfold of Davy Jones from The Monkees, his luscious lips on one side and his heavily browed eyes on the other. I open it up to find a folded piece of notebook paper and two macramé bracelets, one with blue and green beads and the other with black and red. The note says, "For my friend, Ida-Sue (Can-a-lot survivor and best roommate ever!!!): Please write." Underneath is Jody's full name and a Ketchikan address, care of "Mrs. Mildred House." Her grandmother?

Thanks, Jody. I slip the new bracelets on my wrist with the first one she made me, getting that lump that everyone talks about, except that mine isn't in my throat—it's in my heart, knowing I'll probably never see her again.

Wait a minute. What if she was the one who dropped off

my stuff? Nah. They wouldn't let her leave work during the busiest time of the year. On the other hand, my stuff was in our room. I can't imagine anyone else bothering to pack up my stinky, crusty clothes.

A knock, loud and confident. Could it be? Did Fate time this? I hurriedly fumble with the chain lock to open the door.

It isn't Jody.

I scream. Dena screams. We hug and she lifts me off the floor, which hurts my banged up bod, but there's no stopping her. We scream some more before I remember Mom is trying to sleep. I usher her in, her and her enormous backpack/ sleeping bag combo, like she's just spent the last two months camping. For once, she's as ragged looking as I am, no makeup on and her hair rolled up in a sloppy bun. She dumps her load on the floor and flops back in the green chair, arms and legs splayed like a starfish.

"Not to sound rude or anything, but what are you doing here?" I ask.

"Didn't your mom tell you? I'm coming back with you guys. Couldn't hack it. Canning is just too damn gross and boring." She plays with her right hoop earring. "Nice bandage, by the way. Rocks are so unforgiving."

"You heard about my accident?"

Dena rolls her eyes. "Your mom only told *the world*, and this was *after* all the missing posters and phone calls. They thought you were with me." She shakes her pointer finger at me. "You had us all worried. Then you go and crack your head open. But at least we found you. Actually, Sam called your mom."

"I thought so."

"No offense, but I'm kind of glad. I can't get out of here

soon enough." Her eyes sweep around the green and gold room. "I thought Alaska would be so, I don't know, exciting? Ha! The scenery's kind of nice, but half the time it's raining so hard you can't see it. And sliming." She shudders. "I never want to see another salmon for as long as I live."

"I know. Me neither."

"But at least you stuck with it. You weren't calling begging to come home."

"No."

"You're made of stronger stuff than me. So your head's okay?"

"It hurts a little and I'm kind of tired, but the doctor said to expect that. At least I'm evened out now."

"Huh?"

I tap my finger to my slightly crooked nose.

"Oh yeah."

Behind us, Mom's mattress creaks. She's sitting up and digging through her purse in the light from the night-table lamp. She gets a bill out of her wallet. "Hello, Dena. Did you have any trouble finding this place?"

"Nope." Dena straightens up in her chair.

"Good. Here's some money," she says, handing me a ten. "Why don't you girls go downstairs and get a snack in the lounge?"

"You're not coming with us?" I stuff the bill in one of my back pockets.

"No, I'm going to rest some more. But you can bring me up a turkey sandwich."

As we walk down the hall to the stairs, Dena says, "She really loves you, you know."

A heavy sigh betrays my guilt. "I wish people would stop reminding me what a jerk I've been."

"Sorry." Dena's stride slows as she turns towards me. "I just thought you should know what my dad said about your mom when he was helping her find you. He said she was really scared, like *really* scared. I mean, you can see for yourself. She looks terrible."

"I know. I know. I already feel like crap for worrying her, okay?"

She shakes her head. "I didn't say that to make you feel like crap, Ida. It's just that, well, I do it too. We take our parents for granted. We even hate them sometimes. Since your dad, you know . . . I've been appreciating my dad a lot more. And then, being up here at this stinky job, well, it really makes you think about how good you have it."

"I suppose."

The dining room isn't open for dinner yet, but we can get stuff that doesn't require cooking. We slide into a cave-like booth that smells of stale cigarettes and order the boysenberry pie a la mode. There's only one slice left so we have to share. I'm glad I remember to ask for Mom's turkey sandwich to go.

Our pie comes. I dig into its tart-sweet-flaky-creamy-cold wonderfulness like a starved person.

"Do you think we need to experience bad stuff to know what good is?" I ask Dena. "After I was rescued, I was so thankful for everything—not just my life, but the people in it. Sam and Jody, my cannery roommate, and even this weird guy who I thought was a pirate but ended up saving us. It was weird. I just felt all this love. But it took almost dying."

Dena nods vigorously with her mouth full of pie. She swallows and points her fork at me. "Exactly! That's why our dads came up here. It wasn't just the fishing, it was the excitement and the occasional close call. They felt more alive after they cheated death. It's the danger. They get kind of hooked on it."

"So to speak."

"Ha, hooked," she says. "I get it. By the way, did you find out anything?"

"Oh, my God, I haven't told you about Trinity!"

Her fork stops midway to her mouth, dripping ice cream.

"Dad's secret lady friend in Alaska." I fill her in on the note, the letters, our visit to the youth center, and the mystery surrounding Miss Red and Two-Bit.

"Turns out Miss Red was another name for Dad's boat. I didn't get the chance to ask about Two-Bit because, well, Mom kind of beat me to the punch. She asked Trinity about the condoms she found in Dad's pockets."

Dena mouth drops open mid-chew.

"I thought I'd die, but Trinity didn't miss a beat. She told Mom the condoms were for preventing teen pregnancy. She said Dad donated them to the Center. Then Mom got all upset and, like, collapsed on the floor."

"Wow." Dena slowly forks another piece of pie and ice cream and studies it as if she's never seen the two together before. "So . . . if Uncle Steve wasn't using the condoms himself, why was she upset?"

"I'm not sure. During her, um, spell, she said she'd made a mess of things."

"Like what?"

"I don't know."

"Turkey to go?"

I nod as the waitress sets down a box with Mom's sandwich. "Anyway," I continue, "here's Mom laid out on the floor after basically accusing Dad of screwing around, and Trinity's really nice about it. She helps Mom up, gets us water, and . . . Oh, yeah, we're invited to go to this potlatch tomorrow. I think you could come too."

"What kind of a potluck?"

"Pot*latch*. It's a ceremony for a Native elder who died."

"Gee, that sounds like fun," Dena deadpans.

"No, it's actually supposed to be kind of a party, to celebrate a life."

"I guess. Not like I have other plans."

RAVEN must be really important, because he comes up time and again during the potlatch, and that doesn't even count the speeches in Tlingit, which I have to admit are pretty boring. It's Raven this and Raven that, like he created the world or something. Oh, wait, he did. Then he brought water and light, caused all the different animals to form, and created humans out of leaves. Not bad for a scoundrel.

The tall guy playing the part of Raven is a good dancer. One moment, he's skulking about, shoulders hunched, head slowly turning to take in the kids in the front row. The next, he's stretched out to full height with his floor-length robe open like wings as if to grab them. They all shriek and lean back into their parents' knees.

I imagine Geraldine Weaver enjoying the ceremony as

she prepares to cross into the spirit world. She has to be both happy and sad. Trinity said she died a year ago. That's a long time to float around with no place to go.

But then, survivors float around, too. When you suddenly lose someone you love, all that love doesn't know where to go so it drifts around, homeless. It may even change shape, turning to fear and anger, before settling into that hole that never goes away.

Much as I'd like to believe Dad's still alive, my heart tells me he's not. My heart tells me he's nowhere and everywhere. He was on Nagoon to save Sam and me from drowning. I'm convinced of that. What were the chances of Jody and her pirate friends showing up with the boat at just the right moment? For that matter, what were the chances of Mom and me coming to this potlatch?

Thanks Dad. Now that your work is done, are you waiting to be released to the spirit world? I may never know what happened to you, but I do know this: Like Raven spying something shiny, you couldn't resist a good story. You collected and traded them. Stories were your treasure. Maybe you're waiting for ours.

CHAPTER 29

Salty Dog
*Slang phrase with several meanings,
including an experienced sailor*

David was right. This place really is a pub that wants to be a museum. I half expect to see him here, all tanned and gorgeous, hanging out with his fishing buddies. But the dining room is practically empty, making an odd contrast with the surrounding busyness. The walls and ceiling are so packed with stuff you don't notice any one thing, except the hammerhead shark. *That* jumps out at you. If I were the owner, I'd be worried about an earthquake shaking it all down.

Not that the customers would notice, judging from the three guys slumped over the bar on a Monday morning. They leer at us, but Mom doesn't seem to care. I don't know what it was about that potlatch yesterday, but it certainly put her in a good mood. The way she said good-bye to Trinity, all teary-eyed, you'd think they were best friends.

"Do they have ID?"

I follow the voice to a great mound of a man in a Hawaiian shirt behind the bar. Has he been there all this time? I was trying so hard not to make eye contact with the men *at* the bar, I must have missed the man *behind* it.

"They don't, but I do." Mom says. "I'm Christine Petrovich. You may have heard of my husband, Steve?"

The man drops his head. "Heard of him?" His fleeting sadness turns to cheer. "Hell, I named a burger after him."

He puts down a glass, wipes his hands on a towel, and comes around the end of the bar through a set of waist-high swinging doors. "I'm Dwight, the owner. I'm not usually here in the morning, but my cook called in hung over." He shakes our hands. His is round and damp, like dough.

Greetings done, his arm falls limply at his side. He reminds me of a bear, ball-shaped and too heavy to be standing on two feet. "Steve was a good guy, and the best storyteller I've ever had the pleasure of knowing. Believe me, things haven't been the same."

Mom thanks him and introduces us. Then she pushes me forward. "Go ahead, tell him why you're here."

"Yeah, um, I want to know more about my dad, the time he spent up here fishing."

"Well, I can't speak to the fishing, but he always sat in the same chair."

As I leave to follow Dwight into the dining room, I lock eyes with one of the men at the bar. He's turned completely around on his stool to watch us, and now that we're moving out of his sightline, he gives me an exaggerated frown, like a sad clown.

"That one in the corner," Dwight says, pointing.

There it is, the chair under the dusty moose head with the Christmas lights threaded through its antlers. I walk over to it and touch the wood, carved with people's initials and oiled black by their hands. My fingers search for telltale evidence he was here, but there's nothing so obvious as an "S.P." Not that my dad would be so juvenile as to carve his initials.

"Go ahead," Dwight says to me. "Have a seat."

I do. Mom and Dena take the chairs on the opposite sides of the table. It's probably my imagination, but the air around us seems to crackle with Dad's presence.

"You know," Dwight says, "some folks have suggested I install a name plate there in Steve's honor. Put it right on his chair or the table. What do you think?"

"I guess that would be okay," I say.

"Kind of what I thought." Dwight shrugs. "You folks hungry? Can I bring you anything?" He addresses my mother. "Drink?"

She brings her hand to her heart. "Heavens, it's too early! Do you have tea?"

"Sure do. And I'll bring over some menus. We serve breakfast all day."

Dwight comes back with menus and Mom's tea and tells us lunch is on the house. Mom protests, but not very strenuously. This unplanned trip has to be setting us back. I figure if lunch is free, I may as well get something I want. I flip to the list of burgers, and there's *The Tale Spinner: A burger every bit as good and juicy as one of Steve Petrovich's stories. A quarter-pound all-beef patty smothered in fried sweet onions and bell peppers.* I point the menu item out to Dena and Mom. Dena reads it out loud.

"I don't remember Dad liking bell peppers," I say.

"You crave fruits and vegetables when you're on a fishing boat," Dena reminds me. "They don't keep."

I remember one of Dad's impromptu history lessons. "The sailors on the old clipper ships would get scurvy because they ate no fruits or vegetables. Their gums would bleed and they'd break out in sores."

"Thanks, Ida. That really makes me want to eat." Dena closes her menu.

Mom sips her tea. "You girls."

Dena and I both order the Tale Spinner. "Good choice," Dwight says. Mom apologizes for ordering a plain cheeseburger. I tilt Dad's chair back against the wall to occupy the same space he did when he told his stories. Mom pushes on my armrest to get me back down on four legs. But before she does, I notice that the man at the bar has moved to a table in the dining room so he can continue to watch us.

"Don't look now," I whisper, "but there's a man at the front of the dining room staring at us."

Dena immediately turns around. I kick her under the table. "Ouch!"

"Great," I whisper-shout. "Now he knows we know he's watching us."

"What man?" Mom says.

"A man from the bar has been staring at us since we came in. He actually *moved from the bar* so he could watch us."

"The bald guy with the moustache?" Dena asks.

I nod.

Dwight comes with our burgers. They're massive, like he is, with a pile of fries that could be a meal of their own. He asks if he can get us anything else, and when we tell him no, he says, "Bon appetit." The French surprises me, but if Alaska has taught me anything, it's not to judge a book by its cover.

The Tale Spinner is as good as advertised. I like the sweetness and tang of the peppers with the meat, and the dairy-free sauce is amazing.

We eat kind of fast. I think we're all anxious to escape the watching man. Just as we're finishing up, Dwight returns and pulls over a chair from another table. Dena and Mom move over to give him room and he plops down with a grunt. His commanding physical presence is a comfort. If he can't protect us from that weird guy, no one can.

"So, young lady," he says, resting his arms heavily on the table. "What can I tell you about your dad that you don't already know?"

"What were his stories about?"

I think it's a dumb question until Dwight starts in.

"Well, of course, there were the usual one-that-got-away stories fishermen love to tell. But your dad told them so well he'd have us all on the edge of our seats. I think they were 10 percent fact and 90 percent fiction, but we didn't care. He also liked to share the Native folktales. At least, he said they were Native folktales—mostly Tlingit, I think. What made them so special was the way your dad would act out all the characters, like a one-man play. Pretty soon, he'd have half the bar gathered around him, glued to the sound of his voice. You'd think we were a bunch of kids in story circle, except these stories—"

"Weren't for kids?"

Dwight chuckles. "No. But there was always a message or lesson in them."

"Like?" I prompt.

"Oh, let's see . . ." He drums his fingers on the table. "Okay, like, *Don't be greedy. Respect animals and nature.* That kind of thing. *Eye for an eye.*"

"*Don't run off on your wife.*"

Dena and Mom both turn to me in surprise.

"So you've heard these," Dwight says.

"I read the same book of myths he carried around," I say. "And Dad told me some of the Raven tales."

Then I remember the one question I didn't get the chance to ask Trinity. "Did Dad ever mention an Aleut prostitute who went by the nickname Two-Bit?"

"Ida!" Mom recoils.

But Dwight doesn't even blink. "Sounds like one of your dad's fish stories."

"But there really was a prostitute named Two-Bit!" I protest. "She worked on Creek Street. Her own people nicknamed her, but she adopted the name herself to show them she wasn't ashamed."

Dwight gives me a blank look, Dena's eyes widen, and Mom just shakes her head.

"Honest to God, Dad talked about her a lot when he was here with the other fishermen. He and Two-Bit were friends."

"Never heard of her," Dwight says, "but that doesn't mean she doesn't exist. Prostitution on Creek Street stopped in the mid-'50s. The only sporting woman I've heard of by name is Dolly Arthur, because they turned her house into a museum. She's still alive, by the way. As for Two-Bit, you need to know that your Dad was known to, uh, exaggerate."

"You never even heard him talk about her?"

"No. But, again, that doesn't mean anything. He may have talked about her. While I would have loved to just sit and listen to your Dad's stories, I have a bar to run."

"Speaking of which, we should let you get back to it." Mom crumples up the napkin from her lap and sets it on her plate with her half-eaten burger. "Are you sure I can't pay for lunch?"

"Positive."

"Well, you've been more than generous. Thank you, Dwight."

"Thank you for visiting." He starts to walk away, then stops and snaps his fingers. "Before you go, some of Steve's friends have asked me where they can send memorials. They were sorry to miss the funeral."

"We didn't have one." Mom purses her lips together. "I tell you what, if they'd like to support something Steve believed in, tell them they can donate to the Center for Native Alaskan Youth here in town. They do good work there."

"Yes, I'm familiar with them," Dwight says. "And I'll pass that along. It was so nice meeting all of you. Good luck with your research, young lady."

I tell him thank you. As we file out of the dining room, I glance back at the watching man. He starts to rise out of his chair. I quickly turn away. Another round of good-byes and we're out the door and down the street. Just when I think we're in the clear, I hear footsteps running behind us.

"Hey! Hey, you there!"

Mom tells us to keep walking.

"Steve's wife," the man says.

Mom stops. Dena and I hesitate before turning around. Up close, the man from the restaurant is younger than I thought, maybe in his thirties. He smells of cigarettes and alcohol and his eyes are watery, but his stare is fixed.

"Sorry," he says catching his breath. "I heard you talkin' about Steve? I knows a guy who fished with him."

"I think you're mistaken," Mom tells him. "My husband fished alone."

"Steve Petrovich, the one lost west of Dixon?"

WE go back to The Salty Dog with Hank jabbering the whole way. He tells us he's been working on fishing boats since he was fourteen. "I wanna get my own boat, but the money . . ." He shrugs. "Fishing ain't what it used to be. Years of over-fishing, then that quake four years ago. I tell ya, Alaska's future is in black gold—oil—but I'd rather battle thirty-foot waves than work out in the frozen middle o' nowhere."

Mom picks a table near the door.

"Back so soon?" Dwight waddles over, wiping his hands on his towel. He casts a sideways glance at Hank.

Mom explains. "He says he knows someone who fished with Steve."

"Wouldn't be surprised."

Hank orders a cup of coffee. He seems to take Dwight's comment as testimony to his good character because he puffs up his chest and goes into great detail about the biggest fish he ever landed, a four-hundred-pound halibut, and how he lost the tip of his right pinky finger gutting that halibut. I'm thinking he'll never get around to talking about what we want him to talk about, so I finally ask him how he knew my dad. He takes a roundabout path to the answer. Turns out he only knew *of* Dad.

"There's good captains and there's some real assholes, pardon my French. I've worked with both. Fishermen talk. You get a rep, some of it fair, some not. But I ain't never heard anything bad 'bout Steve, which is saying somethin', cuz there's no escape on a thirty-eight-foot troller. You see the good and the bad." Hank gets his coffee. His hand shakes pouring the cream.

"Like what kind of bad?" I want to know.

"Well, it's hard work and you're getting no sleep, so you see people for how they really is. Selfish, mean, horny. Sorry, ma'am." He bows to Mom. She jerks her head away as if hit with a bad smell.

I lean forward. "Did you ever hear about a Native prostitute named Two-Bit?"

Mom glares at me.

"I want to know if there really was such a person."

Hank looks from Mom to me and back again. "I can't recall the name . . ."

"Did you ever go to the Creek Street bawdy houses?" I persist.

Hank actually blushes behind his alcohol-reddened skin. "Well—"

"You don't have to answer that!" Mom whips around to face me. "Ida, stop with this question."

I sit back, fold my arms across my chest, and give her my best pout. Dena tries to stifle a laugh and lets out a squeak.

"You know," Hank says. "My friend talked about this one

thing Steve did. It wasn't bad or anything, but it kinda got on his nerves. He'd hum. Same song. Over and over. My friend heard that tune so much, *he'd* start hummin' it, and he didn't even know the damn song."

"'I'm Beginning to See the Light.'" Mom's eyes fill up with tears. "That's the name of the song. Excuse me." She gets up and runs sniffling to the ladies' room.

She's in there *forever*, leaving me and Dena alone with Hank, who's actually kind of nice. Without Mom, we're free to ply him with so many nosy questions that he finally breaks down and orders himself a real drink. Thus fortified, he does his best to answer, but he says he has no way of knowing a) If Dad was alone when he disappeared, or b) What might have happened.

"Dixon can be bad news wit' a storm comin' from the southwest or even a good northwesterly," he says. "If not a storm, could've been any number a' things: fire, engine trouble, rogue wave, hittin' a snag, fallin' asleep—"

"Falling asleep?"

"Sure. If you're not anchored, ya gotta stay awake for all the things I jus' mentioned. That's why it's good to have someone to trade off with."

I hope Dad was alone when he went down. I'd hate to think there's another family out there grieving over the mysterious disappearance of a loved one. It makes me wonder if Hank's buddy is alive and accounted for. "Your friend, did he fish with Dad last summer?"

"Not sure, but I'll ask around, see if I can find who went out with him."

I write my address down on a napkin and ask him to drop

me a line if he hears anything. He puts the folded napkin in his breast pocket.

Mom finally returns as Hank's downing the last of his drink. Her eyes are red and puffy, but she zeroes right in on his empty glass and hustles us out of there with a hasty good-bye to Dwight and a scowl at Hank.

SO now we're on an airplane drinking 7UP and eating smoked almonds. Dena was kind enough to give me the window seat, but all I can see are clouds. She's between me and Mom, who needs easy access to the restroom in case of another crying jag. The stewardess assumes Mom's fragile state is due to her fear of flying. Every time she passes, she asks her, "How are you doing, dear?"

The ferry trip took three days. Flying the same distance takes an hour and a half, the equivalent of a Walt Disney movie. Still, I have to occupy the time somehow, so I get out my pen and notepad and start a list.

Things I Learned about Dad in Alaska:

1. He didn't fish alone.
2. He and Trinity were probably just friends.
3. He supported a center for Native youth.
4. Miss Red was his boat.
5. He told great stories.
6. He hummed the same song.
7. He probably isn't alive.

Dena reaches over and covers my hand with hers. "You saw where he went. That has to count for something."

I nod. In a weird way, my time on Nagoon told me as much about Dad as meeting Trinity and going to The Salty Dog. I close my eyes.

I wake up and we're fifteen minutes away from the Seattle-Tacoma Airport, where it's clear and 75 degrees. I don't know what day it is—I've lost track—but I do know it's August, and that an anniversary is fast approaching. We found out Dad was missing on the 17th. I remember writing the date down in my notebook of homecomings. Guess I won't be doing that anymore. Without Dad, there's no point.

PART THREE

CHAPTER 30

Chums

A species of salmon, also called dog salmon and fall salmon

My time in Alaska was short, less than two months, but I felt like a different person when I got back to my room in Annisport. Everything—my collection of troll dolls, my stuffed animals, my notebook of homecomings, even my movie posters—seemed to belong to someone else. It was like coming back to elementary school and seeing all the kiddie chairs, tables, and drinking fountains for the scaled-down size they really are.

Aside from this weird maturity warp, it's a relief to be sleeping in my own bed, soaking in a bathtub, and changing into clean clothes. Mom will never be able to get the smell out of the jeans and T-shirts I wore in Alaska, not that I'd ever want to wear them again. I'll definitely need some new clothes before school starts. All my old pants are baggy around the waist and short in the legs. When I look in the mirror, I can't help but admire how fit and strong I am. Even Mom wouldn't call me chubby anymore. Come to think of it, she hasn't said anything about my weight, hygiene, or habits since we've returned, though she did take me out to get my hair cut after I got the stitches removed from my scalp. I no longer have to go around looking like I have a hole in my head. Mom says the pixie cut shows off my eyes, but I just love how easy it is. I can actually use a comb versus an industrial-strength hairbrush. Now Dena wants to get hers cut too.

The two of us, plus Sophie and Gerry, are spending the afternoon on Dena's patio, sunbathing and listening to the radio. Stretching the antenna of her transistor radio as far as it will go, Dena tries to tune in something from Alaska, but the closest she gets is a classical music station out of Vancouver, BC, so we turn it back to KJR and the Top 40.

"I hated it, but now I kind of miss it." Dena rubs Coppertone on her neck, lies back on her lounge chair, and places two walnut shells over her eyes.

She tans better than I do. We put our arms together to compare, and she's always about two shades browner. Sophie is a rosy golden color, and Gerry, being a redhead, just burns and peels. She lets us pull the dead skin off her back in ragged strips.

"I only hated the sliming," I say. "I'd go back to visit Jody." For Gerry and Sophie's benefit, I add, "She was my roommate on Nagoon Island. We stayed in these Army barracks-type houses."

"*You* got Army barracks. I got the Scar. A fish-processing ship." Dena's walnut shells move slightly as she scrunches up her nose. "Its real name was *Star of Alaska*, but it's so ugly, people call it the Scar. It stank, too. And I thought I was used to fish smells."

Dena and I go on to describe every gross detail of canning work until Sophie screams, "Stop!" and Dena snorts, upsetting her shells.

"There go your eyes," Gerry says.

"Don't make me laugh," Dena says, putting them back.

"I'm going to miss you guys," I whine.

"Aww, it's tough being the baby." Gerry puckers her lips and gives me air kisses.

"You can always come visit," Sophie says with a consoling pat on my knee. "See the big city. I'm going to get a place in the U-District. That's where most of the students at the U-Dub live if they're not in the dorms or pledging to a sorority."

"U-Dub?" I ask.

"Short for University of Washington."

"Oh."

"We could all share an apartment." Sophie clasps her hands together like a little girl praying. "You guys could work on the Ave and drive to your night classes in Shoreline," she says to Dena and Gerry.

"The Ave?"

"Oh, Ida, don't you know anything? The Ave is the main street near campus where everything happens. My mom says to watch out for hippies selling drugs on the corners. It's pretty wild. This spring, there was a big student protest against police harassment."

"At least it's not boring," Dena says. "Ida, you've *got* to get your driver's license so you can come down whenever you want."

"If Mom ever lets me drive."

"So how *is* Aunt Christine?"

I make the so-so sign with my hand. "Small things set her off. Like, the other night, she was making soup and just started bawling, and it wasn't the onions."

"Have you tried talking to her?" Sophie asks.

I shake my head.

Dena gives me an exasperated sigh without moving her head. "Why not?"

"I'm kind of afraid of what she's going to tell me."

"This from the girl who went to Alaska looking for answers."

Gerry and Sophie snicker.

"I know."

"Make up your mind," Dena says. "Do you want the truth, or do you want to live in eternal darkness?"

"Eternal darkness?" I giggle. "You've been watching too much *Dark Shadows*."

Dena bites her lower lip to affect vampire fangs.

"Now you look like a rabid squirrel," I tell her.

Dena erupts in laughter. Her shells go flying. Sophie, Gerry, and I all collapse in hysterics. When I'm finally able to breathe, I realize something's different. Joy no longer brings guilt, like I'm betraying the memory of my father. He was a joyful person, after all. He'd want me to be happy and live life. I take a mental snapshot of the flushed and grinning faces around me and will myself to never to forget this moment.

CHAPTER 31

Spawn

The eggs of fish; to deposit eggs in water

om sits cross-legged on her bed, a pile of photographs, letters, and cards spread out before her, a box of Kleenex in her lap. On the floor is the drawer I went through months ago, now empty.

"I never got around to organizing these." She holds up a black-and-white snapshot of me in the tiger costume. "We certainly took enough pictures of you. God, you were cute." She sniffs. "Still are."

I clear a spot on the side of the bed and sit so I'm facing her. Her eyes are red and puffy from crying. The rash around her neck is fading, but she's still way too thin.

"I have that tiger suit somewhere," she says.

I nod. "It's in a box in your closet."

"Of course, you'd know." She picks up some random photos and tosses them aside. If there's any organization to what she's doing, it isn't obvious.

"Can I help?"

"I didn't think this would be so hard," she says, sniffing.

I take that as a yes. As I start to gather up all the letters to get them out of the way, I see photos of Dad spilling out of a manila folder labeled "Departures and Arrivals."

"I was wondering where those were."

"Coffee table drawer," Mom says. "You mean to tell me you didn't look there?"

"I guess I didn't think of checking somewhere so obvious."

She shoots me a sideways glance.

I shrug. "I'm not perfect." I dump the contents of the folder and start lining them up according to date, departures in one row and their corresponding arrivals in another. It's easy to tell the difference. In the former, he's always clean-shaven. In the latter, he's weather-beaten and bearded.

"Why did we do this? Take all these pictures of Dad?"

Mom grabs a tissue from the box and wipes her nose. "That was him. After he got the boat, he wanted photographs."

"But they're all so similar." As soon as I say it, I realize it's not true. Dad's much younger in the earlier black-and-white photos and more like the Dad I remember in the later color photos. It's not a complete timeline of his fishing career because he was fishing before I was born. It's more a timeline of me and him, our joint time on this earth. When I come across the departure photo taken a year ago last spring, I get a chill. I study it for any obvious clues to his fate, something he or we forgot that broke the run of good luck and safe returns. But it's all there—the red sweater, the name of the boat, my dad's smile. He has more wrinkles around his eyes, more gray in his hair. The boat is the only thing that looks the same from the first photo to the last. He was so meticulous about maintaining her.

"His first and last love was that boat," Mom says, as if reading my mind. "Or should I say Miss Red?"

"No!" My outburst makes her flinch. In a quieter voice, I say, "Lady Rose was her real name."

"She was named after you. I think that's what got you started on boat names. Remember how you used to write them all down?"

"I won't be doing that anymore." I place 1962's spring photo above its late-summer mate.

"I'm sure the arrivals, in particular, would be hard to take," Mom says. "Besides, you—we—will be busy doing something else this month."

I look up from Dad's faces into Mom's. She's smiling like she's trying not to cry again. "What?"

"I want to have a memorial potlatch."

For a second, I think she's joking. Then I remember she doesn't joke. "A potlatch? Like the one we went to in Alaska?"

"Well, sort of, but our own version, with fewer speeches and no gifts."

A number of questions fly through my head, including when and how, and what about the fact that we're not Native, but I settle on, "Why? What's changed?"

"Everything. You. Me." She dabs her eyes with the tissue in her hand. "Your running away. Excuse me, running *to*. If you were that desperate to find out about your father . . . well, I figure there's a reason we have these things. Can I count on your help?"

"Uh, sure . . . absolutely."

"At a memorial, you'll hear stories, Ida. You'll learn things you never knew." She purses her lips. "No snooping required."

I blush.

"Well, I'm guilty too," she says. "I went through your room. I was trying to find some evidence of where you'd gone. I didn't find any, but I did find this." She reaches into the breast pocket of her blouse and pulls out the piece of photo I tore off to make our trio a duo. The rip cuts off Mom's left arm. It's just her maimed figure in front of the rose bush.

I cringe. There's no explaining away what I did.

Mom sets the photo down on top of the Kleenex box in her lap. "It hurt to find this. I won't lie. But I can't say it was a surprise."

"It's not . . . I . . ."

She holds up her hand to stop me. "You loved him more. I knew that. Maybe you still do."

Without thinking, I shake my head no, which prompts Mom to place her hand over her heart. "I have to say, I was bitter for a long time about the, um, bond you two had. I felt so left out. I mean, here I was, the one who was home with you. I was the one who saw us through all those long fishing seasons, year after year, but all you cared about was when he would be getting back. You'd ask me that over and over again when you were younger. I got to hear how much you missed him, how resentful you were that he had to go away for so long. We suffered together, you and me, but that didn't bring us together. It seemed to drive us apart. Then when he returned—usually with some ridiculously extravagant gift—you forgot all about me."

The gift-giving. I'd never tried to see it from Mom's eyes before. "Is that why you gave away my coat? The white one?"

"Oh, God. That." She winces. "Not one of my prouder parenting moments, I'm afraid. But, oooh!" She shakes her head. "I was so mad at your dad. A white fox-fur coat for a five-year-old? Honestly."

"You said it made me look ridiculous."

"I know, and I'm sorry. If I could take that back, I would." She sighs. "That coat, besides being wholly impractical, just smacked of pandering."

"Guilt talking, you said."

"Yes. And I should have let you wear it even though it didn't square with the tough, resilient girl I wanted you to be. You're a fisherman's daughter, for Christ's sake, not some spoiled rich kid."

"Is that what you meant by *ridiculous?*"

"I shouldn't have used that word."

"I thought you meant that it made me look fat."

Mom clamps her hand over her mouth. "Oh, no, Ida, no. Have you been thinking that all this time?"

I nod.

"I'm sorry." She removes her hand from her mouth and strokes my arm. "I know I haven't been the best mother to you. I've taken out my frustrations. I've lost my temper. I've been critical." She stops, takes a breath. "If I've been hard on you, it's because I want you to be a strong person in your own right, not someone who can be bought with pretty things or swayed by looks and charm . . . like I was."

"Dad."

"Yes. We possibly weren't the best match." She grabs another tissue to dab her eyes. "I'm going to tell you something that may come as a shock, but I figure you're old enough to hear it now." She takes a deep breath and meets my eyes. "You weren't our first child. We had a son, Jack, who died. You probably saw photos of him when you went through the drawer."

My mouth hangs open as I take in what she just said. Then I remember the photos of Mom and Dad at my grandparents' house with the baby I thought was me. The date stamp was three years before I was born. I just assumed it was a mistake.

"He'd be eighteen or nineteen, right?"

"Eighteen."

"How did he die?"

"Heart defect. We didn't know. He was small, but we thought he was healthy. The day he died, your father was out fishing. I woke up to find Jack dead in his crib. Grandma Grace tried to comfort me by telling me we would have another baby. I remember wanting to slap her." She balls up the tissue in her hand. "Your grandmother didn't understand. When Jack died, I felt my life had ended too."

"Is that why you and Dad never told me?"

"Yes. And, well, I didn't know how or even why I should tell you, to be honest. I didn't know what purpose it would serve. Dad and I didn't even talk about it. Jack's death was hard on both of us, but harder on him. He always dreamed of having sons he could take fishing, just like Grandpa took him and his brothers. I think he saw it as a legacy."

"Ending with me."

"Oh, Ida, your dad cherished you. You have to believe that."

"He never took me fishing."

"He was traditional. Girls don't fish. Alaska had plenty of young men hungry for the chance. I think that may have been why he connected with Trinity. He needed deckhands, and he wanted to help a kid who could really use the job, not some college boy hoping to make big money, not that Dad could pay it."

"But why didn't he tell us?"

"I wondered about that too. Then I remembered something. You see, after we had you, I had two miscarriages before the doctor told me I couldn't have more children. Right or wrong, I felt like a failure—at everything. I couldn't give Dad the son he wanted, and I thought it was too late to start the career *I* wanted. I dreamed of becoming a writer. Did you know that? I was going to go to college and major in English, but that all went out the window when I met him. We were so in love. And naive, as it turns out. I thought our love was strong enough to endure all that time apart, the worry, the not knowing if he would return. I was wrong. We fought— not in front of you so much, but we fought." She stops, grimaces. "I don't know how much of this I should be telling you."

"Mom, I'm not a baby."

"No, you're not." She sucks in her breath. "Well, after we found out you would be an only child, your dad told me he was thinking of becoming a scout leader—of boys, not girls. It wasn't so unreasonable, what he wanted, but it infuriated me at the time. I took it as an insult, to you and to me. I accused him of not being satisfied with the way things were. With us." She looks down into her lap. "I was unfair to your father in other ways, too. We had a . . . loveless marriage. Maybe because I knew I couldn't have another child, I lost interest, and it frustrated him. Then I found that note from Trinity and those condoms, and—"

"You thought he was cheating."

She nods. "I think I was looking for signs of infidelity to make myself feel better, more justified in rejecting him, if that makes sense."

"Um-hum." I think back on my own tendency to look for signs to explain the unexplainable. Alaska, with all its surprises, seems to have cured me of that habit. "The problem with signs," I say, "is you only see what you want to see."

Mom cocks her head and smiles. "True."

"Who did you think Dad was seeing in Alaska? Trinity?"

"I didn't know her name, but yes. And maybe others as well." She sighs. "I think it's fairly safe to assume he and Trinity weren't lovers. As to others? Who can say? There's no evidence of it."

"There was no evidence he drowned either, but everyone assumes he did."

"That's different, Ida. And, to tell you the truth, I struggled with that too. That night you overheard me talking to Grandma? That was all I was saying, that it's hard to accept someone's dead when there's no evidence." The tears that have been welling up in her eyes roll down her cheeks. "Turns out your grandparents were right. I wasn't cut out to be a fisherman's wife. I'm not strong enough."

I lean over to give her a hug and knock the Kleenex,

along with a couple of my baby pictures, to the floor in the process. Neither of us moves to pick them up.

"Maybe you weren't cut out to be a fisherman's wife," I say. "But you're stronger than you think."

CHAPTER 32

Come About
To maneuver the bow of a sailing vessel across the wind so that the wind changes from one side of the vessel to the other

M y head's reeling with revelations, including the news that I could have had a brother, but there's no time to dwell on any of it. We have a memorial service to plan. Mom wants to have it at the Acropolis, the dance-hall-turned-roller-skating-rink north of Seattle where she and Dad met. I think it's a fabulous idea.

"Will there be roller skating?" I ask, just to be funny.

"Of course," Mom says. "But what do we do about Grandma Grace? Can you see her on skates?"

"I can't even see her at the Acropolis."

"Bingo. You've identified our first hurdle. We have to get her to agree to a service outside of a church. I have a plan."

We start with Uncle Pat and Aunt Janet, who helped

Mom search for me when I went missing. There was much fence-mending on both sides, apparently, but they're still shocked to hear she wants a service at all. Once they get over their surprise it's not hard to sell them on the idea, especially given Dad's support of the Center for Native Alaskan Youth.

"A memorial potlatch is a celebration of life," Mom tells them. "It will do more to honor Steve's memory than a long, stuffy Catholic service. The Tlingit have the right idea. Debts are paid, and then they send their loved ones off to the after-life with songs, stories, and a last meal. We won't do the debt or gift-giving part, but we'll do the rest, and throw in some Croatian dancing as well."

"You want to do this in two weeks?" Uncle Pat's forehead wrinkles in doubt.

"Twelve days, actually," Mom says levelly. "But I'm sure we can pull it off."

God, is this the same woman who was afraid to drive? Or have aliens come down and taken over Mom's body? Whoever she is, I like her.

"ABSOLUTELY not!" Grandma Grace literally puts her foot down, sending Lassie skittering off in terror. "My boys were born and raised Catholics, and they'll go out Catholics!"

"But Father O'Neal has already given his blessing and agreed to give a short eulogy," Mom says.

"He has?" She looks so stunned I wish I had a camera. And when Mom puts her in charge of the food, she actually starts asking questions—as in, how many?

I later find out that the Father O'Neal claim was a complete lie when, in a gamble that would have made Dad proud, Mom convinces the good Father to participate by telling him that Bill and Grace Petrovich wanted to have the service in a bigger place.

Now that everyone's on board, we actually have to pull this thing off, which means figuring out the guest list and a million other details. Given how last-minute this is, we use the fishermen-homecoming telephone tree to invite people and get their confirmations. I get the job of contacting people in Alaska, including Trinity, who we hope will provide the Native dancing, music, and storytelling. I also send an invitation to Jody and Dwight, asking that he extend an invitation to Hank.

TRINITY responded right away. She'll be coming with a troupe of young dancers from the Center to perform a traditional dance in robes and masks, the whole nine yards.

Nana will be coming from Montana with her new boyfriend, Phil, and my aunt Corrine, of the many letters.

On the other side of the family are the aunts and uncles and cousins, as well as friends from church, since it's not going to be *at* the church. The list goes on. Fortunately, the Acropolis can accommodate everyone and still have space to spare for a circle dance. Uncle Pat knows a family of musicians and singers who will lead the uninitiated in a traditional Croatian Kolo.

The days whizz frantically by. With only a week to go before the potlatch, I find out that Sam's back from Alaska, so I do what any girl who's been separated from her boyfriend for too long would do: I drop everything and run to his house.

His mother answers the door. I don't think she recognizes me at first because of my short hair, but then she gasps and hugs me. She asks me about my head and I show her the wound. "It's getting better," I tell her.

"That is good!" She pats my shoulder kindly, but there's a nervous twitch in her face when she calls for Sam.

When he walks into the room and sees me, he pretends to stagger backwards in surprise.

"Your hair! It's shorter than mine!"

And it is. After a summer in Alaska, Sam's hair is down past his neck.

"Do you like it?" I ask, biting my lip.

"It's a lot different, but yeah."

He gives his Mom a peck on the cheek, says he'll be back for dinner, and sweeps me out the door. Once we get a safe distance away from his house, he grabs me and gives me a long kiss. "I've missed you."

"Same here!"

He asks what's new, and I tell him all about the memorial potlatch we're planning for Dad. "Of course, you and your mom are invited, if you want to come."

"I wouldn't miss it."

We walk along the waterfront, past the cannery where Sam's mother works. They're already winding down for the season.

"I have a place I want to show you." Grabbing his hand, I lead him toward the bluff. "It's not far from where I first saw you."

"Oh, yeah. I remember," he says without a trace of sarcasm. In fact, there's a hint of sadness in his voice.

We walk in silence, past the turnoff to the lighthouse, along the dirt path that keeps going straight onto the bluff overlooking the mouth of the harbor. I take him into the wind-dwarfed trees to my "old man."

"Sorry, he's really a one-person tree, but if we squeeze together . . ."

Sam laughs, but only faintly. Why is he being so serious? We somehow manage to adjust our bodies around each other so that no one's arms or legs are in danger of falling asleep. Fortunately, the ground is dry and padded with needles. The air in late summer carries the sweetness of sap and evergreen. I rest my head on his chest, inhaling the Ivory soap smell of his skin and listening to the thumping of his heart.

"Ida, I enlisted." The words vibrate in my ear. "In the Navy."

"Wait. What are you saying?" I prop myself up on my elbow so I can look him in the eyes. "You're not even eighteen."

"So I'll have a year. I'll finish school. It's better than being drafted."

I try to understand, but I still can't figure out why anyone would *volunteer* to go to war before they're even draft age. "Why couldn't you wait? Maybe you would have gotten lucky. Maybe this stupid war will end."

"That would be great. My dad would come home, but—"

"That's the real reason, isn't it? You want to show your dad how tough you are! What happened to being the man of the house? What about your mom? What about me?" I slap him on the chest with my palms.

"Whoa!" He grabs my hands so I won't hit him again.

His hands are warm. How is it his hands are always warm?

"Ida, hear me out. I enlisted because I *don't* want to end up on the front lines. There's a wait for Navy spots. If I really wanted to show my dad how tough I was, I would've joined the Marines." He lets go of my hands.

"Why do you have to fight at all? You're going to college, right?"

"The service gives you a way to pay for college. It's called the GI Bill. But you have to serve first." A fat blue vein pulses in Sam's neck. I want to touch it, but I just might strangle him instead.

"You just can't walk away from a fight, even a stupid one!" I'm almost yelling now. "What if your ship blows up or sinks? What if . . ." But I can't think of another what-if. "Damn it. I don't want to lose you!"

"I don't want to lose you either, and I came close on Nagoon." He holds his arms open, inviting me to lie on his chest again. I do, and he squeezes me in a hug. "How's your head?"

"Fine. Don't change the subject," I say, slapping him on the chest again.

"I'm not. When you hit your head, I really thought I'd lost you. Your eyes were open, but you looked like you . . ." He stops, searching for the words. "Weren't in this world. Then you said something that made me think you were dying."

I prop myself up to see his face. "What?"

"You don't remember, do you?"

"Apparently not."

"Ida, you asked for your dad. But not like you wanted him to come. More like he was already there, like you were looking right at him."

A shiver runs through me in spite of the warm summer air and the heat of Sam's body against mine. I don't remember any of this.

"Then you said *my* name," he says. "And I knew you were going to be okay."

"God, Sam, if you hadn't been there to help me off those rocks, I would have drowned."

"If I hadn't been there, you might not have tried to climb the rocks in the first place."

"Maybe, maybe not. Don't underestimate me."

He laughs softly. "Oh, I'd never do that."

I squeeze myself around him and that familiar buzz shoots through me. Now that I'm showered and not collapsing from cannery exhaustion, the electricity is more intense than ever. It's *want*, pure and potent. His body is so lean and strong and perfect. I can't believe I once thought we didn't fit. We fit fine. I turn towards him and kiss that vein. It's smaller now, but his heart is beating fast and hard. His mouth is open and his eyes are closed. I kiss his lips, tasting spearmint. Sweet Sam. I roll over on my back, pulling him on top of me. He buries his face in my neck, working his way down with his mouth to the edge of my bra. I'm glad I wore the pretty one. I grab his hair while his hand slips under my shirt, cupping me gently. He moans. Or is it me? I reach down for his belt but he grabs my hand.

"I'm ready," I tell him. "I want to."

"I don't have anything to put on." He rolls off me and onto his back, panting. "Sorry."

"It's okay." I kiss his cheek, tasting soap and sweat. "We have a whole year for this."

"Longer, I hope."

We lie side by side, letting our breathing return to normal as we stare up at the branches and the shapes of sky in between.

"I told Mom I was going to the library," I tell him. "I don't know why I lied. I think she's okay with us now."

"You have to stop lying."

"I know, but she's still such a worry-wart. It's a habit."

"My mom's too tired to worry about me."

We talk about our families. I tell him about the older brother I could have had. He tells me about the relatives he's never met in the Philippines, a town called Olongapo, or "old man's head." The name comes from the mysterious disappearance of a rich landowner whose body later turned up missing its head. "It's just a story," he says. "I don't know if it is true or not."

I tell Sam that I'm the only thing that the Irish and Slavic halves of my family have in common.

"Petrovich is Croatian. It means 'son of Peter.' Pretty boring, huh?"

"Taposok means 'from my heart.'"

"Really?"

"Really."

"You're not just making that up to get me to kiss you again?"

"No, but you can still kiss me."

And so I do, over and over, until we have to stop ourselves again.

SAM walks me home even though I live about eight blocks past his house. He turns down my invitation to come in for a Coke, reminding me that I've just spent the afternoon at the library but didn't check out any books. I kiss him good-bye, hoping that my mom isn't watching from the window.

She isn't, but she's sitting at the dining room table waiting for me. "Finally!" she says as I walk in. She isn't mad, but I have to wonder if she senses something different about me. I'm so full of sensations of Sam, I don't know how she could *not* notice.

Were it not for the letter, she probably would.

CHAPTER 33

Beacon

A lighted or unlighted fixed aid to navigation attached directly to the earth's surface

"It took all my willpower not to open this." Mom hands me a Scotch-taped envelope addressed to me. It's from Alaska.

I take it up to my room, make myself comfortable on my bed, and settle in to read. The letter is three pages long and written in a child's large, blocky print with different-colored inks, as if it took several days.

DEAR IDA,

HANK SAID YOU WANTED TO KNOW ABOUT YOUR DAD. I FISHED WITH HIM THE LAST 3 YEARS. SORRY I CANNOT COME TO THE POTLATCH BUT THIS IS WHAT I WANT TO SAY.

I DID NOT KNOW A BOOM FROM A CANONBALL WHEN I STARTED FISHING. NOW I SAVE $ FOR MY

BOAT! I HAVE A LIFE THANKS TO HIM. FOUR YEARS AGO I HAD NO JOB AND NO HOME. I WAS A DRUNK AND STOLE THINGS. GOT STABBED BY A MAN FOR MY COAT. ALMOST DIED BUT GOD WAS LOOKING OUT FOR ME. HE SEND AN ANGEL. TRINITY TOOK ME IN NO MATTER I AM NOT NATIVE.

THE CENTER TEACHED ME TO CARVE. IF I WANT A DRINK I PICK UP MY POCKETKNIFE. I GOT REAL GOOD AT THE CARVING BUT MY DREAM WAS TO FISH. TRINITY GOT STEVE TO GIVE ME A JOB ON HIS BOAT. WE WORKED! I NEVER WORK SO HARD IN MY LIFE!!

WHEN WE WEREN'T WORKING, STEVE LOVED A GOOD STORY. HE TELL SOME AND I TELL SOME. NO ONE ELSE LISTENED TO ME EXCEPT HIM AND TRINITY. I TOLD THEM SOME BAD THINGS, BUT THEY NEVER SAID I WAS BAD.

SO YOU PROBBLY WANT TO KNOW WHAT HAPPENED TO YOUR DAD. SORRY I DO NOT KNOW. THE FISHING WAS BAD. WE WENT WAY OUT CAPE SPENCER. DOZEN KINGS WERE A GOOD DAY. STEVE MADE NO $ BUT PAYED ME. WHEN I HEARED HE GONE MISSING I CRIED LIKE A BABY AND I WANT A DRINK SO BAD! THANK GOD FOR TRINITY AND THE CENTER! I GOT THROUGH THE WINTER AND IN SPRING GOT ON ANOTHER BOAT. I HAVE EXPERIENCE NOW THANKS TO TRINITY AND STEVE!

SORRY TO WRITE ALL ABOUT ME. STEVE TALKED ABOUT YOU A LOT. HE ALWAYS WANT TO GET

*BACK TO HOME TO HIS GIRLS. YOU AND YOUR
MOM. STEVE SHOWED ME YOUR PHOTOGRAPHS.
SO PROUD. EVERY YEAR HE ASK ME WHAT TO GET
FOR YOUR BIRTHDAY PRESSENT. LIKE I KNOW
WHAT GIRLS LIKE! I SAY JUST GET BACK TO HER.
THAT IS WHAT THEY WANT. SORRY IF THAT
MAKES YOU SAD.*

*SO I WILL END THIS LETTER BEFORE I NEED MORE
STAMPS! HAVE A GOOD POTLATCH. WRITE BACK IF
YOU WANT TO.*

*SINCERELY,
ARROW*

*PS. TRINITY HELPED ME WRITE THIS LETTER. I
DON'T SPELL SO GOOD.*

*PPS. SHE GAVE ME THE NAME ARROW BECAUSE I
AM GOING IN THE RIGHT DIRECTION NOW.*

I show Arrow's letter to Mom and she cries all over the
last page, leaving wet, blurry blobs in the ink.

MY letter back to Arrow is much shorter than his to me, but
it still takes me several drafts before I get it just right. I know
it's just right because Mom cries over, though not on, my
letter, too.

Dear Arrow,

*I love your nickname! From what you've told me, it fits
you perfectly. I'm just sorry we couldn't talk in person.*

Maybe someday. In the meantime, we can write, if you want. You have no idea how much your letter meant to me and my mom. She cried and cried when she read it, especially the last page. You may find this hard to believe, but your words told me all I really needed to know about my dad. When you're handed a mystery you can't solve, it's tempting to fill in the blanks with all sorts of nonsense, ignoring what you know in your heart to be true. Your letter helped me realize that love has no bounds. Sure, Dad loved fishing and Alaska. He loved Trinity and you and the Center. But he also loved Mom and me. I don't know what happened to him and probably never will, but I do know he wanted to come home, and for now, that's enough. I'll write again soon.

Love,
Ida (my real name)

CHAPTER 34

By and Large
*"By" is into the wind, while "large"
is with the wind; used to indicate all
possible situations*

What Grandma Grace calls a three-ring circus is about to start. Dena, looking fabulous in a long, batik-print dress and huge hoop earrings, helps me usher people to their tables, which almost fill up the Acropolis's rectangular ballroom, except for a space in the middle we've reserved for dancing. On the back wall is Dad's life in photographs, including a timeline of his leaving and arrival pictures from age twenty-six to forty-two.

Trinity sent us her favorite photo of Dad and Miss Red. Turned out she had the negative. Mom had a large print made because it's so beautiful. There's Dad in his red sweater, looking relaxed and happy as he leans on the polished rail of his beloved boat, blue and white peaks behind him. Mom has displayed the picture on its own stand, wreathed in red and white roses and sprays of baby's breath. I now know why sailors consider flowers to be bad luck. They symbolize remembrance.

I stoop down to get a whiff of the roses, but all I can smell is Grandma Grace's buffet, which takes up five tables—I counted—on one side of the room. There are cold cuts and cheeses, fruits and vegetables, salads of every stripe, and six steaming bins of hot food, including her famed pork shank. On a big round table is a whole galaxy of desserts surrounding a giant pink Jell-O-cream mold in the shape of—what else?— a salmon. There's enough here to feed all of Annisport and some of Alaska, too—which is good, because Trinity brought a big dance troupe and Dwight came as well. His suit's a little too small but I'm touched by his obvious effort to look his best, not to mention his coming all this way to honor my dad. Jody said she'd come, but I still haven't seen her.

The Montana contingent is here. Aunt Corrine is an older, brunette version of my mother, and I almost don't recognize the older woman at her side. Nana's hair is no longer orange but a pretty silver-grey. She introduces her boyfriend, Phillip, who shakes my hand and immediately starts talking about music. He's in a bagpipe band, very Scottish, with the same startling blue eyes as someone else I know.

David just got back from fishing with his dad. He came over and gave me that hug, one year late. It was nice, but I'd rather be hugging Sam. Where is he, anyway?

The tables are almost filled when the lights blink on and off and Uncle Pat's voice booms over the microphone asking everyone who hasn't yet to please take their seats.

I find my place between Dena and Mom just as the room

goes dark. The audience grows quiet and I can hear them, the drums and rattles, coming up from behind us. Sound building like passing thunder, they shuffle past our table and climb the stairs to the stage, taking their places. The music stops. The stage lights come on, revealing a circle of robed performers wearing cone-shaped hats. They part, revealing a young man, crouching, head down, so that his beaked mask and shiny, feathered arms create the illusion of a magnificent white bird.

Many years ago, when Raven was born, the world lived in darkness.

The narrator is a woman with a voice so strong she doesn't need a microphone. She stands on the far left side of the stage, all but invisible in her black robe.

Jody?

A rich old man who lived far up the Nass River kept the light just for himself.

Yep, that's her all right. Her voice is clear and smooth—as smooth as this graceful boy in the Raven mask. He unfolds his body, stretching his winged arms wide. Then he starts to dance, pivoting back and forth on alternate feet around three big boxes spaced evenly across the stage. Under his mask and cloak of feathers, he's nearly naked save for a loincloth where it matters most. The other dancers, in contrast, appear weighed down by their elaborate robes, decorated with buttons or woven in designs of black, white, and yellow with long fringe that jumps and sways when they move.

I glance around our table. Mom's looking mighty pleased with herself, no doubt because Grandma Grace, sitting across from us, can't take her eyes off Raven.

Raven flies to where the old man's daughter is picking berries.

He turns himself into a hemlock needle and drops into the stream.

Two dancers unfurl a long blue cloth. Raven disappears behind it and a young woman steps forward. She bends down and cups her hands to her mouth as if to drink.

She swallows the needle and becomes pregnant, giving birth to a baby boy with bright black eyes.

The cloth is lowered to reveal a little boy standing next to the young woman. Everyone goes "ah" because the kid is so cute. And now he's making an adorable fuss as he clamors for the first box.

Raven cries until the old man gives him the box containing the stars. He plays with the box for a while, then opens the lid and lets the stars escape through the chimney.

When the lid to the first box opens, the mirror ball in the center of the room starts to spin, sprinkling us all with spots of light. Mom gets this dreamy look in her eyes like she's a million miles away. Grandma Grace is spellbound. Dena, sitting next to me, is so uncharacteristically still that I almost forget she's there.

Too bad Dad couldn't attend his own potlatch, but then, maybe he *is* here, admiring the way this storytelling girl he once mentored is drawing out the suspense.

Only one box left—the box containing the sun. Raven cries and cries. His eyes turn round and round, showing different colors. The grandfather thinks, Maybe this is no ordinary baby, *but he loves his grandson like he loves his daughter, and so, with much sadness, he hands over the last box.*

The drumming gets louder as the dancers circle around the boy and the third box, their backs to the audience, displaying the full spread of their beautiful robes. "Gr-r-o-c-c-k!"

cries Raven, rising up from the center. The little boy is gone
and the half-naked bird-boy is back, this time in a *black* cloak
of feathers, holding aloft a red lantern the size of a beach ball.
At the same time, the orange and yellow lights switch on
over the ballroom, bathing us all golden.

From that day on, we no longer lived in darkness, Jody finishes.

There's a celebratory dance involving all the performers.
Then they form a line, with Jody and Raven in the middle,
and take their bows. The audience rises to its feet in a standing ovation.

I pity Father O'Neal, who comes next. Jody didn't need a
podium or a microphone, but both are brought out for the
Good Father, who fortunately keeps his words short and his
scripture-quoting to a minimum. Then we sing that song
again, the one from the candlelight vigil with the line I liked
about praying for "those in peril on the sea." This time when
I sing the chorus, I think of Sam as well. I wish he would
have waited and taken his chances on the draft, but I'm kind
of glad he'll be on a ship rather than in the jungle. In spite of
what happened to my dad, boats seem to be the safest option
over there.

Father O'Neal steps aside for my Uncle Pat, the first of
our family and friends to get up to speak.

Looking at him all suited up and clean-shaven, I notice
for the first time how much the past year has aged him. His
forehead's looking as lined as President Johnson's, and he
needs reading glasses to see his pages of notes. He talks about
his and Dad's childhood together, how they used to go down
to the docks to watch the fishermen repair their nets. "From

them, Steve learned how to tell a good story and swear a blue streak. Actually, we both learned to swear at a tender age."

The audience titters.

"But who do you think gets in trouble when I ask Mom to pass the blankety-blank potatoes?" Pat wiggles his fingers in the air, inviting laughter. "Truth is, I couldn't have asked for a better. . . . He chokes up, looks towards the ceiling. "I'll miss you, Bro."

I hear sniffling all around me. Mom's going through one Kleenex after another from the box on her lap.

My uncle Alex goes up and tells the story of that one Christmas when Dad fell off the roof. He was playing Santa. Tradition dictated that he get up on the porch roof and prance around like eight tiny reindeer, then make his grand entrance.

"This was the year it really snowed," Alex says. "There must have been a foot on the roof, which would have been fine, except Steve had had a little to drink. A couple of us gently suggested he not go up there, but Steve wouldn't hear of it. So the kids got their pawing and prancing—as well as a yell, followed by some crashing and snapping, and one choice four-letter word. I went outside to see if Santa needed help and found Steve picking himself out of Mom's rhododendron bush. He brushed himself off, put the hat back on, and then burst through the front door bellowing, 'Ho, ho, ho,' as if nothing had happened, though clearly something had. His beard was askew and his Santa pants were torn."

I remember that Christmas. I must have been about five. I no longer believed in Santa, so it didn't come as a crushing blow to discover Dad under there. What I remember most was the adults laughing their heads off. They seemed to have a secret understanding of events that excluded us. Now I realize there was nothing sinister about it. They reacted to Dad's mishap as they would any pratfall. The humor was lost on us kids because we still saw our parents and uncles and aunts as perfect, always knowing right from wrong, safe from unsafe. That fall off the roof, and my parents' unusually loud fight after they got home, may have been my first glimpse into the hidden world of imperfect adults.

All these years later, his near-disaster is remembered as comically heroic. Of course, no one's going to say anything bad about Dad at his own memorial. Even the fishermen, who aren't known to sugarcoat things, have nothing but praise. My father was committed and caring, a generous man and hard worker, dedicated to his family.

It's not that I disagree with these descriptions, it's just that I know he wasn't so saintly. He took unnecessary risks and was prone to mood swings—long, silent, brooding stretches—that could come without warning and just as suddenly disappear. I guess problems with your marriage would be reason enough to brood and search for love elsewhere. What better elsewhere than Alaska? Of course, Dad was so lovable he could get anyone, even Trinity, to cover for him. That business with the condoms. She didn't really explain why there would be loose ones in his pockets. It took Sam's want of one to get me to wonder if Dad was using them himself. I've never purchased condoms and I'm relatively sure Mom hasn't either, but I saw them for sale at the little store on Nagoon. They're sold in *boxes*. If you were to make a donation to a teen center, you wouldn't remove them first.

I suppose he could have been doling them out to his deckhands and young fishermen friends. David? Or Arrow? I won't jump to conclusions like Mom did, but I suspect Dad's love, while limitless, may have also been imperfect. As a husband, he could be selfish. As a father, he had a bias for sons. I could choose to be mad and jealous, but that would only lead to more hurt. Instead, I'll focus on the good and the love that always brought him home to me.

I'm thinking the eulogies are done when Mom gets up from her chair. My God, is she actually going to speak? Clomping across the stage in her dark blue dress and high heels, she looks so small. She unfolds her written remarks on the podium, and, unlike Pat, actually reads them, her voice starting off shaky but gaining in strength as she goes along. I find myself sitting forward in my seat, silently rooting for her.

"Just over a year ago, I got the call every wife of a fisherman dreads. My husband was lost at sea. A search was underway. As you all know, that search was valiant and thorough, but ultimately unsuccessful. It was as if Steve really had disappeared. That's a hard death to accept, though no death is easy. Without so much as a mayday, without a wreck—indeed, without a trace—I was supposed to accept that he drowned in a fishing accident. And I couldn't. I just couldn't. Obviously, I couldn't accept the thought of a funeral, either. In fact, as many of you also know, I fought it."

"Boy, that's the truth," Grandma Grace mutters.

"I think I knew in my heart he wasn't coming back," Mom continues. "But I wasn't ready to say good-bye. Then my daughter, Ida, ran away. Yes, it's been a hell of a year." Her sarcasm gets knowing chuckles. "But that's what it took to get me to see beyond myself. Ida ran away to Alaska in search of answers about her dad. I only went up there to retrieve her, but I ended up needing that trip as much as she did. We learned things about ourselves. How strong and connected we really are. And we learned things about Steve. I didn't know of his involvement with the Center for Native Alaskan Youth. I didn't know that he'd changed lives by giving young men a chance to fish on his boat. I didn't know he carried around a book of myths and stories, retelling them to help keep them alive. You might say there was a lot I didn't know, and you'd be right. For whatever reason, Steve kept his two worlds separate. Still, I don't think he'd mind if I shared something with you all, a letter from a young man who was probably the last person to see him alive. Arrow couldn't be here today, but he wanted you to know what Steve's involvement in his life has meant to him."

Mom doesn't read all of Arrow's letter. She leaves out some of the grittier details of his life, as well as the entire last page, which was so personal to the two of us. But it's still enough to get most everybody reaching for their handkerchiefs—everybody but me, of course. I'm still praying for Mom, willing her to get through what she has to say without breaking down.

"When I was in Alaska, I got to thinking how important stories are," she says. "How they help us make sense of the world and how they help us heal. I never thought of Steve as a reader. He never had books by his side of the bed like I did or like Ida did. But he knew, maybe more than us, that stories told well, memories passed down, are absolutely vital, so vital that a young girl would run all the way to Alaska to get them.

While we were in Ketchikan, we attended a memorial potlatch for a woman we didn't know—Geraldine Weaver. After
the celebration was over, I had a real appreciation for her
efforts to keep her native Tlingit language alive, though all I
knew of her were the stories that had just been told, some of
them in a tongue I didn't understand. That's what finally
convinced me it was time to have a memorial for Steve, to
say good-bye and celebrate his life instead of mourn it. If stories are so powerful they can turn a modest fish into the biggest one you ever saw"—she waits while the crowd laughs—"
then maybe, just maybe, they can make a sad anniversary a
little less so. That's all."

My mother walks away from the podium. Everyone claps,
and then, one by one, they get up from their chairs until the
entire room is on their feet, including Grandma Grace and
Grandpa Bill. My mother stops walking and just stands there.
I hear someone whistle loudly. She puts her hands to her
mouth and lowers them again. Her lips pucker and widen like
a fish taking a breath.

"Wow," she's saying, though no one can hear her.

And then it finally happens. As I'm silently willing *her*
not to cry, I start. I grab my napkin from the table to mop my
face as the tears keep coming. My aunt Janet puts her arm
around my shoulders and draws me to her. She probably
thinks I'm sad. But the weird thing is, I'm not. I'm happy.
Really, really happy.

"What's this?" Mom says when she gets back to our table
and sees me crying on Janet's shoulder. Janet hands me over,
into Mom's outstretched arms. Bending over to receive her
hug, I'm the ungainly chick that's outgrown its parent. I finally

stop crying, but the hugs keep coming. People *line up* to hug both me and Mom, many of them telling us, with a tone of amazement, that this is the best funeral they've ever attended. "Steve would have approved." I hear that over and over again.

When I'm not being hugged, I watch, still waiting for Sam. People start lining up at the buffet tables, and there's Grandma Grace, gold tooth flashing, as she accepts her accolades for the spread. I'm happy to see the Alaska folks mixing in. Trinity has somehow found her way to Nana, or maybe it was the other way around. I overhear them talking about elderberry roots. Dwight returns from the buffet table with a heaping plate of food. Too excited to eat, I'm scanning the heads for Jody when I get a tap on my shoulder and there she is, back in her jeans and faded baseball cap. We scream and hug like little girls.

"I thought you didn't come. Then I see you on stage!" I have to talk loudly to be heard over the Croatian music that's just started up. "You never told me you were with a dance troupe."

"You never asked." Same old Jody.

I grab her arm. "Come with me to the ladies'. We need to catch up, and I need to tidy up."

"Yeah, you're kind of a mess."

In the bathroom, I splash cold water onto my face. Jody hoists herself up to sit on the counter. I watch her tap out a cigarette. "Those things are bad for you, you know."

"Yeah, yeah." She lights up, takes a draw, and exhales. In one of the stalls, a toilet flushes, and we stop talking until an older woman emerges and washes her hands. She casts a disapproving glance at Jody as she leaves.

Jody shrugs and taps her ash into the sink next to her.

"Ida-Sue, you don't have to protect me from myself anymore. I hereby release you from duty."

"Okay," I tell her. "But I'll never stop caring."

"You're sweet." With her free hand, she reaches over and pinches my cheek. "Just like your dad. I had no idea until Trinity told me. He was such a nice guy. How many commercial fishermen would take the time to hang out with a bunch of Indian kids?"

"I don't know."

She holds up her left index finger. "Your dad. He's the only one. And you *are* like him, you crazy fool. You and Sam are lucky you didn't drown."

"We're lucky you came along in the boat. So where did you go that night? Why did you leave the party?"

"Why do you think?"

"Connor and Murf?"

She nods.

"He's a jerk," I say.

"Nah. He just decided he liked someone else. That doesn't make him a jerk. But I was pretty bummed out about it, so I took a walk on the beach. When I got back, they said you and Sam had gone out to look for me."

I stare at the reflection of Jody's ponytailed head in the mirror. "I guess I kind of freaked out because of Red Beard and his friend. I thought they took you away and . . . you know."

"Eric and Hoggy? They come up from Canada every summer to fish—and party. Eric's full of gas, but harmless. What did you call him, Red Beard?" She snorts.

"That's the name Sam and I gave him because he reminded us of a pirate."

"Ha! That's funny. But we have another name for him. Earache."

I giggle.

Jody fingers the beads on her bracelets. "Sorry to get you all worried. Is your head okay?"

"I was getting headaches there for a while, but it's better now." I turn my head to show her the wound, which is a lot less obvious now.

"That's good. I really like your hair short. It's feisty, like you."

"Thanks." I blush at the compliment. I'd never describe myself as feisty, but I guess actions speak louder than words, as Dad would say. He was friends with someone far feistier than I could ever hope to be. Then it occurs to me that I haven't asked Jody, the one person who might actually know.

"Sorry, this is kind of out of the blue, but have you heard of a Native prostitute nicknamed Two-Bit?"

Jody coughs on her own smoke. "What?"

"So she *does* exist." I follow Jody's glance up to the ceiling, where bored girls have thrown wads of wet toilet paper. The mounds look like insect bites.

"Well, yes and no," she says.

"What's that supposed to mean?"

"Trinity doesn't go by that name anymore."

"Trinity is . . . was Two-Bit?"

Jody exhales. "It's not something she advertises."

I remember Trinity saying something very similar when she covered for Dad. *We don't advertise*, in reference to the Center's need for condoms. She's no longer working as a prostitute, but she's still protecting her customers' identities as carefully as she protects her own.

"That was a long time ago, before she started the Center," Jody is saying. "I don't think her past is any secret, but no one talks about it, out of respect for her. She's Trinity now."

"That would explain why Dwight and Hank said they'd never heard of Two-Bit. Maybe they had, but weren't saying. And what about her new name, Trinity?"

"My grandmother says she took it from Raven's three names. I don't remember the names in Tlingit, but they basically mean White Raven, Black Raven, and Baby Raven. I think she wanted to show that people can change—maybe not their forms, but certainly their futures. It doesn't matter how you start out. With support, you can change your path."

The restroom door swings open. Dena bursts in. "Oh, hello," she says to us before checking herself in the mirror. "It's getting kinda wild out there with the circle dance." She grabs a paper towel from the dispenser and blots her neck and forehead.

"Uh, Dena, this is Jody, the roommate in Alaska I was telling you about? Jody, this is my cousin, Dena."

"Hey, nice to meet you!" Dena turns to Jody and they shake hands. "The Raven Tale Dancers, wow! Just wow. Especially Raven."

"Sorry, he's taken." Jody flashes a grin.

Dena whistles through her teeth. "Lucky girl. What's his name?"

"Cody."

"You're kidding—Jody-Cody? Oh my God, it was meant to be."

"Dena's a habitual matchmaker," I explain.

"Speaking of matches, where's your love?" Dena asks me.

"I haven't seen him. I don't think he made it."

"He better have a damn good excuse," Jody says. "If we could make it all the way down from Alaska." She bounces off the counter. "That reminds me."

She digs into the back pocket of her jeans, pulls out a well-worn envelope and hands it to me. "Your cannery check, special delivery. Bill told me to give it to you."

"But, I—"

"He couldn't bear the thought of you not getting paid for all your hard work."

"Well, this is a surprise." I fold it up and tuck it into the pocket of my skirt.

"Aren't you even going to see how much it's for?" Dena asks.

I shake my head. "Maybe later."

Jody shrugs. "Suit yourself. I got more than nine hundred dollars. Gonna use it to move to Anchorage."

"Anchorage? I thought you wanted out of Alaska."

"Well I did, I do, but Trinity thinks I can get a grant at Alaska Community College. It's changing into a four-year university, and they're recruiting Native Alaskan students who show promise." Jody pats her puffed out her chest with her cigarette hand.

"That's great."

She pouts at my lackluster reply. "You don't sound very happy for me."

"It's just that you and Dena . . . all my friends have *plans*, even Sam, and I can't see past school starting. I've been so focused on my dad, and now, with this memorial, it's all over. I won't know what to do with myself."

Jody shakes her head. "Trust me, Ida-Sue, it's not over.

It'll never be over. Saying good-bye to your dad is a begin-ning, not an end."

Dena fidgets with one of her earrings. "That's really pro-found."

"Yeah," I say. "And I have no idea what it means."

"You will." Jody beams, all calm and knowing, like some wise man—or woman, rather. She stubs out her cigarette in the sink and drops the butt in the standing ashtray. "Come on, I'll introduce you to Cody."

THE dance circle isn't so much a circle as a crazed amoeba snaking around the floor, swallowing unsuspecting bystand-ers in its path. There goes Dena. With everyone dancing, it's easy to spot Trinity, looking beautiful and proud in her white beaded dress. She's sitting with her musicians and dancers, including one little boy, still wearing his Baby Raven robe.

Your secret's safe with me, I think as I accept her bear hug.

Jody introduces me to the others as her "roommate from Can-a-lot," no mention of me being Steve Petrovich's daughter, which is fine by me. She takes a seat next to her boyfriend, identifiable by the black makeup that still clings to the valleys of his face.

"You were amazing!" I sound like a groupie.

He acts embarrassed, like he's not used to compliments, which I find hard to believe. Close up and in full light, I no-tice that his nose is a bit crooked and he has some pimples on his chin, so I guess he's not perfect—but he's still pretty damn cute.

"Cody has been dancing since he could walk." Jody

reaches down and squeezes his knee. I notice that he's traded his loincloth for cutoffs and a tie-dye T-shirt, but you can still see the lines of muscle in his arms and legs.

"It shows," I say, willing myself to look up at his eyes.

For a moment, no one says anything. I blush.

Finally Jody fills the silence. "Cody is doing an internship at the Center. He wants to counsel Native teens, same as me. So, you see, Ida, you really can stop your worrying."

"Never." This is the first I've heard of Jody's plans to become a counselor. I've no doubt she would be good at it.

Cody grins. "I heard about what happened at the cannery, how Jody had you searching for her."

I blush even more. By now, I must match my pink dress.

"Hey, speaking of friends . . ."

Jody's gaze fixes on a point to my right, toward the dancers—and a black-haired boy in a brown suit.

"Sam!"

He turns around, relief spreading across his face. I excuse myself and walk over. He smells wonderful, spicy and sweet.

"You made it!"

"Of course."

"Jody's here. With a new boyfriend."

Sam waves to her but doesn't walk over. He's more interested in the herky-jerky line of people trying to follow each other's steps. "What do you call this dance?"

"The Kolo."

"Holo?"

"K-olo," I say exaggerating the K. "It's Slavic for 'wheel' or 'circle.' We usually do it at weddings."

"Looks like fun," he says.

"Are you being sarcastic?"

"No." He holds his hand out. "Want to dance?"

I don't answer because my eyes have just landed on an extraordinary sight: my mother in a circle of Slav relatives, arm-in-arm with Grandma Grace. They're a study in contrasts, Mom in her dark sheath dress and high heels, Grandma Grace in traditional Croatian white and sensible orthopedic shoes. One big woman, one small; one strawberry-blond, one black-haired (dyed); their heads leaning together as Grandma teaches her daughter-in-law the steps. Mom's movements are slow and unsure, but she's getting it. She tosses her head back to get her hair out of her face, and I think she sees me. I wave. I detect a smirk, as if she's saying, "See? I'm game."

"Your mom looks like she's doing okay," Sam says. "So do you."

"Even better now that you're here." I kiss him on the cheek, not caring who sees. We're standing so dangerously close to the dancers, I'm getting dizzy from the vaporous mix of Chanel No. 5 and Old Spice. There's Dena, cool as ever in her sleeveless batik dress, and Uncle Pat, flushed and sweating in his dress jacket. Next to him is Aunt Janet, holding hands with my cousin Doug, who grew so much over the summer that we've finally dropped the "ie" off his name. Uncle Alex, the only son still fishing full seasons in Alaska, has linked hands with his still-spry father, my grandpa Bill. There are several fishermen (identifiable by their wind-burned skin) and their pale wives, and finally Grandma Grace and my mother. When Mom gets close enough to Sam and me, she lets go of the man to her left.

"Come on, you two," she says, waving us into the circle. I

take her hand. Sam takes mine and the stranger's to his left. Gap filled, we're carried along, mimicking the steps we don't yet know.

ACKNOWLEDGMENTS

Many generous people helped me bring *Leaving Year* to light.

My late great high school English teacher, Ellen McComb Smith, of the purple pen, taught me to delve below the surface layer of clichés and broad sentiments to write what is real. I'm trying, EM.

Friend and fellow author, Anne Leigh Parrish, convinced me that I could and should write a novel (before I die). Then she willingly read and critiqued chapters and drafts ad nauseam. Without her, this book wouldn't exist.

I'm tremendously grateful to beta readers Rebecca Alexander, India Rose Bock, Kay Rae Chomic, Steve Kink, Gabe Castillo, Patricia Paul, Paula Zook, Sharron Nasman Whitesel and, of course, Carol McGaffin, who, unlike other mothers, always gives her honest opinion.

Special thanks go to Steve, Gabe, Eric Hogeboom and Pandora Eyre for taking the time to meet with me and tell me about their fishing and/or canning experiences.

Every writer needs a good editor, or three. Authors Lish McBride and Martha Brockenbrough, of Nothing to Novel, helped me shape, sharpen and summarize my story; and copyeditor Emily Russin saved me the embarrassment of sending out an error-riddled manuscript.

The team of professionals at SparkPress, including Brooke Warner, guided me through the whole publishing process, including cover and page design. I may be biased, but isn't it beautiful?

Of course, my family took this years-long journey with me. My husband, Mark Funk, deserves endless gratitude for his endless patience and support. I also want to thank Carl and Mara Funk for their ongoing encouragement, and my sons, Casey and Charlie, for listening to me read aloud my entire book (without checking their phones too often).

I have to acknowledge some family members who are no longer with us. My parents in-law, Mary Ann and Wallie Funk, championed all creative endeavors, including mine, and had the good sense to buy a beach house on Guemes Island, my favorite place to write. Finally, my father, Robert L. McGaffin, died before he could see his daughter become a novelist, but his estate will help pay for the costs of this book, and, I hope, more to come.

ABOUT THE AUTHOR

Photo credit: Robert S. Bock

PAM MCGAFFIN is an award-winning former journalist who returned to her original passion of writing fiction after a long career in newspapers and public relations. Her short stories have appeared in online literary journals, and her articles and essays have been featured in newspapers and magazines. She and her family live in Seattle. This is her first novel.

Selected Titles from SparkPress

Above the Star, Alexis Chute, $16.95, 978-1-943006-56-4. *Above the Star* is an epic fantasy adventure experienced through the eyes of three unlikely heroes transported to a new world: senior citizen Archie; his daughter-in-law, Tessa; and his fourteen-year-old granddaughter, Ella. In this otherworldly realm, all interests are at war, all love is unrequited, and everyone is left to unravel the truth of who they really are.

The Frontman, Ron Bahar, $16.95, 978-1-943006-44-1. During his senior year of high school, Ron Bahar—a Nebraskan son of Israeli immigrants—falls for Amy Andrews, a non-Jewish girl, and struggles to make a career choice between his two other passions: medicine and music.

Tree Dreams, Kristin Kaye, $16.95, 9781943006465. In the often-violent battle between loggers and environmentalists that plagues seventeen-year-old Jade's hometown in Northern California, she must decide whose side she's on—but choosing sides only makes matters worse.

Colorblind, Leah Bowron, $16.95, 978-1-943006-08-3. Set in the hotbed of the segregated South, *Colorblind* explores the discrimination that an elderly African-American sixth-grade teacher and her physically challenged Caucasian student encounter at the hands of two schoolyard bullies.

Beautiful Girl, Fleur Philips. $15, 978-1-94071-647-3. When a freak car accident leaves the seventeen-year-old model, Melanie, with facial lacerations, her mother whisks her away to live in Montana for the summer until she makes a full recovery.

Blonde Eskimo, Kristen Hunt. $17, 978-1-940716-62-6. Neiva Ellis is caught between worlds—Alaska and the lower forty-eight, white and Eskimo, youth and adulthood, myth and tradition, good and evil, the seen and unseen. Just initiated into one side of the family's Eskimo culture, she must harness all her resources to fight an evil and ancient foe.